# THE BAKING GAMES

*by Rachel Hanna*

# CHAPTER 1

SAVANNAH

I HATE MORNINGS. I have always hated mornings with the passion of a thousand suns. I remember when I was in school, I would set all my clothes out the night before, put on my deodorant before I went to bed, and put the toothpaste on my toothbrush just to give myself ten more minutes of sleep. It wasn't very hygienic, but it got the job done. I mean, no bugs were flying around me or anything.

The snooze button was my very best friend.

Which is why it doesn't make sense that, as a thirty-year-old woman with a brain, I am currently standing in the bakery section of my local grocery store, staring at a clock that says 4 AM. Certainly, I am having a bad dream.

But, no. This *is*, in fact, my life these days. While I would love to be snuggled up in my soft blanket inside my tiny bedroom in the apartment I share with my younger sister, I am instead standing in the cold, stark grocery store that hasn't been updated since God was a child, wearing a black apron and no-slip shoes that aren't going to win any fashion shows.

Why is my life like this? Trust me, it's a question I ask myself hourly, if not minute-by-minute. How I got to this place is baffling, especially for someone who had much bigger dreams for herself.

Like most kids, I assumed I'd grow up to be a ballerina or a famous singer. Sadly, I have no balance and can't carry a tune in a bucket. Taylor Swift needn't worry. I won't be taking her job.

As I got older, I developed a love for baking. It was something I'd done with my grandmother as a kid, and I realized I could actually do it for a job. I would go to some illustrious culinary school, graduate top of my class, and open my own bakery, which I would then franchise around the world and be interviewed by Oprah while we ate cupcakes and exchanged cell phone numbers. My delicious desserts would be featured in her "favorite things" list, and I'd watch my bank account balance soar afterward.

But here I am at the grocery store. Oprah isn't here, and I do not know her number. She's probably asleep in her cushy bed, which is where I'd like to be. Well, in my bed, not Oprah's. I'm sure she's wrapped up in a plush blanket that actually *was* on her "favorite things" list while I'm standing here feeling the overly zealous air conditioning beating down on my pasty white arms.

So, where did things go wrong? I guess you could say things went wrong the day I was born. Okay, maybe that's a bit drastic, but it feels true. I was born to a young mother. When I say young, I mean she was sixteen. I loved my mother, but she always had problems. I didn't know her any other way.

I didn't know the kind of mother who makes you lunch and kisses your forehead before you get on the school bus. I didn't know the kind of mother who cuddles with you on the sofa and watches a movie while you share a big bowl of popcorn.

I knew the kind of mother who passed out on the sofa for an entire day after a particularly bad bender the night before. I knew the kind of mother who regularly got arrested for writing bad checks and then missed your first elementary school talent show. I twirled the baton, by the way. Not well, but I twirled it nonetheless.

Addiction and mental health issues plagued my

mother every day of her life. It was hard to be a kid with a whirlwind of dysfunction swirling around me every day. My grandmother had been my only saving grace, but when she died on my ninth birthday, I was left with my mother again. Alone.

Until she found out she was pregnant. My dad was never in the picture at all. I know his name was Axel, but that's about it. I've never really wanted to know more. I'm fine living in the mystery. I guess I know that any man who was interested in my mother wasn't there to build a family. He was there to take advantage of a broken woman.

My sister, Sadie, was born just a few days after I turned ten. I adored her. She was *my* baby, as far as I was concerned. Her dad stuck around for about six months, but then he went to jail, and that was the last we heard of him. As awful as it was, Sadie and I shared that in common. No dads. But we had each other, and I was determined to make sure Sadie had a normal life, even with our mother regularly getting drunk and embarrassing us at our school functions or forgetting to pick us up from school at all.

My mother had her moments when she tried to get clean, but those demons never let her out of their clutches. Watching someone you so desperately wanted to love… and were supposed to love… fight shadows you couldn't see was painful.

After I graduated from high school, I applied to pastry chef school. I got accepted but couldn't afford the tuition. Mom sure couldn't help me. She hopped from one job to another when she was working at all. During high school, I had to work two jobs just so we didn't lose our crappy little apartment.

I decided to put away the dream of pastry chef school and got into the working world. I spent years saving every penny I could just to get the chance to go to school one day. Unfortunately, my savings ended up going to pay for a funeral when I was twenty-two years old. Our mother's heart just gave out.

That left Sadie and me alone—truly alone. I got guardianship of her, and we tried to start over together. Sadie was just twelve, but I felt like I could salvage her childhood. There was still a chance.

So, I worked two jobs—one at her school cafeteria and one at a diner at night. Our next-door neighbor, Mrs. Copeland, watched Sadie at night until I got home after one in the morning. By watch, I mean she'd fall asleep on our sofa and then go home when I arrived.

When Sadie had parent-teacher conferences, I went. When she had school plays, I was in the first row. I was the shoulder she cried on when she had breakups with boyfriends. I was determined to be everything to her that my mother never was to me.

Once she graduated from high school, I quit both jobs and got this job at the grocery store bakery department. It doesn't pay great, but at least I get to have my hands in icing and buttercream all day. Sure, there's no creativity, really. After all, this is a big grocery store chain, so they have their own rules.

Everything comes in bags of premade mixes. I follow the pictures of the cakes like paint by numbers. I don't get to make up my own recipes. It's restrictive, and I hate the hours, but it fills my soul drop by drop.

Three years ago, I could finally go to pastry chef school since Sadie was old enough to be home alone. After saving and getting a small financial hardship grant, I went to a night school about an hour away. Being with others who wanted to work in this field was wonderful. Well, mostly. Some of the students were downright horrible people, but I guess you will find that to be the case in every school.

Even though I got my certificate, I couldn't find a job locally and needed to be there for Sadie. So, I took this job at the grocery store. Sadie says I need to think bigger, to get out of our crappy little suburb and hit the big city. She believes in me way more than I believe in myself.

"Stop daydreaming, Savannah!"

My boss, who we call Big Thelma, stands behind me with her hands on her hips. Just to be clear, she asked us to call her that. She likes it for some unknown reason. It fits her. Big Thelma is taller than most men, and her shoulders are so broad that she regularly bangs them against the doorway leading to the small office where she sits most of the day.

"Sorry," I say, knowing that arguing with her is pointless. Her voice is booming, and I can't form enough words at four in the morning.

"After you finish the doughnuts, you need to make the retirement cake for Dan Shoals and then the birthday cake for that little girl. The one with the unicorns."

"Yes, I know," I say, a little edge to my voice. Big Thelma seems to think I can't read. She tells me everything I need to do even though I have an exhaustive list right beside me. I get the job done. I'm a good worker, although she never recognizes that. After all these years of working together, she still treats me like I just got hired.

I'm pretty used to working hard and not getting any praise for it. Honestly, it feels more comfortable that way. I don't know what to do if someone compliments me.

"Did you make the scones?" Big Thelma asks, interrupting my daydreaming again.

"Not yet," I say, wanting to let out a groan but worrying that Big Thelma will take one of her giant hands and smoosh me into the ground.

"Get on it, girl!" she says, her voice reverberating around the empty grocery store. Big Thelma does very little work besides ordering me around. Most of the time, she sits in the little rolling chair in the office and plays games on her phone. But she's worked here for almost twenty years, and since everyone is scared of her, she gets away with murder. I'm convinced she could set the whole place on fire, and the manager would give her Employee of the Month.

After I finish the doughnuts, I decide to make the scones before moving on to the first cake of the day. We still have three hours before the store opens, and the cakes aren't picked up until ten, so I have plenty of time.

Big Thelma enters the office and shuts the door, a sure sign she will take a cat nap in that poor little chair. I keep waiting for it to crack and crumble to pieces, throwing her onto the hard, industrial tile floor, but no such luck yet. I imagine one of the screws holding it together, flying out, ricocheting off the wall, and poking her eye out, and it makes me smile. I might be delirious from the exhaustion that is my life.

I take the chance to look at my phone, which I have tucked in the back pocket of my horrible-looking black work pants. By the time I get home, they will be covered in all manner of things. My dog sniffs me down like I'm carrying a kilo of cocaine every time I come home.

As usual, there's a text from Sadie, who always wakes up early for her job, too. She doesn't have to be at the diner until six, but she simply must look good, she says. Sadie is gorgeous, with thick, curly brown hair and the biggest green eyes you've ever seen. I think she needs to be a model, but she poo-poos the idea every time I bring it up.

She wants to go to college, but we can't afford it. *Yet.* I've got to come up with a way. She's been out of high school for two years now, and working at a diner isn't going to get her anywhere. Sadie is smart, although she didn't have the grades to get a scholarship. She didn't test well.

I never expected to have so much weight on my shoulders at this age. I thought I'd be married, have a kid or two, work a good job, and enjoy my life after such a hard upbringing. Instead, I became a mother to my sister, and I can barely rub two nickels together. Okay, now I'm getting depressed.

But I don't get depressed. I'm what one calls a perpetual optimist. It often drives other people crazy, but I'm hard to rattle. I've had so much handed to me in my life that, at some point, I just decided to put a smile on my face and get on with it. Even when I don't feel like smiling, I smile. No matter what my internal voice is saying, my outward appearance is that of an overly positive person. I guess I'm a good actress, too.

Pastry chef school was hard. Working all day and then going to school at night, all while making sure Sadie had what she needed, just about did me in. But I still smiled. I might've cried in my bathroom at night while the water was running, but I didn't let anyone see that.

There was one guy in my classes who hated me. Hated that I was happy all the time. Said it wasn't possible to never feel down or sad or tired. The more he picked on me, the happier I appeared. I wouldn't let that jerk make me feel bad about myself.

I've learned in my life that if I let myself give in to the sadness, I may never climb out. And I don't have time to wallow. I don't have time to let the shadows of sadness fester within me. I have Sadie counting on me. If it wasn't for her, I may never get out of bed again. Sometimes, the ones smiling are the saddest ones of all.

But I digress.

I look back at my phone and read Sadie's message.

*Have a good day at work, sis! I appreciate all you do for me!*

Sadie is the reason I do what I do. I want to see her cross that stage as a college graduate someday. That's what I remind myself of all day as I plod through this life I'm living. After all, not everyone gets to live their dreams. Some of us have to live in reality.

I leave work just after lunchtime, go grocery shopping, and head home. While it seems like a luxurious life to get home before three o'clock, I assure you it's not.

I run my own side business, making cookies, cakes, and other delectables for clients. Well, occasional clients. If I can ever go viral on TikTok or Instagram, maybe I can hit it big. For now, I'm making a birthday cake for a little girl in our apartment building and a batch of cookies for some lady's baby shower. But isn't that how empires start? I'm choosing to believe that.

I walk into our tiny, fairly crappy apartment, my

arms filled with grocery bags. I've learned the art of shopping on a small budget. Coupons, watching the sales, and using store discount cards. These are all important for people who don't have a lot of money.

We mostly buy things like eggs, bread, some meat, and frozen veggies. There is very little eating out around here. Sadie brings home leftovers from the diner when she can. And I sometimes sneak a few pastries home from the store, but just the ones that didn't come out right. Big Thelma won't let us sell those anyway, so why should they go to waste? Plus, I've seen her filling her giant handbag with them plenty of times.

"Let me help you with that," Sadie says as I push the front door open with my foot. She grabs two of the bags. I refuse to make two trips up to our third-floor apartment. "One day, you're going to fall backward down those stairs trying to carry all this stuff. Why didn't you call me to come down?"

I follow her into our tiny galley kitchen and put the bags on the counter, letting out a huge breath. "I didn't know you were already home. How was work?"

"A grind, as usual," she says, starting to put the cold stuff away. "Gary fired Mario, so now our best cook is gone. Julia is cooking, and we both know she can't even boil an egg. So, we got complaints all day about overcooked hamburgers and undercooked fries. My tips were so bad!"

"Why did Mario get fired? He's been there for a long time, right?"

"Yeah."

"So, why was he let go?"

She looks at me, stifling a smile. "He might have taken Celia on a date."

"Celia? Isn't that Gary's wife?" I ask, my eyes wide.

"Yep!"

"Wow! That takes some guts to date the boss's wife," I say, putting the bread on top of the microwave.

"Right? Anyway, he's interviewing new cooks… and divorce lawyers, I assume."

I playfully punch her in the shoulder. Sadie has a great sense of humor. While I'm perpetually happy, she's more realistic. She has more emotions. You know, like a normal person.

"I hate that you have to work at that place. I'm thinking of taking a night job again."

"Sis, I'm not a baby anymore. You don't have to work yourself to death just so I can go to college. Lots of people don't go to college. I'll be fine."

I know she's lying. Sadie has talked about going to "real college" since childhood. She wants that whole college experience where she lives on campus and walks between the giant brick buildings going to classes. She wants to join a sorority and go to parties. At twenty years old, that time is drawing to a close. She doesn't want to be so much older than her classmates.

I feel time moving so much faster with each passing day. I owe her this experience. Her life has been far from easy. Neither of our lives has been easy, but I can still save her. I can still make her dreams come true.

Mine? Well, that is starting to seem like a lost cause, even to a positive person like myself. But you can't have it all, right?

# CHAPTER 2

RHETT

I STAND ON THE DOCK, staring out over the ocean. There aren't many places in the world prettier than the Bahamas. The temperature is perfect today, and there isn't a cloud in the sky.

I've spent all morning doing what I love most in the world—creating visually stunning and delicious-tasting desserts for people who may or may not appreciate all the work that went into them.

This is my life. At thirty-one years old, I shouldn't care what my family thinks about it, but I can admit to myself that sometimes I do. I'm a grown man, but I can't help that it matters—deep down—that I don't have the support most people take for granted.

Even surrounded by all this beauty, it's hard to live with the knowledge that your parents don't accept you. They don't think what you do is anything special. They don't like that a son of theirs has "given up" on being successful by cooking fancy desserts for rich people.

Mom is a respected cardiologist in Boston, and Dad is one of the top entertainment attorneys in the country. He splits his time between Boston and Los Angeles, where most of his clients are. I'm sure that's where he also keeps his mistresses, although no one in our family would ever bring up that topic.

They've been married for almost forty years, and I can't remember ever seeing them hold hands or kiss. They are more of a partnership, I guess. Their marriage is one reason why I will never get married. Sharing your whole life with someone you don't love seems pointless.

Then there are my two brothers—Ben and Liam, the stars in my parents' eyes. Ben is the oldest at thirty-seven. He works with my dad and travels from Los Angeles to New York City on a weekly basis. Liam lives in Boston and is thirty-five. He's a noted plastic surgeon and keeps my mother looking twenty years younger. She thinks no one notices that her hands are sixty-five years old, but her face is forty-five.

"You on break?"

I look up and see my co-worker, Eric, standing before me, smoking a cigarette. Nasty habit. He smells like an ashtray, but the beach winds thankfully keep the smoke away from me. I'm highly allergic.

"Yeah. I scarfed down some tacos, and now I'm regretting it," I say, putting my hand on my midsection.

"It's been a long day, huh?"

"Every day is a long day," I complain. I'm what a lot of people might call grumpy. I call it realistic. I picked the wrong profession for someone who isn't a morning person. Pastry chefs have to get up early, and it's the only part of the job I detest.

"You should take some time off," he says, leaning against a wooden post adjoining the dock.

"Why? I have no family. No wife. No kids. Might as well make money and sock it away so one day I don't have to work at all."

"You're a workaholic, man. You're always going to work," he says in his thick British accent. Eric is covered in tattoos. Both arms are sleeves, and he even has some on his hands. I want to ask what they are sometimes, but then I'm afraid it will cause a long conversation. I'm not built for long conversations.

I shrug my shoulders. "Who knows? Maybe one day, I'll have a good reason to take time off. For now, it's pointless."

"You've got those big dreams," Eric says, taking a long drag off his cigarette and then tossing the butt into the ocean. I want to push him in after it every time I see him do that.

"Stop littering."

"Mate, it's basically paper. It disappears down there."

"Have you watched the videos about trash in the ocean? Stop throwing your butts in there."

He puts up his hands like he does every time we have this conversation. It's the one good thing about being built like a linebacker. People tend to listen to you.

"Fine. Anyway, I thought your dream was to work in a Michelin-star restaurant?"

I eye him carefully. "A three-star Michelin-rated restaurant."

"Right, right. Only the best for Rhett Jennings."

"Don't you have some fruit to prep for dinner?" I say, trying to get him out of my hair. Eric is inherently lazy, but he knew someone who knew someone that got him this job. I expect him to get fired at every port, but here he still is, looking disheveled and smelling of stale ashes.

"You're becoming an old coot right before my eyes," he says, chuckling as he heads back toward the kitchen we share. I pick up my water bottle from the ground, ready to follow him back inside, when my phone buzzes in my pocket. Being out on the water most of the time, I rarely use the thing. I forget it's even there until I want to look at social media and check my email.

"Hello?"

"Rhett? Oh good. I'm glad I caught you. Where are you this time?" There's a hint of disdain in her voice, as always.

"The Bahamas. And where are you?"

My mother sighs. "At the hospital."

"Well, that's a good place for a cardiologist, I suppose."

She pauses for a long moment. "I'm not here for work, Rhett."

My pulse quickens. I rarely see my family, so I'm always out of the loop, but this is the first time I've been worried. I love them all, of course, but it's just easier this way. Being picked apart for all your life choices can get a bit taxing.

"Why are you there then?"

"Your father took a fall." She says it like she's telling me the most boring piece of information she's ever uttered. Like she's reading a lunch menu.

"Is he okay?"

"He will be. He was off work for a few days—we know how rare that is—and he decided *not* to call our handyman, Pete. Instead, he climbed up on the ladder to clean the gutters, and bam! Down he went onto the sidewalk. Broke his leg in two places. He'll be home for a very long time now. I might lose my mind."

I wanted to laugh at that last comment. It isn't as if she spends much time with my father. She doesn't clean the house. She never cooks meals. Even as kids, we had a nanny who took us everywhere, cooked meals, and put us to bed. "Mother" was more of an official title and reason to deduct us from their yearly taxes.

She spends most of her days at her office or the hospital. As harsh as she can be, my mother is a terrific cardiologist. She's known around the country for her innovative treatments and approach to heart disease. She specializes in women's hearts, which is funny because she doesn't have one herself. Okay, that might've been too far. I get it. But it was funny.

"Is there anything I can do?" I don't even know why I asked the question. What can I do? I'm in the Bahamas. They're in Boston. And I'm not a doctor, as my mother likes to remind me on a perpetual schedule throughout the year. It's like she sets an alarm on her watch to remind me of that fact as often as possible.

"Well, dear, you're not exactly a doctor…" Ah, there it is. Now I can set my timer for three months from now when she says it again.

"No, Mother, I'm not."

I've noticed other people call their mothers' names like "Mom" or "Ma." My friend Hal, who is from Tennessee, calls his "Momma". My brothers and I have always called ours "Mother" like something out of a horror movie.

*"Mother is killing a goose in the backyard."*

*"Mother is holding a knife to Father's throat."*

*"Mother drove the getaway car for a gang of human organ thieves."*

*"Mother needs a sponge bath."*

There's a lack of affection in the word, at least how I say it.

"So, what are you up to these days?"

"Well, still preparing desserts for rich celebrities on their fancy yachts." I leave the details out of what I tell her because I've learned that more details equals more questions. And more questions equals more criticism. And more criticism equals more self-loathing. It's not a fun cycle, and I'd rather avoid it.

"I'll never understand you, Rhett."

"What don't you understand?" I use my thumb and index finger to rub the bridge of my nose. It's my "thing" that I do when I'm stressed. I'm surprised I even have a bridge anymore.

"You had everything laid out in front of you after prep school. A full ride to multiple universities, a job waiting for you at the hospital. And now you're traversing the world on someone else's yacht, making them cupcakes."

I roll my eyes so hard I think I can see behind me. "I don't make cupcakes, Mother. I'm a trained pastry chef with skills that are in demand with wealthy people."

"*We're* wealthy people!" She shrieks so loud that I swear I can hear someone's heart monitor going off in the background.

"I'm not doing this with you again," I say in a low growl, hoping she gets my message. My mother never gets social cues. Or maybe she just doesn't care.

"Dear, it's just that we all love you and want to see you do well. If you'd gone to medical or law school, you could have your own yacht and hire a baker."

"A pastry chef."

"Whatever," she mutters. She says it like even the words "pastry chef" taste terrible on her tongue. Oh, the irony.

"Why can't you just be happy that I'm happy?"
Am I happy, though? I don't let the question linger
long before shaking it off.

"Happiness is overrated."

If that isn't the best way to sum up my mother's
life, I don't know what is. She's a brilliant cardiologist. I'll give her that. She helps people daily, and she
saves lives. But she does so with a lack of emotion
that would make a serial killer proud.

"Look, I'm not going to keep having this circular
conversation with you, okay? I love my job, and I
have big plans."

"Oh, really? What kind of big plans can a pastry
chef have?"

"Well, for starters, I want to be the pastry chef at
a top restaurant. Michelin star rated. I want to be in
magazines, maybe on TV. When people think of
desserts, I want them to think of me."

"Oh, good Lord," she groans. "Honey, there's no
way a person can make a good living as a baker.
Maybe just a few people in the whole world. But, if
you went through with medical school and became a
neurologist, as we talked about…"

"Mother, stop! I don't want to be a doctor. I'm
not going to medical school."

"Law school then. It's not as good—don't tell

your father I said that—but it's a decent career if you're good at it."

"I'm not going to law school either. I already went to school."

"Rhett, you went to night school. That's not real college, you know. Nobody in our circle has a child that went to night school."

"That was because I was working at your office to make rent, remember? I could only go to school at night."

She pauses for a long moment. "I have to go check on your father, but I need to prepare you for something."

"What?"

"We've been reviewing our will."

Oh, here it comes. The threats. This isn't new. My mother and father have threatened to remove me from the will if I don't do what they want several times.

"Here we go again," I mutter.

"It's just not fair that your brothers are contributing members of society, and you're doing… well… whatever it is that you're doing. You can't expect to just wait until your father and I kick the bucket to cash in, sweetie."

She adds "sweetie" to soften the blow. It doesn't. My mother uses terms like "dear" and "sweetie" and "honey", but they aren't terms of endearment.

I pause for a long moment and consider ending the call before I finally speak. "Most parents let their kids pursue their own dreams. Live their own lives. They just want them to be happy."

"Darling, you should know by now that we're not most parents."

Oh, I know better than anyone.

## SAVANNAH

I'm standing in the bakery section of the grocery store, staring at a birthday cake I'm making for a little girl's fifth birthday. She picked this princess cake from the laminated book we give customers when they want to order something. Of course, some of them order online, which is great because I hate interacting with customers.

I'm an outgoing, positive person, but customers can be awful. They're often rude and snarky, as if I don't already hate my life getting up at the crack of dawn to make cakes that come in a bag.

Big Thelma isn't here today. Said something about dental work, but I think she just wanted a day off. That's fine with me. I love the quiet mornings in the bakery. I can dream of better days when I run my own bakery in some small town where everybody comes by for a morning bagel and a chat.

Instead, I'm standing in stark fluorescent lighting, smelling the seafood case the next department over. A lobster stares at me from the tank, and I'm overwhelmed with guilt. I'd free him if I had any idea where one would take a lobster on a Tuesday morning in the middle of Georgia.

I understand his plight in a way. We're both trapped here. If I could figure out a way for us to run away together right now, I'd totally be up for it. Me and my lobster best friend, making a life for ourselves on the run.

I look back down at the cake. The little girl's name is Leighton, so I write it out in fancy script, being sure it reads correctly. The colors are purple, hot pink, and white, with thick frosting around the edges. The frosting tastes like someone dumped sugar in a bag. I can't eat it. It's pretty disgusting. Customers would go nuts if they let me make my famous caramel buttercream icing. But no. Everything must be uniform and by the book. Literally.

As I carry the cake to the refrigerator, I feel my phone buzzing in my apron. I carefully set the cake down, not wanting to have to remake it, and then pull my phone out. I take off my thin plastic gloves and toss them in the trash, but not before leaving a dollop of pink icing on my phone screen.

"Sadie? Is everything okay?" She rarely calls this early, so I immediately assume the worst. Even though I'm not her actual mother, I feel like one.

"Everything's fine. I wanted to tell you about something I just found out."

"What?" I sit on a high stool behind the doughnut case.

"I was online checking Instagram, and there's a new reality show."

"Another reality show? Shocker. Isn't everything on TV a reality show?" I say, brushing some stray flour on the metal counter onto the floor.

"No, sis, listen. This is a baking show."

"A baking show? Like a competition show?"

I can hear her clicking around on her laptop. "Kind of. It's a competition for both trained and self-taught bakers, but you're also locked in a house with everyone."

"Locked in a house? What is it? A horror show?"

"They have cameras on you 24/7, so there's the drama between contestants mixed with baking competitions."

"Why are you telling me this, Sadie?" I stand and walk over to today's schedule to see what I need to work on next. Oh great. Another birthday cake. This one's a train cake for Dalton, who's turning three.

"Because I think you should apply."

I let out a loud laugh that reverberates around the kitchen. "Me? Why?"

"Because of the prizes."

"I have a job, sis. I can't just leave my life behind for some reality show."

"It's only six weeks!"

"Almost two whole months? Are you kidding me?"

"I think you'll change your tune when you hear what the prizes are."

"Fine. What are they?"

"One prize is a publishing deal for a cookbook..."

"Okay. That's cool, but not enough to leave for two months." I pull the bag of cake mix off the shelf and look for the blue icing for the train.

"You also get to make the wedding cake for a celebrity wedding."

"Which celebrities?"

"Keaton Mallory and Keira Donaldson!"

Okay, making the wedding cake for two of the most famous actors in the world doesn't sound bad, but it still isn't enough to get me to give up my job for almost two months and risk getting fired. We'd go under in a matter of weeks if I weren't working.

"That's cool, but still not enough to entice…"

"And two hundred thousand dollars."

Sadie lets those words hang in the air like a carrot dangling above my financially broken head. I can barely form words. Two hundred thousand dollars? That would be a life-changing amount of money for us. Sadie could go to college, and I could open a bakery. Maybe. I think I could, though. If I bought used equipment and rented a space in a smaller town…

"Are you still there?" Sadie asks.

"I am," I say, sitting back down on the stool.

"This is our chance, sis." She says the words with such seriousness that I almost start to cry. This isn't just about me. She knows this is her chance, too.

"But what are the odds I'd even get accepted onto the show? I'm sure hundreds of pastry chefs better than me will apply."

"Hey, you're supposed to be the positive one!" She's right unless it's about myself. I'm not at all positive about myself.

"And you're supposed to be the realistic one," I say. "What happens if I get accepted and leave for six weeks? How will you pay the bills? And I will surely lose this job."

"I'll work extra shifts. And Big Thelma isn't going to fire you. Nobody else would work with her."

I laugh. That's probably true. More people have left the bakery section of this grocery store after working with Big Thelma. She's not the easiest boss.

"It does sound intriguing, but what are the chances I'll even get picked?"

"You won't know until you apply," Sadie says. I can hear the smile in her voice. I have a flashback of the begging I had to do at the orthodontist to let me make payments so she could have that dazzling smile. "Come on, sis! This could change our lives!"

I sigh, not wanting to get my hopes up. "Send me the link."

# CHAPTER 3

RHETT

I PULL my rolling laptop bag behind me as I head for the small cafe at the edge of the port. Today, we're in Miami, which means I can take a little extra time to pick up some groceries and get my legs under me again before we head back out to sea on another vessel.

I stop at my favorite cafe, The Salty Flamingo, and set up shop at one of the outdoor bistro tables. This is where I like to work when we're docked in Miami for a day or two. Seeing people other than the ones I serve or work with is vital to my mental health.

I order an iced tea with lemon and a Cuban sandwich with fried plantains and then open my laptop. I start by researching some new ideas for desserts. Nothing related to recipes is exciting me, so I head to my email, and that's when I see it.

There's a new reality show focused on baking. I don't know how I got on their email list, but I barely look at it before I click the link to apply. There's no question that I want as much visibility and experience as possible. This one has three prizes for the winner—a cookbook deal, making the wedding cake for a celebrity couple I couldn't care less about, and most importantly, a fat two-hundred-thousand-dollar check.

My parents could pull that much out of the safe right this very second. I get that. Life would be so much easier—financially, anyway—if I would just go back and finish college, become a doctor, and inherit more money than I'd ever need.

But I can't do it. I just can't.

I'm not like my brothers. Or my parents. I feel like an only child, but an orphaned one. Basically, a guy with no family. I mean, I have them, but the emotional connection doesn't exist. There are expectations, criticisms, and disappointments that could feed the masses, but no real love. Not the kind I'd want.

So, the only way I will build the life I want is to do it on my own, financially and emotionally. And at thirty-one years old, the opportunities are only getting fewer and fewer as time marches on.

I fill out the form, telling the producers about my background, education, and future goals. I don't even care what the show is about or what I must do. That money has my name on it.

SAVANNAH

Two weeks have passed without a word from the reality show people. I knew it was a pipe dream. I'm sure thousands of more qualified people applied. Sadie had been so excited about it but hasn't mentioned it in days. I think she knows it's not happening, just like I do.

And it's okay. I know it will all be okay. Somehow, I always skate by in life, just by the skin of my teeth. I don't think I'm one of those people destined to do big, bold things. I think I'm one of the worker bees. You know, the people who keep things running in the world while other people take vacations, buy expensive handbags, and post about their exciting lives on social media.

But it really is okay. I always land on my feet. I have to believe I will this time. Somehow, I'll come up with a way for Sadie to go to college, and maybe one day, I'll come up with a way to open my own bakery. For some people, dreams just take longer.

I'm exhausted today for some reason. Big Thelma was on a roll this morning, yelling out orders like she was putting me through basic training.

*"Stir that mix better so it won't be grainy!"*

*"Your icing needs work!"*

*"Where's that doughnut I was eating?"*

Mind you, Big Thelma has no real training in the world of baked goods other than eating enough of them to put us out of business. She calls herself "self-taught," which, from what I can gather, means she cooked and baked for her ten younger siblings growing up many decades ago.

And my icing *doesn't* need work.

Some days, I wonder why I put up with her or any of it, really. The early hours. The boring, unfulfilling job. But then I see Sadie's face at night and remember that I'm doing it for her. Sure, she's twenty years old and not a baby anymore, but from the day she was born, she has been my baby. I have to do better for her.

After getting home from work, I fall onto the couch in a lump. I didn't sleep well last night. Applying for that show got my hopes up, and I don't usually allow that to happen. You see, although I'm a positive person, I don't allow myself to get my hopes up about things. Historically, that hasn't worked out for me.

For instance, I got my hopes up about my last relationship. His name was Connor, and he was dreamy… at first. He hung on my every word, told me how beautiful I was, and repeatedly said he wanted to marry me one day. We dated for exactly two years and twelve days before I broke up with him after a particularly bad argument. We only argued about one thing, really. It was always the same.

Sadie.

He thought it was ridiculous that she was over eighteen and I was still "taking care of her." He couldn't understand that we were all we had. Our mother was gone, and our fathers were never in the picture. Sadie was and will always be my top priority.

He blew up when I explained to him that we couldn't get married until he accepted Sadie as a part of our family and someone who would always be close. At that moment, I realized that I didn't want to be with someone who didn't care about my sister like I did.

Sadie is a go-getter; one day, she will show me up in a big way. But for now, I feel responsible for making sure she gets to follow her dreams. She doesn't demand that from me; I demand it from myself. Sadie always tells me to stop giving up my dreams for hers, but I just can't.

Still, despite my recent breakup, I'm an optimist. I'm not sure I always live up to that description, though. I'm positive and practical. Is that even a thing?

My positivity is in the moment. I can fake it for long periods of time before I hide in my bathroom to cry. I've cried in all sorts of places. Behind the counter at the bakery. In my car. Into an empty icing piping bag. That almost suffocated me.

I feel like if I let my emotions bubble to the surface for too long, they'll take over, and I might never get back to baseline. I must stay at baseline to survive. It's funny the coping mechanisms you develop when you grow up like we did.

Just as I close my eyes to take a little nap, my phone buzzes in my pocket, startling me. I sit up quickly and fish it out, answering it on the third ring.

"Hello?" I say, sounding a bit breathless, like I just ran up a flight of stairs. I really need to get to the gym if pulling my phone from my pocket makes me out of breath.

"Is this Savannah Greene?" a chipper woman on the other end of the line asks.

"Yes, it is. Who's calling?"

"This is Amanda Burton, the casting director for *The Baking Games.*"

My heart feels like it literally stalls in my chest. Like I need jumper cables to get it going again. I feel like my tongue won't move. Do you know how hard it is to talk without a tongue? Turns out, very hard.

"Uh huh…" I mumble out, just to make some kind of sound. They don't call you for a reality show unless they *want* you on a reality show, right?

"We were very impressed with your application video. The cake you made looked so delicious!"

For the application, I had to fill out an extensive form and make a five-minute video showing something I made, with clips showing the process. I made my famous coconut caramel layer cake. It's usually a hit at parties. Well, the two times I've been invited to a party and made it.

"Thank you," I say, finally getting the feeling back in my tongue. I take a quick sip of water from a bottle on the end table that has probably been sitting there for a week. Hope I don't die.

"We're in the final stages of choosing contestants for the show, and you made the cut!" She sounds like the hype person who comes out before Oprah gives a speech and gets the crowd excited—not that Oprah needs help getting people excited.

"Wow. Really?" I'm shocked. I'm not all that special, to be honest. Just a run-of-the-mill gal trying to make it in this crazy world. I'm blown away that they even watched my video. "So, what's next?"

"Well, there's quite a lot, actually. More paperwork, interviews with other members of our team, background checks, and psychological evaluation if we get further. There's also a health check to ensure you're suitable for the stress of a competition like this."

"Sounds a little like joining the military or something," I mutter under my breath.

"I know it's a lot, but the prizes are amazing, right?"

"Definitely." The prizes are the only thing keeping me motivated at this point.

"I just need to ask if you're interested in moving along in the process then?"

I think of Sadie and don't hesitate. "Absolutely."

The last few weeks have been a whirlwind. After finishing all the rounds of interviews, background checks, and everything else the producers wanted me to do, I can't believe I'm standing on the sidewalk in front of the airport, one bag of rolling luggage in my hand and a duffel bag over my shoulder.

"I'm going to miss you so much, sissy!" Sadie says for the tenth time since we left the house. I try not to cry each time she says it.

"I'm going to miss you, too," I say, bumping into a man who seems hell-bent on getting to his plane on time, even if he has to take me out in the process. The Atlanta airport is the busiest in the world, and I can see that on full display today. It's early summer, so kids are out of school, and families are heading out on vacation.

I wish I had that. The doting husband carrying my luggage. The two kids running beside me, tiny suitcases in hand. A vacation to a tropical beach or to tour Europe. To make memories. That's what is really missing from my life. Making memories.

I shake my head in an effort to get the thoughts loose so I can refocus on what I'm doing. This is for Sadie. And for me, too, I suppose. I need a way out of the grocery store bakery lifestyle. Big Thelma was not at all amused when I told her I was leaving for six weeks. She would've fired me if anyone else was interested in working with her. Instead, the poor new girl from the seafood section got recruited to take my spot temporarily. Good luck to you, poor new girl.

Sadie could've driven me to Sweet Haven, the little town near Savannah where the show is filming. Ironic that a baking show would be filmed there, I know. She could've driven me, but that would've taken hours out of her day, and I didn't like the idea of her driving back alone.

Instead, I opted to take the hour-long flight from Atlanta to Savannah. I don't particularly love flying, but it felt like the right thing. Anything to keep Sadie safe.

I hug her one more time and then make my way inside without looking back. It's the only way to keep from breaking down.

RHETT

Flying makes me sick. Every single time I fly, I need a barf bag. Yet I can float out on the open ocean with nary a problem. It will never make sense to me.

Thankfully, the flight from Miami to Savannah wasn't very long—about an hour and a half—but it didn't take long to make me turn green and lose my breakfast into the poor airplane nausea bag. I really felt bad for that little girl sitting next to me. She saw some things a child shouldn't see. I think she's scarred for life.

I step into the terminal, happy to be on earth again, and head toward the outside doors. Producers will pick me up straight from the airport and take me to the secure location where we will film.

Apparently, the little town is called Sweet Haven. Well, isn't that cute? I'm being sarcastic if that wasn't clear. I think the town name is silly.

It's about twenty minutes from Savannah, but we won't see much of the town. Just the house and the grounds. We'll be on a pretty strict lockdown during the six weeks of filming so that we don't get any outside influence that could muck up the competition results.

That's fine with me. I'm not what one would call a "people person." I like being alone. I like working alone. I can trust myself. When you include other variables—namely, people—you lose control. As long as I'm in charge, at least, things go well.

I decide to stop by the cafe I see and get a ginger ale. My mom always gave them to us when we were sick as kids. It's one of my few fond memories of growing up with my mom. When I was sick, I got attention. Not for long, but at least it was something.

The server gives me the ginger ale to go, and I

turn around and head toward the outer doors again. And that's when something catches my eye. Something striking and hard to miss.

Red hair.

Sure, I know lots of people have red hair. Gingers, as the young people call them. Well, not that I'm old. I'm only thirty-one, but to actual young people, that *is* old.

I turn my head just in time to see her walk out of the bathroom. She's walking toward a vending machine. Her long, wavy red hair is bobbing as she walks. I can only see her from behind, but I swear that's her. Why would she be here? On the same day as me? In this particular airport? What are the odds?

SAVANNAH

This guy is going to kill us. I don't know who taught him to drive, but he wasn't listening, or they were drunk. He's taking every turn like we're running from gangsters with large guns and fast cars.

"Can you slow down?" I ask for the third time. The producer sitting next to me doesn't seem to notice that our deaths are imminent. She continues staring at her phone, frantically typing. She's probably typing out her last will and testament.

"It's fine," the guy responds in very broken English.

"Isn't this scaring you?" I finally ask Nina, the producer with the big doe eyes and giant fake boobs.

She giggles. Actually giggles. She doesn't laugh. It's a giggle like a cartoon character from the fifties. "Nah. Dmitri knows how to drive very well. He drives me all the time."

"Uh-huh," I mumble, staring out the window. I wish I had my phone right now. This drive is both terrifying and boring. "How much longer?"

"About ten minutes."

Ten *long* minutes.

I keep going back and forth in my mind as to whether this whole thing was even a good idea. Leaving Sadie and my job and for what? The *chance* of winning a prize? How do I know I'll even make it past the first week? And then I've lost everything.

Well, not really. Sadie will still be there, and unfortunately, so will Big Thelma. She'll probably spend her time getting meaner. Doing push-ups and eating doughnuts at the same time. The image makes me smile for a moment. Maybe I'll be here long enough to actually miss Big Thelma, but I'm not sure I have enough time left in my life for that to happen.

I guess I'm overthinking this. Sadie isn't a baby. She's a grown woman with a job and a life outside of me. Parents must go through this when their kids get older and leave the nest. Only Sadie hasn't actually left the nest. Neither of us can leave the nest because we can't afford a new nest.

We pass a sign that says Sweet Haven, which then takes us down a long dirt road with the biggest live oak trees I've ever seen. Swaths of Spanish moss hang from them over the road. It is really beautiful, and nothing like the suburbs. If I lived here, I don't think I'd ever leave.

I guess I imagined Sweet Haven would be an actual town, but it's not. It's a dot on the map.

"Do people actually live here?" I ask.

Nina nods. "A few. It's not overly populated because there's so much marshland. There are a few restaurants and shops; otherwise, it's mostly old family land. Big Civil War era houses and such."

We finally pull up outside of a beautiful Southern home. This place is like something out of a storybook. It's white with black shutters, two stories tall, and covered in porches. It seems like every door and window has a porch.

"This is it?" I ask, craning my neck to look at the house.

"Yep."

"It's big."

"You haven't seen anything yet," she says, giggling again.

I step out of the SUV when Dmitri finally gets out and opens my door. He doesn't seem to get in a hurry unless he's actually driving. Then we're trying to beat the speed of light. Or sound. Whichever one is faster.

But to open my door or remove my luggage? Nah, Dmitri has all the time in the world.

"Thanks," I say, stepping out into the ungodly hot Southern sun. I look around for more contestants. "Where is everybody?"

"Oh, we were very careful to bring each of you at different times so you don't see each other until you're inside."

Hmm. That seems weird. We don't know each other, so what does it matter if we see each other? Oh well. I don't really understand how all this TV stuff works. I'm sure they know best.

Nina and Dmitri walk me up the stairs and then set my rolling suitcase and duffel bag at the front door. They both turn and start walking down the stairs.

"Wait! What am I supposed to do now?"

Nina giggles yet again. "Open the door, silly!"

Without another word, they hop into the SUV

and speed off. This whole day has been one of the weirdest of my life. For all I know, this is all one big prank. Or they've dropped me at a very fancy serial killer's house just to amuse themselves.

I throw the duffel bag over my shoulder and grab the rolling suitcase, slowly turning the doorknob to the big, old house. It's heavy wood and creaks when I open it, which is a bit spooky at first—that is until I see the inside. Good, dear Lord. It's gorgeous.

"Oh my gosh," I say to no one in particular. I crane my head in all directions, looking up and down, side to side. There's a long hallway with original hardwood floors in front of me with rooms on both sides and a huge, wide curved staircase going up to the next level. I don't know where I'm supposed to go.

"Savannah?" A man emerges from nowhere, wearing a nice suit and a flashy smile. Obviously, the host, from his demeanor and the fact that he's wearing a mic.

"That's me," I say, immediately aware that I'm about to be on national television for the next six weeks. Well, only that long if I'm lucky.

"Welcome to *The Baking Games*!" he says in a booming voice, as if I just won a brand-new washer and dryer on a game show. His white, toothy grin almost blinds me. He's probably in his fifties with salt and pepper black hair, a fake tan, and those little crow's feet beside his eyes. Why is it that men get better looking as they age, and women have to work so hard at it? Well, *some* men, I guess.

"Thank you." I stand there like a deer in the headlights as he looks at me. Am I supposed to know what to do next?

His smile falls, and he yells, "Is somebody going to bring a flipping camera out here, or do I have to do it?"

Wow, talk about Jekyll and Hyde. He can turn that smile on and off like a lamp. I just stand there, frozen in place. I'm not somebody who likes confrontation or dramatic situations—perhaps I shouldn't have signed up for a reality TV show—so I hope I can just get to my room and have some downtime.

I don't think that's what's about to happen, though. A crew of cameras comes out of seemingly nowhere, lights click on, and the smile is back.

"Welcome to *The Baking Games*!" he shouts again, holding out his arm like he's about to reveal a puzzle on Wheel of Fortune.

"Thank you," I repeat.

"All of the other contestants have already arrived and are waiting in the parlor."

The parlor?

He waves me to follow him and then swings open a door covered in black film so you can't see through it. The cameras are so close to me that I feel like a celebrity running from the paparazzi.

I follow him into the parlor, and when my eyes adjust to the light, I see a group of people standing there in the small room. I assume these are my fellow contestants. Everyone is holding a glass of wine and smiling. Lights are everywhere, and even more cameras are present. The room is bigger than I thought. It looks like they knocked out a wall and made it larger for the show. That's a shame in such a historic home.

"Savannah, meet your fellow challengers!" He points at the group, and everyone either waves, smiles, or holds up a glass of wine. Except for two people I notice immediately.

My pastry chef school nemesis, Rhett Jennings, and my very recent ex-boyfriend, Connor Kane.

I want to go home.

# CHAPTER 4

RHETT

I KNEW IT WAS HER. I just knew it.

Normally, I love women with red hair, but not this one. She is the most annoying person I've ever met. Not that she's unattractive. Quite the opposite. And in the three years since I've seen her, she somehow got better looking.

But she's perpetually sunny about everything.

*Drop an egg on the floor? No problem! This will clean up in a jiffy!*

*Add too much baking powder? Oh well! We'll add a smidge of this or that, and it'll fix it right up!*

I hated being paired with her. Sometimes, things were just bad. Or they sucked. But not to Savannah

Greene. Nope. The world was just a happy place where everything would work out alright in the end.

I have no such notions. The world often sucks, and people are even worse. I find that people will generally let you down, given the chance. I don't give them the chance. I don't let people get too close to me. If you keep people at arm's length, they can't hurt you. Or at least that's what a therapist told me that I seem to think. Well, the one time I went to therapy.

And I suppose they could still hurt you at arm's length if they had a long enough sword.

She's looking at me like she'd rather be anywhere else but here. I know she doesn't like me either. She never said so because she's so irritatingly nice to everyone, but I know. I can feel it.

Her gaze quickly travels to another person in the room. Some guy I don't recognize. He's tall with jet-black hair. Thin and toned, but not muscular. I could definitely take him in a fight. I'm not sure why I'm considering sparring with a fellow contestant on a baking show, but I'm just going with whatever pops into my head.

She looks nauseous. She looks lost. Why do I care? She's my opponent, and I intend to put my boot on each of these people and smoosh them into the Georgia red clay so I can walk away with those prizes. I didn't come here to lose.

"Alright, contestants, we're going to get to know each other now!"

Oh God. I hate stuff like this. Are we going to go around the room and tell everyone what we hope to do this summer? I hope to win and send all you losers home. Should I say that?

"After each of you introduces yourself, we'll talk about the competition and rules."

Rules. I hate rules.

Before I can think too much about how I hate rules, I hear the first contestant introduce herself. I guess I should pay close attention. If you know things about people, you can use them to your advantage.

"My name is Maggie Roy. I'm a sixty-five-year-young widow..."

Young? Yeah, that's a cute thing to say, but she's the oldest one in the room with her solid white short hairdo and glasses on a literal beaded string around her neck. I bet she has cats. That just feels true in my bones.

"I always wanted to be a professional baker," she continues, "but I cared for my disabled husband for many years. He passed away two years ago."

Everyone bows their heads like we knew him. I do the same because I don't need them to know I'm faking my care right now. I mean, I do care that this woman lost her husband, but I don't know him, so why should I act like I'm in mourning?

The next person takes the microphone.

"I'm Leo Martinez. I'm a first-generation Mexican American from Texas. I am a graphic designer but dabble in baking on the side."

This guy is dressed in what can only be described as a bold-colored suit, with shades of lime green and purple that have not been duplicated anywhere else on the planet. Nor should they be. Still, I think I can beat him. I'm trained, after all. He's designing websites and baking cookies for fun. Next.

"I'm Lainey Loudermilk," a voice says. I lean over to see Barbie herself standing in the parlor. Can't we just call this a living room? "Parlor" seems awfully formal. "I'm twenty-eight years old, although everyone thinks I'm college-age."

I did not think she was college-age. I did, however, think she uses a large quantity of tanning creams and potions that are probably killing her from the inside out.

"And what is your training, Lainey?" our host asks. His name is Dan Carmichael, and he could surely sell you a used car. His teeth can be seen from space, and he looks at Lainey's chest, not her face.

"I went to a prestigious culinary school in Colorado," she says, beaming. I bet she did beauty pageants and twirled a baton that was on fire while wearing a pink dress and stiletto heels. Every man in here is staring at her, drool forming at the corners of their mouths. I'm not that guy. She's attractive but in a *too high maintenance and annoying* kind of way. She's fun to look at, but her personality subtracts massive points, and then she ends up with negative numbers.

Okay, I just met her. Not even. Maybe I'm being too judgmental. It's a flaw. I know this about myself. But I read energy, and I don't like hers. I will steer clear as I wipe the floor with her in this competition. No way a girl named Lainey Loudermilk is taking this prize from me. Next.

SAVANNAH

Oh, my dear Lord in heaven. Hallowed be thy name. Why are these guys here? My rival and my ex. Lovely. There's no way this was an accident.

All sorts of conspiracy theories flow through my head. How did this happen?

They asked me so many questions during the process—about my background, likes, dislikes, and family dynamics. I rack my brain, trying to figure out how this happened to me. How did I end up in a parlor with eleven other competitors, two of whom are guys I loathe?

I have so many questions. The first one is whether I should stay here. They can't force me to stay. I can pitch a fit and walk out of here. Who's going to stop me?

I'm going to stop me, that's who. I can't walk away. I signed contracts. I promised Sadie.

The host is going down the line of contestants, asking each one to introduce themselves. I find myself watching Rhett Jennings. His eyes are dark and smoldering, like he's making notes in his head about each person.

I got to know him after going to pastry chef school at night with him for two years. When we graduated, I was thrilled that I would never have to see his grumpy self again, and yet here I am, trapped in a house with him for up to six weeks. Maybe he'll get voted out early on, along with my ex, Connor, who is staring at me like he's trying to bore a hole through my head.

"I'm Connor Kane." I suddenly hear his voice boom across the room as he continues looking at me. "I graduated from culinary school four years ago, and I have skills outside of baking as well." I swear he winked at me. Gross. "Oh, and I'm single, ladies," he says, flashing a broad smile in Lainey's direction. She bats her eyelashes, and I must force myself to keep my breakfast down.

"Nobody cares." I look up to see Rhett crossing his arms and rolling his eyes like he'd rather be anywhere else at the moment. I can relate to him for the first time.

"Okay, guys, let's keep the smack talk for competitions," Dan says, smiling directly into the camera. Where did they get this guy? "Let's move on. How about you?"

"I'm Zara Ali, age thirty-five. As a food blogger, I've traveled the world and know global cuisines. Graduated from culinary school in Switzerland five years ago. I'm a competitor, and I'm not here to make friends." She sounds terrifying, but she's beautiful. A natural beauty. What I wouldn't give to be one of those. Her medium brown skin tone makes me jealous as I look down at my pasty white skin. Redheads don't tend to turn any shades but white and red. SPF 50 is my best friend.

Zara not only has a cool name, but she also has gorgeous curly black hair with little tendrils hanging around her face. Actual tendrils. Stunning. She's one to watch. I think she's going to give a lot of these cocky men a run for their money.

"Hello, everyone. I am Sophia DuBois, from France. I am twenty-two years old, and I moved to the United States about six months ago." Her accent is very thick, and I must listen closely to understand her. "I am a graduate of pastry chef school in Paris, and I will warn that I am quite competitive."

"Yeah, that's kind of why we're all here," Rhett interjects. Man, this guy doesn't have an unexpressed thought, does he? It's kind of entertaining.

Dan suddenly points at me. "And you are?"

Like he doesn't know. TV is weird.

"I'm Savannah Greene. Thirty years old. I live in a suburb of Atlanta and work at a bakery." Kind of a lie, but whatever. "I attended pastry chef school." Wow, even my intro sounds dull.

Thankfully, Dan doesn't pry further. He turns to another man.

"I'm Nate Winston. I'm forty-five, so y'all are all kids to me!" He laughs loudly at his own joke. No one else does. We all look like deer caught in headlights. "Anyway, I come from a whole family of bakers and self-taught chefs. My grandma just loved making cookies…"

"Great! Nice to meet you, Nate," Dan says, cutting him off. "Sorry, but TV time moves very quickly." Nate nods and then stares at his shoes for a while.

Dan continues pointing around the room, where we meet Hank Dalton, a fifty-two-year-old construction worker who got hurt and did a virtual pastry chef school. I don't know how well he will do, but people can surprise you.

Then there's Bianca Rossi, a twenty-seven-year-old goddess of a woman of Italian-American descent. She specializes in fusing the two cultures and graduated from some fancy culinary school in Italy.

There's also Tanya Cohen, a thirty-four-year-old single mother who runs her own catering business and is self-taught. She's a shy, mousy thing. I'm not sure a competition show is for her.

Finally, it all boils down to Rhett. Mr. Congeniality. This ought to be good.

"And you are?" Dan asks expectantly.

"Rhett Jennings."

"Where are you from?"

"Originally? Boston."

"I don't hear an accent," Dan quips.

Rhett stares at him. "I dropped it."

"I don't think you can drop an accent that easily," Dan says, laughing toward the camera. I don't know why he's poking at Rhett. The guy is at least six foot two with shoulders like a pro football player and jaw muscles that twitch when he's annoyed. I saw that a lot in classes with him. Rhett doesn't like to lose. In fact, he rarely messed up. If he did, that jaw muscle twitched. I never saw him lose his cool, though.

"Well, *I* dropped it."

"Okay then… So, what's your background?"

"I attended pastry chef school, and then I went to work on yachts with celebrities."

"Wait. You're telling me you travel on yachts, making sweet treats for famous people?"

Rhett stares at him once again. Gosh, he could set you on fire with one look. "That's what I said."

How did he get on this show? He's the grumpiest person I've ever seen. Part of me wants to hate him, and part of me wants to know what hurt him so bad that he became this way. Babies don't come out ornery like this. Did he come out of his mother's womb and just shoot his doctor the bird?

Sadie would say I'm too empathetic, and I take on other people's junky emotions when I should just focus on myself. She's probably right, but I will never stop doing it. It's just who I am.

"That sounds like a very exotic life! Why did you decide to leave that to come on a competition show?"

Rhett sucks in a breath and blows it out slowly. "I like to win."

Connor lets out a laugh, which causes Rhett to turn his attention in that direction. It's like watching a nature show on TV. The lion has now noticed the small kitten wandering across the desert. Okay, maybe not a kitten, but I don't know what would wander across the desert, so let me have my imagery.

Now, see, the lion could play with the kitten. Bat him around a bit. Make him think he might live to see the next day. That's Rhett Jennings. He'll play around with you. Make you think you might get the best of him, and then bam! He gobbles you up without missing a beat. Connor should tread lightly. Rhett is not to be played with, lest you want to be eaten by a lion.

RHETT

That was tedious. I want to get to the competition, and I don't care what school people went to, how old they are, or if they're single. I'm not here for love. I'm here for money.

But Dan has more to share, so I try to pay attention since this is the part I care about: the rules, the prizes, and the competition itself.

"Okay, folks, let's get down to the nitty-gritty! As you know, this is a competition show lasting six weeks. There will be a panel of three judges, all experts in the area of culinary arts. You'll meet them tomorrow at your first challenge. Voting during main competitions will also involve the audience, although judge votes will weigh seventy percent and viewers will count for thirty percent. Now, each week, we'll have two competitions. One is a reward comp, and the other is a main competition. Rounds will also be solo, but we'll also have partner rounds sometimes…"

He keeps droning on and on. I can't imagine viewers at home will be interested in all the minutia this man is spewing out of his giant, toothy eating hole, but I try to stay awake. This has been a long day, and I really want some food and a nap. I may be "hangry," as the kids call it.

"As you know, the prizes are amazing! One contestant will win two hundred thousand dollars, a cookbook deal, and the job of making a wedding cake for Keaton Mallory and Keira Donaldson!"

Keaton and Keira are this year's *it couple.* At least, that's what my Internet search told me. I don't follow a lot of celebrity gossip, but I'm not telling anyone that. After all, as far as these people know, I'm on yachts with celebrities all day long.

Apparently, they met on a silly reality TV dating show and got engaged, but everyone thinks these two lovebirds will make it. They have the love of a lifetime. Gag. I give them six months tops, if they even make it to their wedding day. I need them to make it there so I can make the cake, of course, so all my blessings and prayers go out to Keaton and Keira. May you make it to the altar so I can get famous for making your cake. Amen.

"You will all share this house, obviously, with several people in each bedroom. There is a large industrial kitchen at the back of the house, with multiple stations, allowing for this type of competition."

An industrial kitchen with multiple stations? In this beautiful home? Somebody is going straight to hell for doing that to this house. People are awful. It's like when developers mow down huge forests to build ugly condos that all look alike and have terrible HOA presidents.

"You will have camera crews all around you during all waking hours. There are also cameras mounted in every nook and cranny of this house. There is no privacy, so assume everything you say and do will be broadcast across this country."

"Wait, how will we use the bathroom?" Lainey blurts out, sounding like a complete fool.

Dan looks at her for a long moment. "Of course, there won't be cameras in the bathroom. That would be inappropriate." He looks at the camera. "I just want to clarify that we do not film competitors while they're in the bathroom."

Everyone is getting restless. Even Savannah has her arms crossed now. I'm sure everybody is hungry and tired and annoyed. Dan had better speed this whole thing up or risk an on-screen bloodbath.

"Okay, I think that's enough for now. Why don't we let you choose your rooms so that everyone can have some downtime to get a bite to eat? We'll have a little meet-up to get to know each other better tonight. Here are your room assignments," he says, handing each of us a colored card. I guess the colors match up to rooms and roommates. The first thing I notice is that Connor has the same color. Great, just great.

I don't know what his deal is with Savannah or what her deal is with him, but there's a story. I don't want to care what it is, but I kind of do. There's not much else going on at the moment, so a little gossip might fill the time.

Within seconds, people are running like a hippo is chasing them. Hippos are fast, if you didn't know.

To be so overweight, those suckers are scary. I was obsessed with them as a kid.

Up the curved staircase, the contestants go, like little kids hunting Easter eggs. Well, if little kids were on methamphetamines while hunting Easter eggs. I walk up the stairs slowly. Why run if your room has already been assigned? It's me, Maggie, and Hank hanging back. The two oldest people and me. It's fine. Maybe it will make people underestimate me.

"You're a hulk!" Maggie says, looking over at me as we walk up the stairs. She's favoring her right leg.

"Thank you?"

She laughs and waves her hand at me. "I didn't mean anything by it, honey. Just that you're a big guy. I'm sure you've heard that all your life."

"Most of it," I say. "I had a growth spurt in between my freshman and sophomore years of high school."

"Quite a growth spurt."

"I suppose so."

"I played football in high school. Did you?" Hank suddenly asks.

"I did for one season. Then, I hurt my knee, and that was that."

"Sorry to hear that," Hank says, as if we should all be in mourning that I didn't play more.

"It's fine. If I'd kept on, I wouldn't be here. I'd be in the NFL."

Hank laughs loudly. I'm not sure if he's laughing because he thinks I couldn't have made it into the NFL or if he's laughing because I'd be making so much money there that this little piddly show wouldn't even be on my radar. I decide not to press further. Again, I'm not here to make friends. I'm here to obliterate every one of these people.

When we arrive up the stairs, which takes twice as long because of Maggie's bum knee or hip and my inability to run ahead of her, we see a long hallway. We split up into our respective rooms. I glance as Maggie walks into hers. The walls are painted pink, and there are three twin beds around the room. Savannah is in there, and I think that Lainey chick is, too. Good luck, Savannah. You're gonna need it.

I walk into my room, which is thankfully painted a light shade of gray. Very masculine. Of course, I don't care if ballerinas are painted on the walls. I'm still going to stay here and win this thing. Done and done.

"Hey, man. No hard feelings, right?" Connor says, walking over and reaching out his hand to shake mine. I don't shake hands. I find it gross. I don't know where his hand has been.

"I don't shake hands."

"What?"

"It's just something I don't do."

Connor stares at me. "You're a weird guy." The camera crew is feet from us, capturing each and every word for TV viewers. This is strange. I couldn't have imagined how weird and awkward it would be to have cameras in my face.

"Good that you figured that out all by yourself," I say, walking past him to the last empty bed. I toss my duffel bag down beside it and lie down, looking up at the ceiling.

My other roommate is Nate, the talkative Southern guy. He seems nice enough, but I hope he doesn't decide to chat me up all the time. No such luck.

"Hey there! I'm Nate. You're Rhett, right?"

"Yep," I say, not sitting up. Nate doesn't get the message and continues standing beside my bed.

"Great name. My momma loved *Gone With The Wind*. Is that where you got your name?"

"No, actually. My mother got it from our family tree that stretches back to England. Apparently, it was a surname there."

Yeah, it's more boring than it sounds. I'm not nearly as interesting as Rhett Butler.

"Oh. Gotcha. I was named after my grandfather's cat, if you can believe that!"

Yes, Nate. I can believe that.

I might be overly ornery today. Honestly, I wish I could fast-forward this game to the end so I could win the prizes and get back to my life, as dull as it is.

Like others here, I have some secrets—things I don't necessarily want to get out, places in my life I've failed, and things I don't necessarily want the world to see. This ought to be interesting.

# CHAPTER 5

SAVANNAH

WELL, this is hellish. While I think Maggie is
wonderful and reminds me of my own grandmother,
Lainey is awful. She's like a caricature of herself.
Why the Universe is choosing to punish me by
having to share a room with her is beyond me.

No, I choose to think positively. Maybe I just
haven't gotten to know her well enough yet. Maybe
she gets judged all the time based on how she looks,
so she lashes out. Maybe we'll become best friends
and laugh about first impressions later.

Maybe.

"I want this bed," Lainey says, standing beside the
bed I rightfully picked first and am now sitting on,
unpacking my suitcase.

"Excuse me?"

"I want this bed," she says again, slower this time and emphasizing each word. Maggie looks at us from across the room.

"Well, I'm sorry, but I picked this bed, and I like it." I'm not someone who enjoys confrontation, but I also don't like bullies.

"I need to be on the wall." Maggie has one bed on the wall, and then there's a bed between her and me. That means Lainey doesn't want to be in the middle.

"Again, I'm sorry but…"

She crosses her arms. "Why are you being such a witch about this? It's just a bed."

"Now, girls…" Maggie says, walking over, trying to be the peacemaker.

"This is ridiculous," I say, standing up to face her. I can feel my heart starting to pound in my chest. I've had panic attacks in the past, although not in a few years. I hate this feeling. "We're grown women, and fair is fair. I chose this bed, and I'm keeping it." I stand my ground, staring into her icy blue eyes. I can see her lips pursing, and I swear one of her eyelids is twitching so hard that her giant fake lashes might fly off and put my eye out. I wonder for a moment if she's going to hit me. She definitely looks like she wants to, but she'd probably break a nail. One of the camera people gets so close that I think the lens will bop me on the nose.

"Fine!" she suddenly shrieks and stomps to the middle bed. I'm in shock. I've never seen a grown woman act this way. It's like she got stuck at age thirteen. Or four.

Maggie looks at me from across the room, stifling a laugh. I already like her.

A few moments later, Lainey leaves the room, evidently heading for the communal bathroom in the hallway. Maggie walks over to my bed.

"What on earth was that all about?"

I shake my head. "I have no idea, but I wasn't giving in. I want you to know I'm very nice, though. I don't get into arguments with people."

"Oh, honey, this place will bring out a side of you that you didn't know you had."

I wave my hand. "No. I won't let it. I stay positive, or I would have a daily mental breakdown."

Maggie sits on the end of my bed. "I'm positive too, dear, but this is a competition. Don't you want to win?"

"Of course! But do we have to argue and fight to get there?"

She turns and looks behind her toward the door. "Yes, I think we do. These people are the best of the best. They're not gonna go down without a fight, I do believe."

"Can I tell you something?" I say, without thinking.

"Of course. What is it?"

"I know two people in this house, and both of them hate me."

"What? You know people?" The camera crew is lingering around us. It's so weird to have the feeling of being watched all the time.

I look at the camera. "Yes, and I don't think it was an accident."

Suddenly, the camera turns away, and a producer comes running into the room. That's definitely not supposed to happen. Producers and contestants stay away from each other. The producer, who I think is named Andy, motions for the cameras to leave and then looks at me.

"What are you doing?"

"Excuse me?"

"You can't divulge behind-the-scenes secrets about the show. You signed paperwork, you know."

"What did I say?"

Maggie looks as confused as I feel. She scurries away back to her bed. Well, as fast as a woman with an apparent hip problem can scurry.

"You looked at the camera and said you didn't think it was an accident."

I stand up, putting my hands on my hips. "Well, I don't think it was an accident. You obviously brought my ex-boyfriend and the guy I hated from pastry chef school and stuck them in a house with me." It's even more infuriating to me when I say it out loud.

His face turns a shade of red I haven't seen before. "Look, it's fine to say that you know people in the house. It adds drama. It's not fine to speculate on the workings of the show."

I look up to see Rhett standing in the hallway, looking into our room. I glare at him, and he continues walking. How much of that did he hear?

RHETT

Something's going on in Savannah's room. First, I heard what sounded like yelling, and then I saw Barbie doll stomp out of the room. Has the drama already started?

I can't help myself, so I walk down the hallway and peek into the room. Sure enough, producers are in there talking to Savannah. What did she do? I can't imagine she started drama. She's the least confrontational person I've ever met.

That was one of many reasons we couldn't stand each other in pastry chef school. Granted, I was a bit prickly at the time. I hated going to night school. It felt like defeat. I wanted to spend my days learning the craft at some fancy school, but my parents refused to help me financially unless I agreed to attend medical or law school.

So, that meant I worked during the day to pay for those classes. But did that get me any points with my parents? Did they see me working hard and think, *"Wow! Our son really wants this, so we should support his dreams!"*

Nope.

As I'm thinking through all of this, I don't realize that I'm standing in the doorway of Savannah's room now, staring at her like some kind of lunatic. She glares at me, and I quickly continue down the hallway. I have no place to go in particular. I just want to see what this house has to offer. I head back downstairs to investigate.

I had hoped my mother would be excited for me when I called to check on my father and tell her about the reality show. She was most definitely *not* excited for me.

*"You're doing what?"*

"It's a great opportunity. I could win a huge money prize, a book deal, and I get to make a wedding cake..."

"Rhett Jennings! You must get out of this whole thing immediately!" Her screeching voice made my ear drums twitch.

"Why would I do that?"

"Do you even care about your family?"

I don't know how to answer that one.

"Of course," I say, underwhelmed.

"Then you have to get out of it!"

"I'm not getting out of it, Mother."

"Rhett, please. This is embarrassing! Our friends are going to see this. Oh goodness, we'll have to skip the Summer Formal at the club. I can't show my face there."

"Because of the facelift?" I know I shouldn't say it, but I can't help it. My mother's recent plastic surgery has made her look like she got stuck in a wind tunnel for a few weeks, and her face never went back to normal. Or like one of those dogs with big flappy cheeks sticking its head out of the car window.

"You know exactly what I mean. I don't want to be too harsh, but..." Since when had she not been harsh? "Well, I'm just going to be blunt like I am with my patients. Like Susie Coleman, who came in this morning and won't take her blood pressure pill regularly. I said to her that she's going to die."

"And you think I'm going to die? By going on a reality show?"

"You're going to ruin any chance you have of getting into a good school or working as a doctor or lawyer."

"When will you get it out of your head that I'm ever doing those things? Because I'm not. I've repeatedly told you this, and you don't listen. I sure hope you listen better when your patients talk to you, Mother. For their sake, I hope you listen."

"Rhett, I'm not supporting you in this. Any of it. This has all gone too far."

I pause for a long moment. "You're right. It has gone too far. I'm done being judged and criticized for following my passion. Goodbye, Mother."

When I hang up the phone, I fully accept that phone call might be the last time I'll ever hear my mother's voice. I should feel sad, but what I actually feel is free.

SAVANNAH

I might've gotten myself in over my head. Now that I finished getting berated by one of the producers, I want to hop the next bus back to my tiny, crappy apartment and hug Big Thelma.

Well, maybe that's a little too far-fetched, but

still. I don't think I thought this whole thing through. I just saw dollar signs. I saw Sadie waving at me as I dropped her off at some fancy college. I saw myself signing a lease on my new bakery.

I did not see myself locked in a house with my arch-rival and my ex-boyfriend. Don't even get me started on Lainey. I would love to meet her parents and see what kind of people raised a woman like that.

I can't stay in the room anymore. Maggie is taking a nap despite all the noise of people talking and shouting at each other up and down the hallway like a bunch of college students moving into their dorm rooms.

Lainey has disappeared, but when I enter the hallway, I see her talking to Connor in front of his room. She seems fine now, with her huge smile and her index finger touching his chest. Weird.

I go in the other direction and down the staircase. I don't know where I'm going. This house is huge. I just need some air, so I look for any exit I'm allowed to go out of. A cameraman is following me the whole time, so I can't get a moment's peace unless I tell him I need to pee.

Only I do need to pee. I have a very small bladder. It's one of many endearing yet annoying qualities about me.

I find what appears to be a bathroom near the kitchen and smile back at the cameraman. "I'll be right back." I'm trying not to talk directly to him because the producer told me we need to pretend they aren't there. He claims after a few days, we won't notice them. Okay, sure.

I walk into the room and flip on the light, only to find Rhett sitting in a chair in the corner of the room. "Oh my gosh!" I say, putting my hand up to my chest. "What are you doing? Are you trying to watch people going to the bathroom?" He quickly jumps up and reaches around to turn off the mic pack that's attached to my lower back before he sits back down.

He rolls his eyes. "Oh, come on. Seriously? You think I want to see people pee? Or worse?"

"Then why are you in here?"

"Lower your voice, Greene."

"Why?" I say in a loud whisper.

"I needed a break from all of… *that*," he says, waving his hand toward the door. "If you keep screeching like a barn owl, they will know I'm in here."

"How did you lose your camera guy?"

"He had a technical issue, so he said stay there, and he'd be right back."

"And you didn't stay right there?" I say, which is a

stupid and obvious statement I immediately wish to take back.

"Right on top of things, as usual, Greene."

I hate that he calls me Greene. I repeatedly reminded him in school that my name was Savannah, and I didn't want to be called by my last name. That made him do it more.

"Whatever. Well, I actually do have to pee, and my camera stalker is right outside, so…"

"So?"

"I have to use the restroom. Get out!"

"But I'm not done hiding from the chaos out there," he says, leaning back and crossing his arms. This man is infuriating. And built like a truck. In school, I only saw him in our requisite white aprons. Today, he's wearing a tight gray t-shirt and jeans. I want to say I find him ugly, but I can't say that. He looks like someone chipped him right out of a large piece of marble.

"There's going to be a puddle on the floor in a second."

He stands up, and I think he's leaving. Instead, he turns around and presses his face to the wall. "Fine. Go ahead."

"I'm not peeing with you in here! You'll hear me!"

"I've heard people pee before, Greene. It's no big deal."

I can't afford to argue anymore. That huge iced coffee I had on the plane is ready to make its landing. "If you turn around, I swear…"

"I won't. I'm a man of my word." The way he says it makes me believe him. "So, are we going to talk about the elephant in the room?"

"What do you mean?"

"They set us up."

"They set *me* up, you mean."

"How so?"

"Well, they put me in here with my archnemesis and my ex-boyfriend, so it seems I was the target."

"Wait. Your ex-boyfriend?"

I finish, quickly pull up my capri pants, and then walk to the sink to wash my hands. Before I can answer him, there's a knock at the door.

"Savannah, are you in there?" It's my cameraman.

"Yes. I'll be out shortly," I call back. "I have… a stomach issue."

No response. Nobody wants to ask follow-up questions when you say that.

Rhett turns around, a slight smile on his face. "Nice save. Although, now everyone thinks you have diarrhea."

I can feel my face flushing. "Did you mention me during your interviews?"

He laughs. "Absolutely not. Why would I?"

"I was just wondering." Why did I ask that question?

"Wait. You mentioned me?"

"No, of course not."

"That's how this happened. That's why I originally got the email application. I just figured the school gave them my info, but it was you. What did you tell them about me?" he asks playfully. He's so amused with himself.

I glare at him for a moment. "I told them I loved pastry chef school except for a jerky guy in my classes." I might have gone into more detail, but that truly was the gist of it.

"I feel like there's more to that story, but I'm very interested in the ex-boyfriend part. Who is it?"

I sigh and lean against the wall, really wishing I hadn't wandered into this bathroom. "Connor."

"My roommate? Yuck. I don't like that guy at all."

My heart suddenly swells a bit. "You don't?"

He shrugs his shoulders. "He seems like a tool."

"He *is* a tool."

"So he dumped you?"

My mouth drops open. "Excuse me, but he did *not* dump me!"

"Sure…"

Now I remember why I can't stand this guy. So smug and sure of himself. Probably because he's fifty feet tall with shoulders like a line of tanks. I wonder what they would feel like under my hands. Gosh, I really need to date more.

"I'm not doing this with you. I refuse to let you or Connor ruin my chances here. I'm going to win this competition, and both of you are going home," I say, standing in front of him with my index finger pressing to his chest. Dear Lord in heaven. It's like touching a piece of stone. It's warm, and I feel his heartbeat, but I have to remind myself that although he's incredibly drop-dead gorgeous, he's just a robot. He's not a real human with emotions. He's Rhett Jennings, the guy who will do anything to win this competition.

He looks down at my finger and then slowly looks me in the eye. Smoldering is what I'd call his blue eyes. They're flanked by black eyelashes that are way better than mine. His thick black eyebrows arch upward as we stand there. Why haven't I moved my finger? It seems to be magnetically stuck there. I can hear my breathing. I can see his lips curving upward.

"You done here?" he finally says, looking at my finger. My face flushes as I quickly pull it back.

"Yes, I'm done. I just wanted to get my point across, and I think I have," I say, backing toward the door, trying to maintain even the slightest bit of dignity. I hate this guy. I hate this guy. I must remind myself that I hate this guy.

"Turn the light off when you leave," he says, sitting back down.

"You're staying in here?" I ask, incredulous.

"I got interrupted. I just need a few minutes of quiet time before I go out there and start eliminating all of you one by one."

I no longer have to remind myself that I hate this guy. I leave the light on, open the door, and yell, "A contestant is hiding in the bathroom!"

# CHAPTER 6

SAVANNAH

AFTER I RAN AWAY from the bathroom, convinced
Rhett was going to come out and squash me under
his giant foot, I ended up in the foyer. I didn't want
to go back upstairs. I wanted to find the kitchen, but
I wandered onto a side porch with cushy furniture
instead.

My cameraman was hot on my trail the entire
time. I don't know how Rhett got away from him for
so long, but I bet he won't do it again. They're
watching him like a hawk now. The thought of the
look on his face when I yelled that makes me laugh
every time I think about it.

I walk over and sit down in one of the wicker

rockers, with its ivory-colored cushions. The swing across from it is made of solid wood and has a colorful striped cushion on it. It's got to be almost dinnertime now, but I don't have my phone, and I never wear a watch, so I'm a bit disoriented about time. All I know is that I'm starving. Are they trying to kill us?

"Well, hello there."

Ugh. I know that voice. I dated that voice for two years.

I turn in my chair to see Connor smoking a cigarette in a darkened corner. I always thought it was a nasty habit, and I warned him about the health implications over and over, but Connor is stubborn and stuck in his ways.

"Why are you sitting there?"

"Just taking a little smoke break," he says, blowing smoke rings into the air like I'm going to be impressed with that. "Fancy meeting you here."

"Yeah, totally coincidental," I say, deadpan.

He stands up and walks closer, sitting down in the chair opposite me. I never thought I'd have to look at this man's face again, and I have to say I was okay with that.

"So, were you surprised to see me?" He grins like he's enjoying this immensely.

"Sure. Kind of like the way I'd be surprised if a bag of dog poo landed right here next to me."

His smile fades. "I didn't know you'd be here, either. Trust me."

Connor used to be so nice. When we first met, he wooed me like nobody had been wooed before. That lasted about six months before I could see cracks. I could look past much of it except for how he interacted with Sadie.

He was often rude. Mean, even. We were constantly at odds over it. He didn't want her around. He wanted more time with me alone. He wanted her to move out of my apartment. On and on it went until I couldn't take it anymore.

Sadie offered to leave. She wanted to see me happy, but I explained to her right before I broke up with him that being with Connor was not the version of happiness I wanted.

So I dumped him. Connor is attractive, and I don't think anyone had ever broken up with him before. He was not happy about it.

But now he looks like the cat that ate the canary, and I can't figure it out.

"I have a hard time believing you didn't know I'd be here," I say. The camera guy behind Connor shakes his head. Apparently, I'm treading on thin ice again, talking about production stuff.

"Believe what you want, Red," he says, standing up and putting his cigarette out on the ground. I guess he figures all the little people on set can clean up behind him.

"Don't call me that, Connor. You know I hate that nickname."

He smiles. "Yes, I know."

RHETT

The news that Connor is Savannah's ex was shocking. The guy really seems like a jerk, and I don't care for jerks. Sure, I may sometimes come off as one myself, and maybe that's why I recognize it in Connor. I don't like him and plan to get him out of this competition as soon as possible.

I walk back to my room, pondering their relationship in my mind. What else do I have to do but think right now?

Why would Savannah even date a guy like that? She always seemed so "sunny" and bright. He seems annoying and irritating. I'll never understand women and the choices they make sometimes.

I'm not a huge fan of overly happy people, but I can admire that trait in them. How they go through life with all its ups and downs and still come out smiling every day is beyond me.

Of course, Savannah annoyed me greatly in pastry chef school. She was always so positive. Seemed to want to be a teacher's pet. Always answering questions before anyone else. Raising her hand like we were in grade school. I never raised my hand. I just answered the question like a grownup. She'd give me a glare when I answered before she could. I found it funny and made it a bit of a game to pass the time when I was bored.

If something fell apart, she shrugged her shoulders and said oh well. She started over and didn't complain. I never saw her raise her voice or even get flustered. She just kept going with a smile on her face,

See? Annoying.

Okay, okay. Most people might find some of that endearing, I guess.

"Come on, man! Didn't you hear the intercom?" Nate stands before me, waving his hands like he's landing a plane. Apparently, I was so lost in thought that I missed something.

"What?"

"It's dinner time!" Nate darts out the door like he hasn't eaten in years. I'm hungry, but there's no need to get all excited about it.

I walk down the curved staircase, which makes me feel like I'm in a scene from Gone With The Wind. Yes, the irony of my name isn't lost on me.

It's weird to be in a house with a bunch of people I don't know. Of course, I'm normally on boats with people I don't know, but at least I know my crewmates. I know the people I work with each day. When I look at these people, they're all strangers. Well, except for Savannah.

I don't see her around. Maybe she quit when she realized she was going to be stuck here with me and her loser ex-boyfriend.

"Everyone gather around!" Our host, Dan, is standing at the door to some room I couldn't get into earlier. He's so over the top on the hosting thing that I kind of want to smack him. His teeth are even too much. His dentist really did him a disservice with those things.

"Are we ever going to eat?" someone says loudly, but I can't see who.

"That's what I want to talk about. First, I hope everyone is adjusting to the house and your new rooms. This is the last time you'll see me until your first challenge." Someone cheers, but again, I can't see who it is. "Thanks a lot," he says, flashing a fake smile toward the camera. "Anyway, we know you're hungry, and it's almost dinner time, so behind this door, we've had a whole meal catered by the area's best chefs!"

The small, sad crowd cheers. Well, I don't.

"From now on, you're responsible for your own meals. You'll find a fully stocked pantry and refrigerator. Our helpers will come in while you're at competitions and refill things daily. You will also be called in for confessionals occasionally, so if you hear your name called, please go to the room over there with the red door." He points down a side hallway. This house is huge and has the weirdest layout I've ever seen.

"Keep your mics on. You are being filmed at all times, except when you're in the restroom. Aside from that, assume America can see and hear you. You'll have access to the communal kitchen and dining room behind this door tonight. During competitions, we'll use our state-of-the-art industrial kitchen with multiple stations, which has been built behind the house as a separate structure."

*I. WANT. TO. EAT.*

"Finally, remember that America is watching. They get a vote, too." He winks as if that's a secret code we're all supposed to get, and then he opens the kitchen door. Everyone runs in like a herd of buffalo. Haven't these people seen food before?

As usual, I'm the last one in, and the only seat left is across from Savannah. She's sitting beside Maggie, chatting away and laughing. She does have a nice smile. I didn't remember that. During school, she just irritated me. I'm sure she'll do it again as soon as the competition starts tomorrow, but I can appreciate her for tonight.

"Greene," I say, sitting down across from her and putting a white cloth napkin in my lap.

"Don't call me that," she says through gritted teeth, a smile still on her face. See, I know she's got a temper under all that positivity, and I'd love to see it. I've always wondered what it would take.

"Fine. I'll call you Sunny then."

She reaches over to take a yeast roll from a basket between us. "Why would you call me that?"

"Because you're always smiling, and it's annoying."

She smiles even bigger. "It's only annoying to grumpy people."

I shrug my shoulders. "I don't think so, but whatever you say."

"Do you two know each other?" Tanya asks. She's the single mom with the catering business, I think. I try to remember everyone. You should always know your competition.

Savannah rolls her eyes. "Unfortunately. We went to pastry chef school together."

"Oh, so he's the jerk you couldn't stand in school? That makes sense," Connor interjects from the end of the table where he's seated himself like he's the king of our group. I'll be setting him straight on that soon.

"You called me a jerk?" I ask, smiling.

She smiles back. "Oh, I called you way worse than that. Trust me."

I can't help myself. I'm enjoying this barbing back and forth. Maybe I'm just tired, but I find it entertaining.

We continue eating the subpar lasagna they've served us as everyone chats amongst themselves. I stay as quiet as possible, opting to listen in to their conversations. People have no idea what they reveal when their defenses are down.

For instance, Leo said his biggest challenge is being timed. It makes him nervous. I can use that information in challenges by trying to divert his attention. Is it mean? Maybe. Will it help me win? For sure.

When dinner is over, we all head back upstairs to our rooms. Dan said our first challenge is tomorrow at lunchtime, so we all need to rest up. I'm not nervous; I'm looking forward to it. Tomorrow is day one of the rest of my life.

SAVANNAH

I lay in bed for hours, staring at the ceiling, watching the live oak trees dance in the moonlight on the ceiling above me. I have learned a few things since coming to *The Baking Games* just a few hours ago.

One is that Lainey Loudermilk is one of the most annoying people on the planet. She has an entire bedtime routine that takes over two hours. She was constantly plucking, tweezing, and scrubbing her face and had some sort of contraption she put on her head to ensure her hair didn't fall during the night. It was a very strange thing to see such a young person do. I try not to engage with her, fearing that I might sock her right in the nose. That's not my personality. I'm a happy, positive person. I get along with just about everybody. Well, except for three of the people who are currently in this house with me.

I also noticed that Maggie, the sixty-five-year-old widow on the other side of the room, snores quite loudly. I like her. She seems very nice. I think we're going to be friends. But her snoring is keeping me awake already, and I can't imagine how I will handle this for several more weeks.

Well, if I'm lucky. If I stay in the competition. It's something I'm trying not to think about. You can get very psyched out coming into a house full of people who are just as qualified as you are, if not more. And then when you're stuck in there with your horrible ex-boyfriend and your rival from school, well, let's just say this isn't the most comfortable spot I've ever been in.

Unable to sleep, I get up, slip on my fluffy cat slippers, and decide to walk down to the kitchen. I put on my robe beforehand because I don't need anybody seeing me in my short little nightgown. I can't sleep with a lot of clothes on, but I would never sleep naked. After all, what would happen if the place caught on fire? I'd have to run right out into a street full of people I barely know, wearing nothing but my birthday suit. No, thank you.

I'm proud of my body. It's a good one. It's keeping me alive and everything, but it's definitely not super-model status. I don't need to show this thing off on the street outside the house, so I wear the least little bit I can, which is my short little nightgown with puppies and kittens on it. It looks like something a third-grader would wear.

There are two kitchens in this house. The

kitchen that we ate dinner in is the communal kitchen. It's much like a regular kitchen would be in a house and probably came with this one when it was built years ago. It has been remodeled to make it bigger and more functional. Then there's the industrial kitchen, which we haven't seen yet. From how it was described, it has multiple stations so that everybody has their own workspace with all their own equipment.

I'm looking forward to getting in there. I love working in an industrial kitchen, but the one at the grocery store where I work isn't exactly that. Half the time, the oven doesn't work, and Big Thelma smacks it with her size ten shoe to get it going.

Yeah. I've really been living the dream.

I had anticipated when I got out of pastry chef school that I would go to work at some fancy restaurant, get all the experience I needed, and then open a chain of bakeries. I never imagined that I would find myself getting up at the crack of dawn to go make cupcakes for some little girl's birthday party while being under the tutelage of Big Thelma. It's not exactly the dream I had for myself when I was working all those nights in pastry chef school.

I'm slightly hungry because of the terrible lasagna they fed us for dinner. I don't know who made that, but they obviously had not attended a quality culinary school. It tasted like somebody who had just learned what lasagna was earlier in the afternoon made it.

I go into the communal kitchen and am surprised to see no one there. Maybe I'm the lone night owl in the house. Of course, I'm being closely followed by my cameraman, Vinny. He doesn't say much, but he's always on me like a duck on a June bug, as my grandma used to say. Dan told us that sometimes we'd just be filmed by the stationary cameras, and other times the cameramen would follow us. So far, I haven't seen any camera women.

The thing about the cameras is we aren't allowed to talk directly to them unless they ask us a question. We're supposed to pretend they aren't there. That's impossible to do so far. Having someone tail you wherever you go is much weirder than I thought it would be. Maybe I'll get used to it eventually, but I highly doubt it. Still, I'd rather be here in this house with my rival and my ex than at the bakery tomorrow with Big Thelma and her huge oven-whacking shoes.

I look around the kitchen for any kind of snack. There's a pantry area that appears to be locked. No idea why, and I can't ask anybody because we can't talk to producers unless we want to leave the competition. They said we'd have a fully stocked pantry, but what good is that if they lock it after hours? Some of us like to eat in the wee hours of the morning to cover up our emotions, thank you very much.

From what I understand, we'll start doing something called "confessionals" tomorrow. They'll take some of us, one by one, into a little soundproof room and ask us questions about how things are going.

So, I'm on my own in my efforts to find food. I feel like a raccoon searching the local dumpster behind the gas station. I open each cabinet and the refrigerator, but the pickings are slim. Then I see what I think is the edge of a bag of chips peeking out of one of the upper cabinets in the corner of the kitchen.

I can hear them singing to me, calling my name, ushering me to them. I walk over and stand on my tippy toes, trying in vain to get my hand to even come close to the red bag, but no such luck. I'm not a tall person. I decide the best course of action is to climb up onto the counter and get onto my knees. Vinny doesn't seem like he's planning to stop me. I assume he'd watch me fall to my death off the roof if it made for good ratings.

First, I have to reach the counter. I find a small, foldable stepstool wedged between the refrigerator and the cabinets, so I slide it out and unfold it. I glance at Vinny, who isn't making eye contact and probably hopes to get the day's best footage of a small red-haired woman falling from the counter and splitting her head in two.

I step up onto the stool and then raise one knee to the counter, followed by the other knee, all while holding onto one of the cabinet pulls. Those chips are within my grasp! I can already taste their salty goodness on my tongue.

I carefully maintain my grip on the knob and pull myself up to a standing position on the countertop. Don't worry, I'm wearing socks. And I will wipe the counter with a disinfectant after I get my prize. I'm not an animal.

I open the cabinet, and that's when the devastation starts. It's not a bag of chips. It's a bag of those little square cheese crackers, which I hate. I think they taste like feet.

"Ugh," I groan, closing the cabinet and starting to make my way back down. But God, or the Universe, or perhaps even the devil himself, has other plans. I feel it happening in slow motion. Socks are not the thing you wear on a slippery granite countertop. It seems very logical now that I think about it, just before my imminent death.

I'm petite. Short, actually. Short people shouldn't

be high up. We have to fall further. It's just science, I think.

First, one foot slips from under me, and then the other foot is like, *Oh, cool, we're gonna kill her today.*

I fall, seemingly hanging in mid-air, going backward straight for the original hardwood floors that stretch around the huge house. Wonder how hard they really are. I'm about to find out.

But then I don't find out. Someone catches me. Someone large and strong and warm. Someone who smells like my favorite men's cologne from high school.

I land with a thud in these foreign arms, the breath knocked out of me for a second, and that's when I finally look up.

Rhett.

He's looking at me, and I'm looking at him, and it feels like time has stopped. Where did he come from? How did he catch me so quickly?

I glance and notice Vinny coming in for a closer shot. Thanks for the help, Vinny.

No words are exchanged as Rhett slowly lowers me to the ground. He sets me down and backs up, leaning against the island, crossing his gigantic arms.

He's wearing a white t-shirt and baggy sweatpants that hug him in all the right places. This wasn't the Rhett I saw in school. That guy dressed like he was going to the stock exchange afterward but with a white apron on.

"Thank you," I croak out as he continues staring at me.

"What in the world were you trying to do?" His tone is accusatory.

"I thought that was a bag of chips."

"So you decided to kill yourself for it? Wearing fuzzy socks?"

I look down at my feet. "I didn't say it was a *good* idea."

"And was it chips?"

"No. It was nasty cheese crackers," I say with a sigh. Why do I feel like I'm being scolded by my large older brother?

"Why didn't you just ask somebody?"

I laugh. "Who? Everyone is asleep."

"Me."

"As far as I knew, you were asleep. And we're not exactly friends, Rhett. It's not like I'd come to you for my potato chip needs." I walk around him and look in more cabinets, like someone with a tapeworm needing a snack.

"Well, I'll let you get on with your chip search," he says, walking toward the back patio. For some inexplicable reason, I follow, grabbing an apple from the fruit bowl. It's not what I want, but it'll do for now.

"Hey, thanks again for catching me."

He waves a hand behind his head. "No problem."

I follow him until we're outside in the large courtyard they've created for the show. There's a hot tub, hammocks, a grassy area, and some outdoor sofas. There are foosball and pool tables on a covered patio area. He walks to the grassy area and pulls one foot behind his very nice rear end, stretching his quad.

"What are you doing up, anyway?" I ask, taking a bite of the apple.

"Running."

"Running? At this hour? We have our first competition tomorrow. Why aren't you sleeping?"

He drops his leg and turns to me, his dark eyebrow quirked up above his pale blue eyes. "Why aren't *you* sleeping, Sunny?"

I forgot he'd given me a nickname. I choose not to engage with him about it. It's not a bad nickname. He thinks it's a putdown. I think it's a compliment.

"As I said, I was hungry."

He turns to stretch the other leg. "I didn't peg you as a junk food eater."

"I didn't peg you as a midnight runner."

He chuckles. "I think it's closer to one now, actually."

"You still didn't explain why you're running this late the night before our first competition."

"I didn't know I owed you an explanation," he says dryly before he jogs away. Now I remember why I don't like this guy. He's rude and sarcastic. He's competitive. I can't trust him no matter what. Well, unless it's to catch me.

# CHAPTER 7

MORNING CONFESSIONAL

*Producer: So, tell us what happened in the communal kitchen last night.*

*Rhett, sighing: Is this really interesting TV?*

*Producer: Our viewers are going to be curious as to how you ended up with fellow contestant Savannah in your arms.*

*Rhett: Are they? Okay, fine. I think this is going to be a letdown, though.*

*Producer: What happened?*

*Rhett: I was walking to the courtyard when I saw her standing on the kitchen counter in her sock feet. First off, gross. Who does that? But still, I thought it unchivalrous of me to let her die of a head injury before the competition even started. So, I waited and watched for a few seconds before, sure enough, she toppled over backward and was falling to the floor.*

*Producer: And you caught her?*

*Rhett, rolling his eyes: Yes. You saw me, right?*

*Producer: So, Rhett, is there something there? Do you think you might start a relationship with Savannah?*

*Rhett, pausing for a moment: I don't do relationships.*

## SAVANNAH

I think I might throw up. That should go over well during a baking competition. Nothing says a "yummy dessert on the way" like a woman retching into a trashcan nearby.

We're being taken to the industrial kitchen where most of the competitions will take place. I can feel the nervousness in the air. Or at least that's the energy I feel. I have anxiety. Pretty bad anxiety, actually. I hide it well behind my smile, which is probably why I seem like the most positive person most people know.

As I step into the kitchen, I'm stunned. This place is huge!

The early morning sunlight floods through these

huge skylights in the ceiling, casting a striking glow across the gleaming stainless steel surrounding us. Everything is polished and shiny like a brand-new penny. Well, if pennies were silver.

I can't believe how big this place is. It's so sprawling and industrial. It looks like a high-tech culinary arena, and it's way better than any kitchen I've ever been in or worked in. Certainly better than the one in the grocery store where we can hardly get the microwave or the oven to work, and don't even get me started on the toaster.

Every station is a testament to modern baking, equipped with the latest in culinary technology. Brand-new mixers gleam like new cars on the show-room floor. Ovens are already humming softly in the background, just waiting for us to put something inside them. Rows of brand-new utensils are lined up with military precision at each station. I take in the grandeur of it all, the way the studio lights hang like distant stars above each station.

There are cameras mounted on silent tracks around the room. I assume they can move and capture any angle of us as we create drama for the television viewers. I can tell that the other contestants around me are either nervous like I am or are completely confident in their ability to send the rest of us home. There are murmured conversations that

I can't make out because I'm too focused on this kitchen's beauty.

A few seconds later, Dan walks into the room with his wide grin and confident stride. He stands in the center of the kitchen and looks into the camera. I swear his teeth are a shade too white, and he has that demeanor of a ringmaster who is ready to show the audience the greatest spectacle of their lives.

"Welcome, bakers, to your very first challenge on *The Baking Games*," he announces, his excited voice echoing through the space. His clear and commanding voice seems to fill every corner of the kitchen. "Now today, not only are you starting your journey toward that big grand prize package, but you will also start to prove to yourselves and the world that you have the capability to be a top pastry chef."

My heart is racing in my chest. There's a mixture of anxiety and excitement, but mostly anxiety. I start to second-guess myself. How did I even get here? Why did I even think I was worthy of doing something like this? Maybe I should quit right now before I embarrass myself on national television.

Before I can think too hard, everybody around me starts clapping, so I just clap along, not knowing what we're clapping about. My hands are just mechanically coming together over and over, while inside, there's a storm of anxiety raging. *"Imposter,"* it tells me. *"You're way out of your league."*

But Dan's voice cuts through my spiraling thoughts as he introduces our judges. There's Chef Alain Laurent, whose stern gaze and imposing presence are very well-known in the world of baking. He has uncompromising standards and makes the most innovative desserts I've ever seen.

Next to him is Tessa Brighton. She's an entrepreneurial powerhouse who owns a chain of trendy cake pop stores, which have made her super-famous online. From what I hear, people stand in line for hours just to get her cake pops, which she makes in all kinds of crazy combinations and decorations.

Marco Santini completes the trio. He's a dessert influencer and globetrotter who goes on adventures around the world and makes viral videos showing various restaurants and bakeries he finds along the way. He has put many small-town bakeries on the map.

"These titans of the culinary world will be your judges," Dan says, sweeping his hand toward them with a flourish. "Their expertise is unparalleled, and they will expect nothing less from you than perfection."

Again, I hear murmurs of awe - and maybe

anxiety - sweeping across my fellow contestants as the reality of all our challenges settles in. Not only will we be judged by these three people, but also by the audience who will expect an interesting show. For the first time, I realize that this isn't just about baking but also about being entertaining. And I don't find myself to be all that entertaining. I wonder why they chose me for this.

"Your challenge, should you choose to accept it," he says, winking at the camera, "is to create one dozen unique chocolate truffles. Each one should be a masterpiece of flavor and a spectacle of design. Now, this is your reward challenge, and it will include your skills as a chocolatier and your ability to dazzle and charm the audience with elegance and sophistication. These dozen truffles will be no ordinary truffles. They must be fit for the most glamorous black-tie event."

He pauses for dramatic effect, letting the weight of the challenge sink into each contestant, and then turns back to us with a mix of mischief and encouragement. "Each truffle should be the perfect blend of flavor, texture, and visual appeal. I want you to think that you're making these for clientele at a high-end gala, mingling under chandeliers, everyone wearing evening gowns and sharp tuxedos. Your creations need to compliment a gathering such as that."

He gestures to a display table laden with exotic ingredients, luxurious flavorings, and various decorative elements. "You have at your disposal ingredients that range from the finest Belgian chocolate to rare spices and edible gold leaf. Your truffles should not only taste exquisite but look that way, too. You will have just two hours to complete this task. That clock will be relentless, so use all of your creativity and precision."

A large screen in the corner of the space suddenly lights up, displaying a countdown clock set to two hours. Its red digits are stark against the bright backdrop. I can feel the tension ratcheting up a notch.

"The winner of this challenge," Dan says, his voice rising with excitement, "will get an invaluable advantage at this week's main challenge. You'll get thirty extra minutes, which could very well be the difference between victory and defeat. Although no one goes home during the reward challenge, someone will go home at the main challenge, so these extra minutes are critical."

He points to where each of our stations are. I look at my station quickly, the array of tools and ingredients laid out like an artist's palette, and despite the turmoil inside of me, I suddenly feel a spark of determination. I know how to do this. I'm trained. I *can* do this. I have to. It's for Sadie.

Dan's next words snap back my focus. "Bakers, please take your positions." He holds his arm up in the air like he's standing on a racetrack, about to tell the cars to take off.

I move to the edge of my station. My heart is pounding in sync with the ticking clock. As I reach for my first ingredient, I realize this will be a real challenge.

"Let the games begin," he suddenly yells and slams his hand down on the corner of one of the stations as the timer starts up above.

I steel myself, ready to transform my fears into something sweet. I'm not just going to survive the competition; I will prove to myself and everyone else that I belong here among the best of the best.

RHETT

After the initial shock of how giant this kitchen is, I go to work on planning my truffles. As I do with every project, I start to sketch it out in a notebook that I always keep with me. I simply cannot make any food item without drawing it first. Call it some kind of a quirk or whatever you want, but it works for me. I draft them much like an architect drafts blueprints.

When the challenge starts, I spend the initial few moments sketching my designs and planning each detail because I want to win. I need to win. Maybe it's ego, but I need this like I need blood in my veins.

My concept is inspired by the architectural elements of Art Deco. It's known for its rich colors, bold geometry, and decadent details, which will go well with these truffles. I want each of them to represent an Art Deco design.

They will be tiny edible sculptures. Some will be sleek and geometric to match the streamlined shapes of 1920s architecture, and then a few of them I will embellish with lavish ornamentations from the table, creating characteristics of the era, such as fans or chevron patterns. For my geometric truffles, I decide to incorporate a marbled effect, using dark chocolate and white chocolate to create sharp, contrasting lines.

After sketching, I get to work. I want these to be ornate and luxurious—the perfect dessert item for a black-tie affair. I might even use some of the gold dust and edible glitter from the table. They've given us a lot to choose from, which is nice. I don't always have these sorts of things at my beck and call out on the open ocean.

But just as I'm starting to focus on the delicate task of creating these truffles, with my hands working almost independently without my input, I notice something. Savannah is at the station next to mine, and I can't help but watch her. She's always been interesting to watch, even in school, the way that her fingers are so deft in the way that they mold the chocolate.

She's petite, which is to say short, but she has long, slender fingers that are hypnotizing if you look too long. I can tell she's putting her heart into this challenge. I don't know much about her background. We haven't had long, deep talks about our hopes, dreams, and families, and I definitely don't want to.

But what's catching my attention is Connor, her ex-boyfriend, who is staring at her from across the room. His workspace is directly across from hers, and he's craning his neck as he watches her. He's pretending to look for his ingredients, but I can see what he's doing. His presence is like a dark cloud in this bright kitchen.

There's something about the way that he watches her that sets off my alarm bells. It's not just a casual observation; there's some kind of intensity there, suggesting that maybe he's not just watching her, but he's assessing her, planning something. I shake my head, trying to refocus myself. Why should I care if Connor has ideas about sabotaging Savannah? It is a competition, after all. Every contestant for themselves. If she gets tripped up by whatever he does, that's just one less baker I have to worry about in the race for the prize.

As I temper another batch of chocolate, I find myself looking back over at Savannah. She's deep into her work, not looking at anyone else. There's such an earnestness about her efforts that commands respect, no matter who she is. I can't help but admire it. Again, why do I care? We're competitors; we're supposed to be rivals. We hated each other in pastry chef school, and we've barely exchanged more than a few words, except for when I caught her falling off the kitchen counter last night.

But I don't like the thought of Connor playing dirty; it doesn't sit well with me. I don't like bullies. I might seem like a bully to some people, but I'm not. I'm just pointed, direct, and honest, but I don't bully others. And if Connor tried to sabotage or bully his ex-girlfriend, he would do anything to anyone in this competition.

I try to shake off the uneasy feeling and bury it under my work, but the discomfort lingers whenever I see Connor looking her way. It's more than just competitive spirit or some kind of fair play. He's watching her in a way that tells me he's planning something.

I force myself to turn my back and perfect my truffles. I am going to stay here. I want to win this round. But I also feel this unsettling realization that maybe I don't want her to fail completely, at least not at Connor's hands. It is a competition, and I'm ready to win at any cost, but not if it means that I'm watching someone like Savannah get sabotaged by an ex-boyfriend who's a complete jerk. Even if I don't particularly like or understand her, I like him even less.

As the clock is ticking down, I set my last truffle on the tray and take one final glance at Savannah. She's finishing up. I can't tell what she did with her truffles, but she looks proud of herself. I can see her smiling. I turn and see Connor looking at her again, and this time, I force myself to make eye contact, lowering my eyebrows, a warning look on my face. He scoffs and turns around, returning to his work as if he did nothing, but we both know he's up to no good.

## SAVANNAH

As I stand at my station, I wipe my hands on a towel and feel my heart racing in my chest. I have a mixture of nervous anticipation and dread. We just finished the reward challenge, so there's nothing else I can do but stand here and wait to be judged. It wasn't until now that I realized I don't like to be judged, but here I am anyway.

The judges—Chef Alain, Tessa, and Marco— begin their rounds. They start with Connor's sleek, modern truffles. I can see them on the big screen in the corner of the room. His creations are displayed in high definition. Each truffle has a perfect glossy shine to it. They look like something out of a gourmet magazine. A knot tightens in my stomach.

For so long, I thought I was in love with Connor, but he has turned into a very negative, spiteful man. He glares at me momentarily as the judges walk to his station. I can't hear what they're saying, but he's smiling like a Cheshire cat, so apparently it's good.

I don't know why he has such a terrible attitude toward me. Yes, I broke up with him, but it was he who didn't want my sister around. Maybe we could have had a strong relationship, but not if he wouldn't accept my sister in our lives regularly.

Finally, they turn up the volume so we can hear

what the judges say at each station. Chef Tessa critiques Connor's flavor balance, which gives me some comfort and reminds me that appearance isn't everything.

Next, they move over to Rhett's station. His truffles are a stark contrast to Connor's. They're intricate and ornate, meticulous and creative. They're based on an Art Deco architecture theme, which I think is incredibly creative. As much as I couldn't stand him in culinary school, I still have to appreciate his talent.

I can see his sketchbook sitting on his countertop, and I crane my head a bit, trying to see what it is, but I can't see much. He always carried it with him in school, but he kept it very close to him so no one could ever see what he was writing or drawing.

Each one of his truffles is a tiny masterpiece of marbled chocolate and gold dust. I can feel his confidence even from here. I wish I had some of it.

Chef Alain praises Rhett's craftsmanship, but he mentions there's an overpowering amount of gold dust on the truffles. I breathe in a small sigh of relief. Even the best have their flaws, I guess.

Then it's my turn. My cheeks warm. It's one of those things that being a redhead does to you. I know my face must be very crimson-colored right now, but there's nothing I can do about it. The screen changes to my truffles. I have showcased different seasons in all of them.

A few are summer-themed with bright pink and green coloring. Others are fall-themed with intricate leaves painted on them and gold dust. The spring-themed ones have tiny flowers painted on them, and winter is dark and spattered with white edible dust like snow.

I'm proud of them, but seeing them next to Rhett and Connor's makes me feel like they might be too simplistic or childish. Perhaps I didn't realize just how talented the people around me are.

Marco compliments the concept, but he critiques my summer truffle and says it has too much thyme, making my stomach knot. I knew I should have been more restrained with it. Less is more when it comes to using herbs in baked goods.

Then Chef Alain looks at them, and my heart sinks when I see the expression on his face. "These are for a black-tie event?"

"Yes, sir. I was trying to think a bit outside of the box."

He stares at me for a long moment. "Sometimes, the box is the right place to be, my dear." And then they all walk away. I want to melt into a puddle.

As they move on to Lainey, I try to gather the little bit of confidence I have left. Her truffles are the epitome of luxury. They're covered in gold leaf and laced with exotic flavors. They even sparkle under the camera and look extravagant.

Tessa's feedback, however, highlights that Lainey's might be stylish, but the substance is not good. The combination of an odd truffle oil in a sweet setting doesn't go over well with her.

Finally, they reach Sophia, who has created Paris-themed truffles that steal the show. Everybody in the room immediately realizes that she will win this thing. Each one is a delicate balance of aesthetics and flavor, capturing the essence of Parisian charm.

Chef Alain smiles as he tries one of them. A few moments later, she is declared the winner of the round, and my heart deflates a little.

I stand there with a fake smile on my face, knowing that Sophia's victory is actually well-deserved, but it stirs a resolve in me. If I'm going to be here, away from my job and my sister, I'm determined to learn, improve, and gain more confidence. I want to win this thing.

Dan reminds us that the main challenge will be in a few days but that we will have some things to do between now and then. He doesn't tell us what they are.

I wipe down my station, still trying to shake off the feelings of inferiority.

"Focus, Savannah," I whisper to myself. "It's not over."

I feel the room buzzing around me. That's what anxiety will do. But for now, I need to be happy for Sophia and double down on the fact that I have to figure out how to become one of the best and win the prize at the end. It's all for my sister, and I just have to keep that in mind.

# CHAPTER 8

SAVANNAH

AFTER THE COMPETITION is finished and we all return
to the house, everyone gathers in the courtyard to
eat lunch. We aren't eating as one big group like we
had done before. Everybody is in their own areas
with their new friends, chatting and eating chicken
salad sandwiches that have been catered for us once
again. A big bowl of potato salad and pasta salad is
sitting on a long table in the corner. Of course, they
can't leave it out here long because it would get too
hot, so everybody scoops what they want onto their
plates and sits down.

My fellow contestants are chatting and laughing,
which is a stark contrast to the morning's competitive atmosphere. Of course, Sophia is still beaming

from her win. She was gracious and grateful when she accepted the round of congratulations that came her way. Her truffles really were beautiful. Watching her, I felt a mix of admiration, but it also kindled a fire in my own competitive spirit. I want to feel that rush of achievement, too.

I settle on the sofa outside next to Maggie, who is crunching on a potato chip when I sit down.

"You did well today, Savannah. I liked your idea of the seasons."

"Thank you," I say, my stomach tightening a little. "I wish the judges had liked it. I loved your little bow-tie truffles. Maybe it's just me, but it's hard not to feel outclassed here," I whisper.

Maggie laughs. "Imagine what it feels like to be sixty-five years old and a self-taught pastry chef. I'm sure everybody sees me as the easy one to beat. But, you know what? We're here to grow," she says, shrugging her shoulders.

That might be easy for her to say. Maggie has already lived most of her life. She doesn't have anyone to support but herself. She's not trying to start a new business or make a name for herself in the culinary world. She's just having fun and doing something she's always wanted to do. I'm doing this so Sadie and I can finally start our adult lives. So we can hopefully get a leg up in this crazy world.

"I suppose so. It's just hard because this competition is very important to me."

"Oh, I imagine it's important to all of us," Maggie says, smiling.

"I know you're right, and I'm glad to be here. A lot of people probably applied."

"It's just the first competition. Nothing to worry about if you didn't win. You did well, and that's all you can hope for."

"Why did you decide to come here, Maggie?" I ask, leaning back against the cushion and taking a bite of my sandwich.

"What, because I'm old?" she asks, laughing.

"No, I just meant..."

"Oh, it's okay. I was just messing with you. You know, when you get my age, and you've lost a spouse, and you're trying to figure out where your life is going, sometimes you do crazy things like apply for reality shows."

I smile. "So it was just a crazy thing you did on a whim?"

"I suppose you could say that. I'm a lot older than you, and sometimes people my age feel like their lives are over. Like they can't do anything else but sit around and wait to learn to knit, do crossword puzzles, or go to weekly bingo night."

I smile. "You don't strike me as somebody who will sit back and wait."

"No, I suppose I'm not. I want to squeeze every ounce of fun out of my life. After all, many people would've loved to make it to my age. I want to cherish every moment, even the cruddy ones. And I suppose I'd like to inspire women of my age to get up and do scary things. So why did you come here, Savannah?" She takes a long sip of her sweet tea and then puts it on the table beside her.

"I came here because I feel responsible for my sister."

"Your sister? How old is she?"

"She's twenty."

"I hope you don't mind me asking, but why do you feel responsible for an adult?"

"We didn't have the best upbringing. Our mother was sort of, well, it's hard to explain. But when she passed away, I became Sadie's guardian. She was just twelve years old then. I haven't been able to help her get the funds to go to college, so when this came along, I thought it was a good opportunity, and she encouraged me to do it."

"Ah, so you really do have a big reason to be here."

"Yes, I do," I say, looking down at my sandwich before taking another bite.

Maggie turns her head and looks over toward the pool table, where Connor and Lainey are outwardly flirting with each other. They're laughing loudly, a bit too loud and forced. Their body language is obviously flirtatious, and Connor keeps looking in my direction.

Maggie notices my gaze lingering and then raises an eyebrow. "What's the story there?" she asks, nodding toward Connor.

I hesitate, but then I think, why hold back? "Connor and I used to date pretty seriously. It ended just a few weeks ago. It wasn't the best breakup."

Her expression softens. "Ah, I see. And who broke up with whom?"

"I broke up with him. He was always bothered that my sister was around and that I was so focused on making her life better. He didn't like it, and so I had to break up with him."

"So, he's over there trying to show off with Lainey?"

"Yeah, it's complicated. He never really understood why I work as hard as I do and why I need to push myself to help my sister. He thought my dreams were just hobbies."

"Even though he's a pastry chef, too?"

I laugh. "Yes, it doesn't make a whole lot of sense, does it? He's never really loved doing this as much as I did. He wanted us to get married soon, and he wanted me to stay home and raise kids while he worked. I wanted to live out my dreams. I want kids one day, but I feel like a woman can do both, you know?"

"Well, I think you're doing exactly what you need to be doing. Don't you let anyone, Connor or anybody else, make you doubt your path. You're here for a reason, Savannah. You hold onto that."

For a moment, it feels like motherly advice. She pats my knee, which makes me ache for the type of mother Maggie probably would be. I never had that kind of mother, and I will always wish I did. I'm grateful to have made a friend in the first few days of this competition because something tells me that I will need it.

RHETT

Nothing will wake you from a dead sleep like hearing Dan's booming voice come over the speakers throughout the house. I'm sure I jumped two feet up off the bed early this morning when he said we needed to meet in the competition kitchen in an hour.

Then there are all of us running in and out of the

communal bathrooms, trying to get ready. He said that we wouldn't be officially cooking or doing any kind of challenge, so we could wear casual clothes. That meant my normal T-shirt, shorts, and athletic shoes. It's pretty much my uniform when I'm not dressed for my official duties.

I make it downstairs into the kitchen and see everybody else already standing there. Savannah looks like she's going out for a summer picnic, wearing a red sundress and white sandals. Her long, red hair cascades over her shoulders, and she put on red lipstick this morning. It's a little distracting, I have to say.

She's definitely the most attractive woman in the house, although she probably doesn't realize that. I'm sure she thinks it's Lainey, the one who looks like a Barbie doll—and not even a good Barbie doll—like some kind of off-brand Barbie doll that had too much plastic surgery and lip fillers.

"Contestants," Dan says in his loud voice yet again, startling me and probably getting me caught staring at Savannah, "today, we're going to be doing something as a community service, but not the bad kind that you get when you've had too many speeding tickets," he says, winking at the camera like he's funny. He's not funny, although he seems to think he is. He should keep his day job, whatever that is, probably a pharmacist or an insurance salesman or something like that, because he is definitely not a stand-up comedian after hours.

"You're going to break into teams of three and bake your favorite cookies. Really, go all out. We will be going on a little field trip to the local assisted living center later today, where you will deliver the cookies to the residents and then spend some time with them."

Spend time with people at the assisted living center? What kind of competition is this? I thought we would be cooking, perfecting our art, and showcasing our skills. I know we don't have our main challenge until later in the week, but is this the kind of thing we will be doing to fill the time? I was looking forward to just relaxing, playing pool, practicing, and doing some workshops. Now, I have to do community service like a criminal?

I look over at Savannah, who is smiling from ear to ear and talking with Maggie. The two of them seem to have gotten closer. Maggie is really the only person I ever see Savannah talking to. Then I glance over at Connor, who, of course, is watching Savannah and snickering with Lainey. It's like middle school. I don't know what this guy's problem is, but it's really starting to get on my nerves.

Again, I have to remind myself that this is a

competition. And what do I care if he's planning to sabotage Savannah somehow? That's just one less person I have to beat in the end. And I have no doubt that I will beat each and every one of these people. That's who I am. That's how I do things. I don't allow myself to fall into the bottom tier. I am at the top of what I do.

Sure, maybe I'm not getting recognized for it yet, and I'm not working at the job that I would like to work, but I know I have the skills. I know I can do this. And every one of these people will have to go home for that to happen, no matter how much I might grow to like some of them.

I don't make friends easily. I never have. I've always felt like I was competing with people, which makes for very difficult friendships. Sometimes I miss it, although I don't know that you can really miss something you've never had. But I do see other guys hanging around together, playing golf, hanging out at a bar, having a drink, and just talking about life. I've never really done that. I've always kept to myself, done my work, excelled at whatever it was I was doing, but I guess I just don't trust anybody enough to call them my friend.

I don't even know what it would be like to have a best friend, so I suppose I have missed that in my life. I guess when somebody doesn't have the approval of their own family, it makes it really hard to trust outsiders.

I don't want to think too hard today. These thoughts tend to take me down a dark path, so for now, I have to do what Dan says I have to do: choose two other partners to bake cookies together with like a bunch of ten-year-olds. Cookies—not even something hard. Cookies are the most basic thing a pastry chef should be able to make. If you can't make good cookies, you really should quit while you're, well… behind.

I suddenly see everybody scrambling and realize they're picking partners. I haven't really connected with anyone here yet. The only person I actually know is Savannah, and she hates me, so I'm at a loss for who I'm supposed to pick. Before I can think much further about it, I realize that Savannah and Maggie are standing alone in the center of the room while everybody else is already paired up.

Savannah glances over at me. I can tell that she wants to be my partner just about as much as she would want to hang out with a rabid raccoon this afternoon, but we don't have much choice, so I walk over and stand beside them without a word.

"I guess we're a group," I say without making eye contact.

Maggie chuckles. "I guess we are." She reminds

me of my grandmother, the one I used to bake with and who accepted me for who I am. "I suppose they think I'm too old to be any kind of a partner. Although I don't know why they wouldn't have picked you two. You did great in the reward challenge, Savannah."

"Thank you, Maggie," Savannah says, smiling and then looking away from me again. I can't stop glancing over at her dress. It hugs her petite form in all the right places. I'm attracted to her, but I think that's just because I'm a man. It's hard not to notice a beautiful woman, especially one who doesn't seem to know she's beautiful. We couldn't be any more different. She's all sunshine and rainbows, and I'm all, well, reality. That's what I am, just one big heaping dose of reality. It's probably why I'm not tons of fun at parties.

"Contestants, choose your station and go ahead and start talking about what kind of cookies you're going to make. You have ninety minutes to get your cookies ready. Make as many as you can. The assisted living home can definitely use them. Anything they don't use today will be frozen for use in the days and weeks to come. Remember, this is a service you're doing for the community, so try to think about the people that are going to eat these cookies and what would be appropriate."

We walk over to our station, and Maggie looks at us.

"I think he's saying don't do nuts."

"Don't do nuts?" Savannah asks.

"Well, as an older person, I can tell you that nuts can be challenging for older people; those with dentures, maybe people with allergies, digestive issues, swallowing problems."

"Okay, okay," I say, waving my hand. "We don't really need to go into everybody's medical history. No nuts. Remember, we're being timed."

Maggie turns and looks at me. "What crawled up your hind end today?"

"Excuse me?"

"You're a nice-looking young man. Don't be such a grouch," she says before turning back to the mixing bowl in front of her and gathering a whisk and a spoon from the other side of the counter.

Savannah looks over at me, a quirk of a smile. "Well, I guess she told you."

I nod. "I suppose she did."

## SAVANNAH

The whole kitchen is buzzing with activity, but at our station, we are having a small culinary debate between me and Rhett, of course. Maggie quietly observes as she preps our baking tools. The smell of sugar and flour floats through the air from each of the ovens while we stand here staring at each other, me with my hands on my hips.

"I really think that we should stick with chocolate chip cookies," I say, reaching for the large container of chocolate chips and holding them up as if Rhett doesn't know what they are. "They're a classic, beloved, and we can churn out a bunch of them really quickly."

He raises an eyebrow. "Savannah, 'beloved' doesn't have to mean boring. We're here to impress, not just participate. How about we make something a little more distinctive, like hazelnut-flavored white chocolate caramel cookies?"

I put my hands back on my hips again, tilting my head. "Rhett, this is not a competition. This is community service. We're supposed to be making these residents smile, not trying to overwhelm them with over-the-top flavors. They're not going to be judging us."

He scoffs, crossing his arms. "Everything is a

competition, and we're always being judged. If you're not cooking to impress, you're just standing around stirring."

"Well, that's a rather cynical way to look at baking for a good cause," I say. I scoop up a handful of chocolate chips and let them cascade from my fingers back into the container. "Besides, do you really think that we have time to fuss over your fancy cookies with caramel and whatever else it was that you said?" The corners of his mouth twitch, a telltale sign that he's holding back a smirk. I very rarely see a smile out of Rhett.

"I think you might just be scared of a little challenge, Sunny."

Maggie looks at me like she doesn't understand why he has suddenly started calling me by a different name.

"Oh, believe me, it's not a challenge," I say, leaning closer. "It's the chaos when you realize we've bitten off more than we can chew, literally and figuratively."

Before he can say anything else, Maggie steps between us, her voice slicing right through our banter. "Kids, we're baking cookies today, correct? Or is this going to go on for a few more hours?" She looks back and forth between us, a look that was a mix of exasperation and amusement.

Rhett and I exchange a glance. "You know what? Maggie's right," I say. "Let's just find a middle ground. How about we do a little bit of both? Make some chocolate chip cookies with caramel or hazelnut as a second flavor. That way, we can cater to all tastes."

Rhett sighs and nods. "Fine, but I'm making sure those hazelnut cookies are the star of the show."

"Right. And I'll make sure that the chocolate chip cookies remind everyone just how great simplicity can taste," I say, turning around.

Maggie laughs, shaking her head as she measures the flour. "You two remind me of an old married couple, always bickering but wouldn't know what to do without each other."

Rhett and I both exchange quick, embarrassed glances. We return to work without talking because what else is there to say?

# CHAPTER 9

RHETT

As the shuttle bus hums along down the road toward the assisted living home, I'm holding a giant bowl of cookies in my lap. They're a mixture of Savannah's chocolate chip cookies and my chocolate hazelnut cookies that I finally settled on after a while. The mingling scents are oddly comforting, giving me a little bit of a distraction from the competition. Looking out my window, my thoughts drift not to the competition, which is usually the thing at the forefront of my mind, but to the banter that I had with Savannah in the kitchen.

There's just something about her persistent optimism that's less grating when you work alongside her rather than against her. Maybe it's her competence showing through, or maybe it's just the fact that she's familiar to me, having known her from school. Either way, I find myself begrudgingly starting to respect her a bit more, even if I'm not ready to admit anything beyond that or call it a friendship.

The bus takes a corner, and the cookies shift slightly in their container. I adjust my hold, my thoughts temporarily focused on the task ahead. We will be delivering a bit of joy, which is an aspect of the competition that feels slightly refreshing. It makes me think of my grandmother, who was in assisted living in her later years. I hated that she was there, but at the time, I was in school and couldn't do much about it. My mother and father were way too busy to care for her, and instead of hiring someone with the vast amounts of money they have, they chose to put her in a nice, assisted living home, out of sight, out of mind for a lot of that time. It made me sad.

As I think about that, I overhear a snippet of conversation from where Connor sits two rows ahead. His voice is laced with sneer, and it cuts through the hum of the bus engine.

"You know, if Savannah thinks playing the sweet and simple baker will get her the win, then she's dumber than I thought. This isn't some charity bake sale." He's talking to Lainey, who is sitting next to him, and he's doing very little to keep his voice quiet. He's obviously trying to rattle Savannah while also playing up to the camera recording him. This guy wants to be "reality TV famous." I do not. I want to win the money and move on with my life.

My grip on the bowl tightens, and a hot flash of anger suddenly surges through me. It's one thing to compete, but it's another to belittle someone's efforts and intentions, especially someone who seems as genuine as Savannah. I hadn't realized until now just how low Connor could stoop or how much his words about Savannah would bother me.

Savannah is sitting just behind him and just in front of me. She shifts quietly. I can see her silhouette stiffening as she looks out the window. Are her eyes watering? She doesn't respond, or maybe she didn't hear. It doesn't matter. The fact that Connor would say such a thing so publicly suddenly stirs something protective in me. I've always been competitive. I've always believed in playing hard but fair, but Connor is underhanded. It's not just poor sportsmanship. It's downright disgraceful.

The bus pulls into the assisted living home's parking lot and I set the bowl aside to prepare to get off. The simple task of delivering these cookies has taken on a new weight. Today isn't just about bringing joy through baking but also about showing who we are, not just as bakers but as people.

Whatever my feelings about Savannah, she doesn't deserve Connor's words, and though I'm not about to start singing her praises, I do find myself hoping that she'll prove him wrong somehow in a spectacular way. Today, I'm just here to help deliver cookies. I'm not here to stand up for somebody else in the competition.

As I walk to the front to step off the bus, I notice that Connor is taking a moment to get out of his seat. I might have let my shoulder bump him rather hard, causing him to drop his container onto the floor. His cookies didn't scatter, but I sure hope his confidence did.

SAVANNAH

As we walk through the doors of the assisted living center, a wave of warmth greets us, not just from the people who work there but from the bright smiles of the residents lined up in the lobby.

Their excitement is palpable. Their eyes light up as we enter with our large containers of cookies. They seem so genuinely happy to see us. It makes me slightly sad because I wonder how many of these people never get visitors. How many of their families have just dropped them off here and barely come to see them? I'm sure there are some good families that are coming constantly to check on their relatives, but everyone knows that some of these people probably never get a visitor at all. I take it as a great responsibility today to make sure that I interact with as many of them as possible and bring positivity and light into their lives today.

The sweet aroma of the cookies probably precedes us, weaving its way through the room and drawing out some eager glances from some of the residents.

"Welcome!" A woman with silver hair and a name tag claps her hands together. Her voice is as cheerful as the colorful cardigan wrapped around her shoulders. "We have been looking forward to this all week. Our residents can't wait to get their hands on some of those sweet treats you're holding."

I step forward, balancing the bowl of cookies that I've taken from Rhett. "We are so excited to be here," I say. "And we hope the residents enjoy these as much as we enjoyed making them."

She smiles and takes the bowl of cookies from me before walking over to a table and opening them. Several other contestants take their bowls and trays of cookies and put them on the same table. They already have milk and coffee set up for anybody who wants to enjoy the cookies. And several of the residents make their way over there very quickly.

As I move among them, I watch them choose between the different types: chocolate chip, peanut butter, hazelnut, caramel, and colorful sprinkle cookies. There's just about everything you can think of.

I listen to their stories in snippets of conversation as I walk. One man, whose hands tremble slightly as he reaches for a cookie, tells me about his grandchildren and how he used to bake with them when they were little. He hasn't seen them in a while, he says. They live far away. I try not to well up with tears when I hear him and how sad he is that he hasn't seen them in so long.

Another resident is a petite little lady with sparkling blue eyes that still stand out among the well-earned wrinkles on her face. She regales me with tales of her youth in a small European village where she used to make pastries with her mother.

Each story adds a little thread to the rich tapestry of all the lives gathered in this room, and I feel immersed in sharing the cookies and these moments. I believe that good desserts can bring on good conversation. They draw people together in happiness.

Out of the corner of my eye, I catch Rhett watching me several times. His gaze is curious. Instead of his usual stoic demeanor, he seems a little softened by the interactions that are unfolding around him. He's not talking to anyone, of course. He's just quietly observing.

Maybe he's going to use it in the competition somehow. Who knows what that guy is up to? Having him observe me like this is an odd but not unpleasant feeling. Perhaps he's noticing a side of me he hasn't seen before. But what do I care? Inspired by a spark of spontaneity, I approach the activities coordinator who introduced herself to me earlier.

"Do you happen to have any nail polish?" I ask her. "I thought maybe it might be fun to offer some manicures while we're here."

Her face lights up. "Really? What a wonderful idea. The residents would love that. Let me bring you what we have."

Soon I settle at a small table with a rainbow array of nail polishes spread out before me. A line forms, mostly women, but a few men chuckle and join in the fun, requesting a clear polish or just enjoying the activity. To my surprise, Rhett approaches me with a bottle of pink polish in his hand.

"Need help?" he asks, and I can't help but laugh.

"Really? You would do this? I don't know whether to be amused or impressed."

He shrugs, a half-smile tugging at the corner of his normally straight mouth. "Why not? It might be good for my dexterity," he says, moving his fingers around.

I nod, and he walks over to a table nearby and takes a chair, pulling it up beside me to share the same small table. We handle two people at a time, and to my surprise, Rhett is pretty good at painting fingernails.

"What made you think of doing this, Sunny?"

I let him call me that at this point because it could be worse. When the guy you hated in school gives you a nickname, it could be something terrible. Sunny isn't so bad.

"When I was in the fifth grade, I volunteered at our local nursing home. I'll never forget the place. It was so sad and dreary and smelled of orange and lemon cleaning liquid. The people there looked left behind, you know? Like someone just dropped them off one day and never came back. Anyway, my teacher said she'd give us extra credit if we volunteered one day a week at that place. Most of the kids went once and then decided they didn't need extra credit that bad. I ended up going three days a week.

I'd eat with them, listen to their stories, and paint the ladies' nails. I guess I've always been way too sensitive and empathetic."

"I'm impressed," he says quietly.

"Why?"

"Most kids wouldn't give up their extra time to spend it with elderly strangers in a nursing home. I know I wouldn't have."

I laugh under my breath. "Well, if you knew how I was raised and what was happening at home, you would've wanted to escape, too," I say the words before I can think about them. Rhett doesn't need to know about my personal life. He'll somehow use it against me.

"I want *that* color!" the woman in front of Rhett suddenly says loudly, like she's purposely trying to get his attention. When he looks at her, she bats her lashes. I want to laugh but somehow keep myself from doing it.

"Yes, ma'am," he says, glancing at me and smiling. It's actually a very nice smile. He should do it more often.

"So, where did you get these skills?" I ask him as he paints the nails of a woman whose hair is pulled up into a tight white bun on top of her head. She looks like she could have been a ballerina in another life.

"I used to do this for my grandmother when she was in a place like this. I was just a teenager back then, but I was pretty good at it. I like to think it's one of the reasons why I'm so detailed in my work."

I smile and continue working on the woman in front of me. She has bright orange hair that is obviously dyed and is wearing some of the most obnoxiously loud jewelry I've ever seen. She's quite a character.

I start to notice that the women are lining up more in front of Rhett than in front of me. They seem to be coming from all around, and then I realize they've never seen such a tall and handsome man willing to paint the fingernails of the women at the assisted living home. Before I know it, he's handling everything, and I'm sitting back, relaxing.

"Aren't you going to do something?" he finally asks me as he tries to keep up with the long line.

I shrug my shoulders and laugh. "I *am* doing something. I'm watching you."

RHETT

I am delicately painting the nails of Mrs. Johnson, who seems to be one of the feistier residents here at the assisted living center. Suddenly, the sound of a microphone squealing breaks my concentration. I look up and see Connor strutting toward the karaoke machine that is set up in the corner, pulling a reluctant-looking Lainey behind him.

"All right, everybody, who's ready for a performance?" Connor yells into the microphone, holding his mouth too close to it, flashing one of his over-the-top cheesy-looking grins. A few of the residents perk up, but most of them seem happy snacking on cookies or watching Savannah and me work our manicure magic.

Most other contestants are sitting with residents, chatting or playing checkers and chess. Only Connor is trying to become the center of attention.

Savannah leans over to me. "You're not going to believe this," she mutters, with an amused shake of her head.

I stifle a laugh. She clearly knows what's coming.

The opening beats of *Shallow* from *A Star Is Born* blare out, and Connor immediately launches into one very exaggerated stage act, clutching his chest dramatically. Lainey joins in, or at least tries to, her voice grating and terribly off-key from the very beginning.

I honestly can't tell if Connor is trying to be

funny or if he really sings like that. I'm hoping it's the former.

They're making a mockery of the people that they're trying to entertain, which kind of annoys me, but it's hard to pay attention to that when you can't take your eyes off the train wreck right in front of you.

*"Tell me something..."* Connor warbles, missing every single note as he starts gesticulating wildly. I shake my head in disbelief at what I'm seeing. Savannah just smirks, as she continues applying the final coat of polish to Mrs. Palmer's bright-red fingernails.

"His singing could use some work, couldn't it?" I murmur to her.

"Oh, you have no idea," she confirms with a laugh. "You know we dated, and I had to endure way too many overly enthusiastic car sing-alongs from him."

I raise an eyebrow at her. "I guess I don't understand why you dated that idiot."

"I dated him for a whole two years until a few weeks ago."

"So what finally made you see the light and dump him?"

Then I notice something like a flicker of sadness

that crosses her face before her jaw sets in determination.

"He couldn't handle how close I am to my little sister, Sadie. We had a pretty terrible childhood and a neglectful mother, who passed away several years ago. So I got guardianship of Sadie when she was twelve, and I basically became her parent. She's twenty now, and Connor couldn't stand that I treat her like my own child instead of putting him first. I'm a protective big sister. I care about her more than anything else. She's all I have left. He didn't want that. He wanted it to just be him and me and one day our own family, but not with Sadie. I missed out on college because I couldn't afford it while I was taking care of her, and then she missed out on college because I couldn't afford it while I was just trying to keep us both afloat. So this competition is my big chance."

"Well, this Connor fella sounds like an idiot to me, dear," an older woman says. She's waiting for glittery nail polish. Savannah smiles at her graciously.

The singing continues in the background, and it's apparent that Connor couldn't carry a tune if it had two handles. I suddenly feel a surge of respect for Savannah's resilience and selflessness, and I admire her ability to put her younger sister first despite the obstacles she's faced.

I can't relate to it, of course. I've always had two parents with plenty of money and a very stable family structure. But she seems closer to her sister than I am to my entire family. Of course an egomaniac like Connor would be threatened by the unshakable loyalty to someone other than him.

Connor hits a particularly sour note, which shatters any charm he might've once had with the residents. An elderly man puts his fingers in his ears in protest, making Savannah and I laugh.

"Boy, he's really working hard to get those extra minutes of camera time in," I mutter, looking back at the hand in front of me.

Savannah smiles wryly. "Don't worry, this sideshow won't last long. His little tantrums were always short-lived, just like his talent."

That makes me laugh. Sure enough, after several more excruciating minutes, Connor finally runs out of breath from his failed attempt at hitting notes far too high, and his voice starts to crack and croak like a frog. He dramatically bows as Lainey gives a few awkward claps and follows along behind him. The karaoke machine is mercifully turned off, and I can't help but feel relieved that the painful audition is over. It's like he thought he was at a nightclub karaoke night instead of an assisted living home.

I look over at Savannah, who has refocused on the resident sitting in front of her, and Connor's pathetic bid for fame is left in the dust. For somebody who's already overcome so much, I wonder if her empathetic heart and sensitivity will let her go far in this competition.

For a fleeting moment, at least, the pressures of the competition have faded into the background. I suppose there are worse fates than getting momentarily upstaged by your rival's tone-deaf ex-boyfriend and his fame-hungry partner. Like realizing that you're actually starting to enjoy the company of the person you're supposed to be competing with.

SAVANNAH

The digital clock's bright red numbers feel like they're burning my retinas. It's after midnight. I sigh and roll onto my back, staring up at the ceiling. My mind just won't shut off. It's a whirlwind of thoughts, making sleep completely elusive to me.

Tomorrow is the main baking challenge.

Someone is going to get sent home. The pressure is mounting, and it's only the first week.

I also miss my sister so much—her smiling face, her stupid jokes, and just the comfort of having someone around who loves me. Not being able to call her or contact her at all while sequestered in this house is already taking its toll.

I can't help but feel guilty for abandoning the person I raised for this opportunity, even if it's just temporary. Even if she's the one who wanted me to go. But this is my chance, our chance. I have to tell myself that multiple times daily, and I'm still not sure I believe it.

Winning this competition would mean financial security and so many opportunities for both of us, but that doesn't make being apart from Sadie any easier right now.

I know I won't get any rest while my mind is whirling like this. I quietly slip out of my bed, pull on my swimsuit, and throw on my robe. Maybe a soak in the courtyard hot tub will help me clear my head before the long day of baking tomorrow. The house is silent as I tiptoe down the hallway and go through the doors into the courtyard area.

The warm night air blows across my skin as I make my way across the fake grass toward the hot tub. It's tucked over in the corner beside some potted palm trees and flowering hibiscus plants. To my relief, the area is completely deserted. Everyone is asleep, getting ready for tomorrow's activities. I will get some precious solitude to soak and hopefully clear my racing mind. I shrug off my robe, bend down to do a forward stretch, and then step into the hot tub, sinking into the steaming water with a contented sigh. I let the heat slowly unknot all my tense muscles, including my lower back, which has been bothering me since I fell off the kitchen counter into Rhett's arms.

I lean back and look up at the stars in the night sky. It's the only sense of the outside world that I have now. Our windows are all covered, and we can't leave the house without being chaperoned. We're completely sequestered like a bunch of prisoners, but we all signed up for this.

This quiet moment is just what I needed after the chaos of the week and the excitement of the nursing home visit. My mind goes back to the unexpected scene of me and Rhett sitting there, diligently painting the fingernails of elderly ladies. Most of them just wanted to see him up close, I think.

Who would've thought that the brooding ice man had such a gentle side? The tranquil silence is suddenly shattered by the sound of footsteps on the grass behind me. I turn with a startled look, my hand to my chest, when I see none other than Rhett himself appear. He's dressed for a run, wearing his sneakers and shorts but no shirt.

Dear Lord in heaven, he has a nice chest. I never considered what might be under that clean apron he wears in the kitchen.

I forgot this is something that he apparently likes to do regularly at night. So much for my solitude. Our eyes meet, and he looks at me with a half-smile, clearly as surprised to see me here as I am to see him.

RHETT

The digital alarm clock numbers had been mocking me for what seemed like hours. I couldn't stand to hear Connor talk in his sleep anymore. He laughed, flung his arms in the air, and occasionally snored. I don't know anybody who could sleep next to that man.

I don't get much sleep these days, anyway. I haven't slept more than four or five hours in a row in ages. My mind will never turn off. It's constantly strategizing, analyzing, and fixating on something.

With a frustrated sigh, I throw off the covers and

quickly put on my running gear, minus my shirt. The nighttime summer air is hot and humid. A late-night loop around the courtyard is my go-to solution for insomnia. Okay, not one loop, probably dozens of loops. I like to hear the rhythm of my feet pounding against the fake grass and let it drown out the endless stream of thoughts.

I lace up my shoes and quietly leave the room, going downstairs through the courtyard doors. It's a warm night, and it hits me as soon as I walk outside. I begin to stretch my calves in the corner of the courtyard area, and that's when I see her—Savannah. She's slowly making her way across the grass with a robe loosely tied around her slender figure. She must be having trouble sleeping, too. I halt mid-stretch because I can't stop my eyes from trailing over her as she unknots that robe and lets it slip off her shoulders. She bends over and stretches for some inexplicable reason, and I feel my cheeks flush.

In the dim moonlight, I can make out the curves of her petite body in a modest, pale blue bathing suit that somehow manages to be both insanely alluring and totally casual at the same time. I have to actively force my eyes away before they linger too long, cursing myself for even noticing her. Thankfully, she doesn't seem to see me as she settles into the steaming hot tub. I should just continue on my usual route, not make this awkward, but then her eyes suddenly look over and meet mine.

"Well, well, look who's up burning the midnight oil," she says, raising an eyebrow. "Don't you need your beauty sleep?"

I chuckle, crossing my arms in a feeble attempt to seem unbothered. "I think I'm already beautiful enough."

She lets out a low laugh, sliding further into the hot tub and sighing. "I'll keep my opinions to myself," she says. "Soaking in these steamy bubbles is such taxing work. Way worse than running around in a circle." I open my mouth to retort, but I can't think of anything to say. She finally speaks again. "In all seriousness, I can't sleep knowing the big competition is happening tomorrow."

"Trust me, I get it," I say. "My mind doesn't exactly hit the off switch these days."

"Well, if you want to stop pacing around like some kind of jungle cat and actually relax for once, you could join me," she points toward the hot tub.

Everything in me wants to take the invite, the alien desire to let my guard down, even if just for a moment, but my tough guy image and self-preservation win out. "Yeah, I think I'll pass on that," I say dismissively, trying to ignore how her damp red hair is curling adorably around her face.

"One of these days, Rhett Jennings, you're going to let your guard down and actually have a relaxing moment. I hope I'm there to see it."

"I appreciate the invite," I say dryly.

"Your loss, but I do appreciate you gracing me with your sparkling presence, even if just for these few moments."

"Don't mention it," I mutter, waving my hand.

I turn and start my laps around the courtyard. I can still feel her amused gaze following me as I run round and round. This is the first time I've ever felt like a complete idiot running in circles. She is so easily seeing through my prickly exterior, and I don't like it one bit. I might need to run a few extra laps just to work off the restlessness she has firmly planted under my skin.

# CHAPTER 10

SAVANNAH

WHEN I SLEEPILY MAKE MY way into the communal
kitchen, the smell of freshly brewed coffee and
sizzling butter fills the air. Despite it being very
early in the morning, the space is filled with activity
as my fellow contestants mill about making their
breakfasts before our big challenge day ahead.

I tie on one of my favorite vintage aprons that I
brought with little embroidered strawberries on it
and start gathering ingredients. Eggs, milk, flour—
the fixings for my favorite pancake recipe. I've made
it a million times for me and Sadie over the years.
Sometimes, I like to throw in extra things like blueberries or chocolate chips, but this morning, I think
I'll just make them plain and use some of the maple

syrup I saw earlier. As I whisk together the batter, my mind drifts off to Sadie like it does all the time these days.

I wonder what she's up to right now. Is she awake? Has she eaten breakfast? Did she make it to work on time? A pang of sadness twinges in my chest. We've never been apart for more than a couple of days in our entire lives. One week into this competition, and I already miss her sunny smile, her stupid jokes, and her giving me one of those trademark big bear hugs every morning when she meets me in the kitchen.

"Pancakes? Can I help?" I glance over to see Tanya giving me a warm smile as she also ties on an apron.

I haven't talked to her a lot yet, and she's not much older than me. Maybe she could be another friend to me in this competition. So far, it's just Maggie, and while I love talking to her, we're about thirty-five years apart in age, and it's a little bit hard to relate on some topics.

"Sure, I would enjoy having some help. I'm missing my sister right now. She normally helps me with pancakes."

"Oh, yeah. How old is she?"

"Twenty. But I've been her guardian since she was twelve." Tanya smiles slightly but doesn't ask any further questions. "You must miss your family, too," I say.

She lets out a sigh. "Terribly. It's always just been me and my kids. I'm a single mom. I've raised them on my own, and I'm doing all this for them. I'm thankful my brother and his wife could care for them while I'm away. I know they're cheering me on from afar, but it is hard not to call and check on them."

I nod. "Yeah, you're right. The only thing keeping me motivated is knowing I'm doing this for my sister and for our future. Otherwise, I would've already called for a taxi to take me home."

Tanya laughs. "There's nothing quite like family, is there?" she says, pouring batter onto the griddle. She starts talking about her kids, their names, their ages. Unfortunately, I'm not paying much attention. I'm just going through the motions of the pancake recipe like I always do while thinking about all the different times I've made it with Sadie by my side.

All the fun we've had, the times that we've tossed batter at each other from across the kitchen, the talks over a big stack of pancakes covered in butter and warm maple syrup. The subtle tang of the buttermilk, the warmth of cinnamon and vanilla.

Tanya is right about one thing. We have to push through the loneliness by channeling the love we have for our loved ones. I have to be determined. I pour another dollop of batter onto the sizzling griddle and think about the challenge tonight. I need to do everything I can to try to win it for me and for Sadie.

RHETT

I chalk up my pool cue, looking at the tightly racked balls with an intense laser focus. I don't do anything halfway. Even a pool game is a major competition. My mind is worrying about the baking challenge ahead, and I think it's making me slightly more uptight this morning. I can't afford any mistakes or sloppy execution on this first shot.

"Don't get distracted," I mutter, forgetting Nate is standing beside me.

"You know, we don't have to take this so seriously." He's infuriatingly calm and breaks the tense silence as he runs the chalk over his own cue. "This is just a friendly game of pool, man. Before tonight's big challenge, I think we should relax a little bit, don't you?"

I glance over at his solidly built forty-five-year-old body and grunt. Despite being just a little bit older than I am—well, about fifteen years—Nate has the most peaceful, centered demeanor of anyone. He's like everybody's relatable buddy. He doesn't get ruffled by much of anything, and he's always trying to impart some philosophical nugget of wisdom to the rest of us.

"Easy for you to say," I respond, lining up my shot and decisively sinking the break. A couple of solid balls drop cleanly into the pockets. "I guess when you come from a long line of bakers, this culinary stuff is second nature. You're probably not even worried about the challenge tonight."

He watches me thoughtfully as I circle the table, sizing up my next move. "You'd think so, but that legacy cuts both ways. There's a lot of pressure to live up to in my family. My grandma started the McBee's Cookies brand. Everybody knows that name. I'm supposed to do even better, at least according to my family."

I stop for a moment and look at him. "McBee's Cookies? Really? I didn't know that."

"Well, I don't exactly advertise it. Ironically, I have the hardest time making cookies," he laughs.

"How are you so calm about all this then? If you have such a legacy to live up to?" I'm genuinely interested in what he has to say.

He shrugs his shoulders. "I learned a long time

ago that no matter what we do in life, we will disappoint somebody. And most of the time, it's their baggage to carry. Not yours."

I just shrug, not looking up from lining up my next shot. "Well, I guess it's better to have something to live up to than nothing to live up to at all," I say. The words are out of my mouth before I can rein them back in.

I just gave an unintended glimpse behind the curtain of my life, my upbringing, my family history, or lack thereof. It's not something that I want to unpack willingly in front of a competitor. To Nate's credit, he doesn't really even blink at what I said. He just leans back against the wall casually, like he's waiting for a bus.

"Sometimes the fire for greatness comes from unexpected places, doesn't it?" He nods his head like one of those therapists who's waiting for you to answer something. Not that I've ever been to therapy, but I've seen them on TV. I stiffen at his attempt to be philosophical about my past. Who gave this guy a couch to start psychoanalyzing me?

"And what is that supposed to mean?" Nate seems completely unfazed by my prickly tone. He gestures calmly at the table.

"Nothing meant by it. Just an observation from someone who's been around the block a few times in the baking world. The drive to be the best usually isn't sparked by having an easy stroll through life."

I grit my teeth and bend over to take my next shot, but the cue ball over-spins, causing me to stumble slightly. Nate's carefully casual words threw me off kilter more than I want to admit, got under my skin, and dredged up some memories and unresolved feelings I work hard daily to compartmentalize. But he's right.

This obsessive need for me to be the best and seize my own success with both hands without anybody helping me was born from tougher stuff than some idyllic family bakery business like Nate had. I'm desperate to prove my worth. I'm untethered from any legacies or connections in my own family. I just live with the gnawing pit of something to prove, and it all came from the lowest of lows that I have felt in my life, trying to make my own way by simultaneously living up to the opinions of others.

I suck in a sharp breath and straighten. "Save the couch therapy for someone who cares about that crap," I say flatly. "I'm here to bake circles around everyone and win this whole dang thing, plain and simple. I'm not interested in group hugs or swapping hard luck stories."

Nate simply shrugs as usual, smiling slightly and then taking his turn to smoothly pocket a couple of balls without breaking his laid-back facade. "Suit yourself, man. But you might find this whole ride a lot easier if you let a few folks in along the way instead of constantly trying to prove yourself as some kind of a tough guy lone wolf. I've been there, and it never ends up anywhere good."

I snort at that, already looking back at the table as he continues taking his shots. I'm temporarily lulled into calmness by the rhythmic cracks of ball against ball, but I will not drop my guard here. There's a fat chance of that, not when there's finally a shot at seizing a victory for myself and by myself. No, I'm going this one alone. Same as with everything else in my life up until now. Letting people get underneath my skin has only ended up in disappointment every other time before. This baking competition is my chance to prove myself on my own merits.

Nate pockets the final ball, and I stalk around the table, racking up for another punishing round. He's a lot better at this than he let on.

I'll show everybody here what I can do with my own unvarnished grit and determination, starting with nailing this first challenge tonight, like it's the only challenge that I've ever had in my entire life. I've been waiting for it.

SAVANNAH

The competition kitchen is buzzing with nervous energy as we all get situated at our stations. I look around and do one last check to ensure I have all the tools I think I'll need, trying not to let my shaky hands give away just how nervous I really am. Someone will leave after this first big challenge, mostly based on what the judges think of our work. It's enough to make my stomach twist into knots.

"Bakers!" Dan's over-the-top announcer voice reverberates around the room, cutting through the tension like a foghorn, as he strides with his big, long legs over to the center of the room. I swear it looks like he has stilts inside his pant legs. "Welcome to our very first main challenge. We're bringing the heat right out of the gate with a real scorcher, folks." I have no idea what he means by that. I think he just likes to say things for dramatic effect. I almost laugh but manage to hold it in.

He rubs his hands together under the bright lights. "For your first true test, you'll have just three hours to design and construct an edible masterpiece out of chocolate."

I look over and catch Rhett's intense glare. He

gives me the tiniest of nods, probably imperceptible to anyone else, and I can tell he's already in competition beast mode from that furrowed brow. Somehow, his laser-focused determination actually helps me feel more confident.

"But hold onto your whisks," Dan continues with an exaggerated wink at the cameras. "This is just the beginning, folks. These chocolate showpieces must embody the theme of *movement* in their design. Our very discerning judges over there," he gestures toward the stern-faced panel, "will be critiquing your craftsmanship, creativity, technical skills, and, of course, the most important, taste factor."

Crap. That last part really cranks my heart rate up another notch. I look around at my fellow competitors. They all look stone-faced. How are they not dissolving inside? This high-pressure first challenge is finally hitting home for me. One of us gets cut today. Just like that. Goes home. It's all over. End of the line. I can't let that happen. Still, I feel like screaming, bursting into tears, and running out of the kitchen. Anxiety is a beast.

"Before we get those mixers revving and crown our first winner, I want to address a couple of questions from the viewers at home on social media." Dan suddenly whips out a blue card from his jacket pocket, clearly milking the dramatic pause for all it's worth. He turns toward Lainey across the aisle. "This first one's for you, Lainey. Seems the audience can't get enough of those beautiful lashes and that perfect blowout. What are your beauty secrets?"

Lainey lets out a high-pitched giggle as she touches her hair extensions. I mean, come on. We all know they're extensions. "Oh, you know, just a lot of time and effort goes into looking this glamorous every day."

She bats her artificial eyelashes like two giant spiders stuck to her face. "I'd love to share all of my tips and tricks for achieving perfect hair and make-up." Suddenly, she starts droning on, detailing an excessive multi-step routine that probably costs more than my rent. I can't resist turning and looking at Rhett, rolling my eyes.

Her vapid answer finally stops, and an awkward silence settles over the room before Dan pipes up again. "Yes, well, that's fascinating stuff, Lainey. Now let's move on."

This is a live show. All the main challenges will be live. I'm sure the audience at home has fallen asleep or turned off their televisions. As he scans the next card, I can feel Rhett's eyes burning a hole in the side of my head. I throw him another glance, finding him smirking slightly, clearly assuming he's about to be the next target of Dan's interrogation.

But that amusement vanishes in a flash when Dan suddenly turns to me with a sly grin. "And this one's for our lovely Savannah, the only redhead in the bunch. Seems the viewers at home have already picked up on some potential romance brewing on the set." He wags his eyebrows as a few cat calls erupt from around the room. "So, the big burning question is, what's the real story behind the little hot tub incident the other night when Rhett may have caught you in a rather compromising position?"

What is he talking about? I feel the heat rush to my face as I'm instantly transported back to the hot tub just a couple of nights ago. I was in the hot tub by myself and noticed Rhett in the courtyard. Purely innocent so I don't really understand the big deal.

Again, I look over at Rhett, who looks just as uncomfortable as I feel. I can tell he's mortified to be forced to talk about anything like this on national television. I clear my throat and try to figure out what I will say. This is ridiculous. Nothing happened. Everybody watching on TV or their phones could tell that. Surely, people don't think something is going on between us. I can also tell that Rhett does not find this amusing. The idea of a romantic entanglement with me seems to be repulsive to him.

I suck in a breath, square my shoulders, and face

the camera. "There is absolutely nothing romantic going on between Rhett and me. I can assure you of that. We can barely stand each other, much less have any kind of chemistry." Rhett's posture relaxes a bit, and he gives the smallest of nods. "The hot tub thing was just an awkward incident. I didn't know he was already out there. I slid out of my robe. I was wearing a bathing suit, as anyone could see, and I got into the hot tub. Sometimes, a girl just needs a break to gather her bearings. No scandal here, folks."

Rhett remains stone-faced, his earlier intensity already back now that the conversation is hopefully moving on. He's just as eager to put that awkward non-incident firmly in the past. "Well, that's not all. Viewers said they also saw Rhett holding you in his arms in the kitchen."

I feel like I want to throw up. How are these people misconstruing everything they see with their own eyes? "I fell off the counter while looking for a snack, and Rhett just happened to catch me."

Dan looks at the camera and winks again. "He just *happened* to be there."

They cut the camera to Rhett, who just stares at it like a deer in the headlights. He obviously has nothing he wants to say, so they cut back to me again.

"He kept me from busting my head open on the

kitchen floor. For that, I'll always be appreciative." I say, looking over at him quickly and then back at the camera, "But nothing romantic. I hate to break it to everyone, but you won't see any falling in love between me and Rhett Jennings. We're both experienced pastry chefs who are here to win a competition. Plain and simple."

It's at this moment that I realize this reality show is not at all about baking. Sure, we are all pastry chefs or self-taught bakers, but this is really about locking a bunch of people in a house and waiting for drama. And if they think they will get drama from me, it won't happen.

# CHAPTER 11

RHETT

THAT MORTIFYING QUESTION from Dan about Savannah and me is still ringing in my ears as the challenge kicks off. Why in the heck would viewers think there was anything romantic going on between us? We can barely stand to be in the same room most of the time. What kind of a vibe are we giving off that American viewers think something is happening?

I shake my head, trying to force myself to put it out of my mind. I need total concentration right now to knock this ambitious chocolate sculpture out of the park. Only three hours to create this intricate masterpiece that somehow looks like it's moving. That's way easier said than done.

I pick up my sketch pad and start drawing, which is always the first thing I do before I create anything. It's just part of my process. Although some other people think it's strange, I need to see it on paper to make sure that what's in my mind can actually be created.

The base of this will be a solid, wide disc that anchors the piece. From there, the tornado will spiral upward, growing thinner and thinner and more twisted as it reaches the top. I hope to add some debris and smaller elements like branches and leaves to give it a realistic look. That will add the needed illusion of movement.

Once I have the design clear in my mind, I start the process of tempering the chocolate. I need it to be perfect. It has to be glossy, smooth, and strong enough to hold the shape I have in my mind. I carefully melt the chocolate, bringing it to just the right temperature before I cool it on the marble slab and then reheat it slightly. This process requires precision, but it calms me. I enjoy the repetition.

As the chocolate cools to the perfect consistency, I prepare the molds for the base and the initial spirals of the tornado. I pour the chocolate into the molds and make sure to get rid of any air bubbles that could weaken the structure. While the base sets, I will start on the tornado's body. I use a rotating platform and begin building the spiraling structure. I pipe the chocolate in a continuous motion, starting wide at the base and gradually tightening the spiral as I move upward.

Every layer needs to harden a bit before I can add the next to ensure stability. I use a hairdryer on the lowest setting to cool the layers faster without causing them to crack. Once I turn on the hairdryer, pretty much everybody in the kitchen turns to look at me, wondering what I'm doing. I will use anything at my disposal to win this.

As the tornado takes shape, I add those smaller details to enhance the sense of motion. Thin strands of chocolate are draped around the sculpture that look like swirling winds. I attach my pieces of debris, which are tiny branches and leaves that I've made out of fondant and dark and white chocolate, making them appear as if they're being sucked into the vortex. All of it is intricate work. I can't believe this is week one. What will the other weeks be like? I use tweezers to place the elements precisely.

The kitchen around me is just a blur of activity, but I stay focused on my own creation. I can hear the sound of mixers, the clatter of utensils, and the talking of other contestants. All of it fades into the background. My entire world is narrowed to focus on the sculpture before me.

Just as I'm feeling confident about my design, I finally glance around the kitchen at my fellow contestants. Most of them have already descended into that laser-focused baking zone, their heads down on their own projects.

I look over at Savannah's station and nearly laugh out loud. She's battling with an industrial mixer like it's a wild animal. I can see the sweat glistening on her forehead, and her full lips are pressed into a determined line.

I should be focusing on my own work, but I can't help but look over because of all her frantic movements. I'm sure the cameras are catching all of it, and it will be great television.

The thing is, this isn't the Savannah I knew in school. She was calm, cool, and collected. She didn't show fear or worry or angst of any kind. That's why I refer to her as Sunny. But this woman? This is a whole different level of panic I'm seeing.

She's cranking the mixer speed knob up and down, and the metal bowl is rattling like it's about to leap off the counter. There's chocolate spattering everywhere, and I wince when I see thick ganache spraying out in big globs.

Her face is full of frustration, her fingers jabbing at the controls with increasing desperation. I'm way further along in my project than she is. I don't know how she'll even finish this. I tell myself to mind my own business. She's not my problem. We're not friends, and this is a competition, but seeing her struggle like this pulls at something in me.

With a sigh, I grab a side towel and make my way over to her station, dodging all the curious glances from other contestants. "You have to stop assaulting the mixer controls like that," I whisper loudly as I walk toward her, trying to keep my tone neutral.

She jumps at the sound of my voice like she's had an adrenaline rush, turning to face me with wide eyes. "What? Oh no, it's fine. I've got it under control."

"Clearly you don't," I say, stepping over beside her. "At least let me take a look."

"I don't need your help, Rhett," she says quietly, a hint of panic in her voice. "People already think there's a romance between us. Go back to your station."

Ignoring her protests, I gently nudge her aside with my hip and then swipe my towel across the controls. "The key to this one is steady, even pressure on the speed lever. You were just jackhammering it back and forth, which is probably how you gummed it up." I adjust the speed dial with a smooth, controlled motion, and the bowl finally begins to whirl, the ganache churning into a perfect consistency. "See? Easy as that." She glares at me, her eyes flashing with a mix of gratitude and possibly annoyance. I look at her. "What? Any idiot could have figured out what you were doing wrong after watching you for ten seconds."

She huffs and puts her hands on her hips. "Oh, really? Then why did it take you so long to come over and help me?"

"Maybe I was paying attention to my own project, or maybe I'm not supposed to be helping my competition."

She rolls her eyes, but I can see a small smile tugging at the corners of her mouth. "Well, thanks for the help, I guess. Not that I needed it."

"Sure you didn't," I say, stepping back. "And don't go breaking any more mixers. Those things are expensive."

She squares her shoulders, lifting her chin defiantly. "I'll be fine, Rhett, but please don't let me keep you from your masterpiece."

"You're very welcome," I say with a tight smile, remembering that cameras are watching us. To ward off any thoughts about romance with the audience, I quickly add, "But good luck not screwing anything else up in the meantime."

Her eyes narrow, and for a moment, I think she will throw something at me, maybe the mixer, but it's too heavy. Instead, she turns back to her work, her shoulders stiff but determined. I walk back to my station, but I can't help but glance over my shoulder. Despite her fiery attitude, something about her makes me want to see her succeed, even if it means putting up with all her stubbornness.

SAVANNAH

Things are not going well. I slam the heavy stainless-steel bowl down on the counter with a deafening clang, the sound reverberating around the kitchen. Of course, it draws the attention of everyone around me, and I can feel everybody staring. My face burns with embarrassment. I want to crawl under my workstation and disappear.

"Dang it," I whisper loudly, my voice cracking. Of course, the cameraman comes in for a closeup of my meltdown.

I slam my hands down on the counter, my shoulders heaving as I try to catch my breath. Tears threaten the corners of my eyes, but I refuse to let them fall. Not here. Not on camera.

I also refuse to look over at Rhett. I'm sure he's enjoying this. The last thing he will do is come over here and help me again. The entire kitchen falls silent, and I can feel the weight of everyone's stares like a physical pressure on my chest. I squeeze my eyes shut, trying to block out the humiliating reality of the situation. I take a shaky breath, my hands still gripping the edge of the counter.

Everything is falling apart. It's just week one. My project is a mess. I have no composure. I feel like I'm crumbling under the pressure, and it's terrifying. I never thought my anxiety would hit me like this, and yet here I am on national television, basically having a panic attack in front of everybody.

"Savannah, honey, take a deep breath."

I suddenly hear Maggie's soothing voice cut through the haze of my panic. I don't know how she got to my station, but she's standing there looking at me with an expression of concern.

"I can't do this, Maggie. I just can't," I whisper. I don't know why I'm whispering since we have microphones, but I do.

"Yes, you can," she says, gently placing a reassuring hand on my shoulder. "You've come this far; don't let one setback make you quit."

I look at her, tears blurring my vision. "But everything's falling apart. *I'm* falling apart."

She looks around at the other contestants who are still watching us. "Hey, everyone, let's get back to work. There's nothing to see here." Her tone is firm, and everybody returns to what they were doing. Slowly, I hear the noise level in the kitchen start to rise again as everybody gets back to work.

She looks back at me, her eyes locking onto mine. "You're not falling apart, sweetheart. You're just having a rough moment. We all have them."

I sniffle, wiping my eyes with the back of my hand. "I've already ruined everything. There's no way that I can fix this."

"Maybe not," she says, looking around at the mess I've made on the counter, "but you can start over. You're good at this, Savannah. Really good. Don't let one mistake take you out of the game."

"Why do you care, Maggie? You're competing with me," I say, laughing.

She smiles softly. "Because I've been where you are, and I know how hard it is to keep going when everything feels like it's falling apart. You have to remember why you're here."

"You sound like a grandmother."

"I'll take that as a compliment," Maggie says, giving my shoulder a squeeze. "Now, why don't you get this mess cleaned up and then start working on how to salvage your project."

I take another deep breath, nodding slowly. "Okay. Thank you."

"Don't mention it," she says, handing me a clean bowl. "Now I've got to get back to work. We both have a competition to win."

As she walks back to her station, I feel a sense of gratitude and determination. She's right; I can't let one setback ruin everything that I've worked so hard for. I won't give up, not right now. I take a deep breath and steady myself. I can do this for Sadie and for me. For all the dreams that we've put on hold for so long.

I start cleaning up the mess on my counter. The broken pieces of my project might be unsalvageable, but I'm not. I refuse to be.

I try not to, but I steal a glance at Rhett who's still working at his station, completely absorbed in his project. I have a competition to win, and I'm not letting anyone, including Rhett, stand in my way.

SAVANNAH

I had a temper tantrum on national TV. This is the thought that I keep reminding myself of repeatedly as I mentally kick myself in the shin while I wait for the judges to walk around the kitchen and make their judgments about each of us.

I might be going home. I can feel it in my bones. I don't see any way around it.

Everyone else at least has something to show for the last three hours of work. I, too, have something to show, but it certainly isn't something I would normally put out for all the world to see. I had these grandiose plans and ideas to make a movement sculpture out of a rose. I don't know what I was thinking. Flowers don't typically move all that much. My heart is thundering in my ears as the judges make their solemn procession around the kitchen.

I've watched a lot of those baking reality shows on TV. They always seem so happy and peppy. The judges are always friendly. Well, these three judges are not friendly at all. They are all business all the time. They barely crack a smile. They don't hand out compliments.

I suddenly flash to the early version of Simon Cowell, who was on American Idol. Everyone who stood before him was harshly judged, and some-times, his comments made me laugh. These judges are the early Simon Cowells who don't hold back on what they think. It's not as entertaining when it's pointed at me.

This is like being back in school, only with the worst set of professors I could have ever thought of having, but I have to stand here and wait for them to come to my station and tell me how much I suck. Then I can go upstairs, lay down in my bed, and sob for the rest of the night like a normal person.

I'm trying to look like someone with poise while I wait for my judgment, but I swear sweat is dripping down my back as they get closer and closer to my station. This intimidating trio is a team of the most formidable figures in the entire modern dessert world. I could only ever dream of reaching their heights if I worked the rest of my life. The worst one is Chef Alain. He's always got this stern look on his face as if it might break if he actually smiles. Next to him is Tessa, the social media queen. You would think she would be social, interactive, smiling, but no, she's very serious about her job.

She has a multimillion-dollar business empire, and rabid fans line up for hours just to sample what she creates. I don't think I could get a line of three stray cats to stand here and eat what I've got on my station.

And then, of course, there's Marco, the dashing international man of mystery who travels around the world eating at different places. How is that a job? How did someone get so lucky in all their life choices that what they do for a living is travel the world and eat?

Anyway, the intimidating brain trust of the

dessert elite continues walking around the kitchen. I can't hear everything they're saying, but they seem pretty impressed with what most people have done. That shall change as soon as they arrive at my station. Everything fell apart, so I had to abandon my original design vision for the chocolate rose sculpture and settle on a sleeker, more minimalist approach.

A series of gravity-defying curved panels that were to be balanced on a sloping wave-like structure. It was supposed to look like perpetual motion. Basically, it was what I could do in the time I had left, but now I find the judges standing right in front of me, Chef Alain with his narrow eyes silently looking at my lopsided curves and imperfect chocolate work. Chocolate is not what I'm good at. I'm a talented pastry chef, or at least I think I am. You give me a cake, and I will wipe the floor with you, but you give me a bunch of chocolate, and well, this is what happens.

I can't help but see the flaws in everything I'm looking at. Tessa's gaze roams over my design, giving no hint as to whether she thinks it's innovative or just completely ridiculous. The knot of dread in my stomach is clenching tighter as Marco picks up one of the rippling wave pieces and looks at it closer. Kind of a strange thing to do. They normally don't pick things up, but mine isn't completely together, so he figured no harm was done.

"This was an intriguing approach," Chef Alain says in a clinical, detached manner. "I suppose you were trying to capture perpetual movement, which was certainly ambitious." I brace myself. I know this isn't going to be good. "To be honest, the execution is very much lacking in precision. These warped curves and uneven layers don't achieve the sort of meticulous mathematical flow that you would need. Very imprecise to convey the intended visual." It's like listening to a thesaurus come to life and speak to me. Lots of big words, and I have no idea what he means.

I can't help but flinch as he continues to tell me everything wrong with what I've done here. But then Tessa decides to join in. "Yeah, I'm not feeling the kinetic energy that you were going for here, and these overlapping wave patterns just look chaotic and muddy."

Her feedback strikes yet another humiliating blow to my already severely lacking confidence. They suggest how I could have improved this, but what do I care? I don't ever plan to do this again.

Marco steps forward with his eyebrows knitted together. He traces his finger along one of the curved panels, and his expression sours. "There's just textural issues here beyond the shape problems," he says. "The chocolate seems over-tempered, wouldn't you agree? It has an almost grainy look, and I ate a piece of it, and I just... well, let's say I wouldn't want to eat it again."

My cheeks flush like someone has poured scalding hot water on them. My rookie tempering mistake has just been called out in front of everyone. I hazard a glance over at Connor, who has a smirk on his face as if he's enjoying this more than Christmas morning.

At this point, I just want them to leave my station. I would like to go upstairs and pack my bags since it seems obvious that I'll be going home tonight. They continue walking around, and they land at Bianca's workstation. As bad as my sculpture looked, Bianca's looks even worse. I cringe with secondary embarrassment for her when I can see that tears are already visible on her face. Her design missed the mark big time, and she looks like she created some sort of a sphere of chocolate that just fell apart all over her station.

I don't know exactly what she was trying to do. Tessa looks at it in disgust. "Was this even supposed to be recognizable as some kind of architectural inspiration? I can't even find a design pattern or theme here at all. It just looks like a big, melted blob. I'm so confused."

Yikes. I feel bad for Bianca. I haven't talked to her often, but she seems nice enough.

"Yes, I'm very confused," Marco says. "This consistency is absolutely unacceptable for professional-level work. Very sloppy and broken down. It's essentially inedible."

Her head hangs, and I want to give her a hug. They say a few more comments, none of them being any better, and then mercifully move on to the next station. I can't help but feel some relief. Maybe I at least have a chance to stay. Of course, when the at-home audience votes after seeing my temper tantrum, they'll probably want to vote me off. I can't blame them.

They finally reach Rhett's station, and sitting there in its immaculate, breathtaking glory is nothing short of what I would call a sculptural chocolate masterpiece—a towering, spiraling vortex that I can't understand how he even made. It looks like something out of an art gallery.

Every component is exquisitely executed, and it makes me mad to even say so, but I can't help it. It's something to really behold. There's a seamless, glossy surface polish to the chocolate that I don't understand how he accomplished, and that was with him coming over to my station a couple of times to try to help me... or maybe taunt me. I still don't know.

"Now, this is what I'm talking about," Chef Alain says loudly. He's still not smiling, but he seems excited. "The impeccable craftsmanship and the visionary scope here. Bravo!"

"That glossy finish is unreal," Tessa says. "And capturing this with such clean architectural style. Very nice."

Even Marco seems at a loss for words for a moment. Everyone is staring at it with rapt fascination, and there's Rhett himself, a gratified pride glowing through his striking blue eyes as they cut over to me briefly. I am, of course, staring at him mortified. I can see the barest hint of a smirk or a smile. It's hard to tell with him.

Chef Alain turns around. "Make no mistake, as far as the judges go, there is a clear winner in today's challenge. Of course, we still have to wait for the audience to vote on who's going home, and their votes will be combined with ours. We already know who we think should leave the challenge today, but the audience might be able to change that decision. We will be back shortly to announce. For now, start cleaning up your stations."

I assume this is when they go on a commercial

break, so I quickly start cleaning up, knowing that this could be the last time I'm in this kitchen. Bianca's masterpiece was no such thing, but neither was mine. It could really be either one of us. It could actually be anyone. The audience does have quite a bit of say-so in this situation.

"Congratulations," I say in Rhett's direction. He turns and smiles slightly.

"Thanks."

*Thanks.* Is that all he has to say? I expected him to stick his chest out and walk around like an egomaniacal rooster or something, but instead, he just begins to wipe down his station.

He had the undisputed victory here. Why isn't he playing it up more?

A few moments later, Dan arrives again in the kitchen with the three judges behind him. They stand before the cameras and announce that Rhett is the winner, and we all clap. Well, except for Connor, he pretends to clap. You can tell he's not actually touching his hands together. He wanted to win, and he didn't, and for that much, I'm thankful that Rhett got it.

"After reviewing the judge's votes and then adding in the audience participation, we have our first contestant who will be leaving *The Baking Games* for week one, and that contestant is..."

There's a long pause for dramatic effect.

"Bianca."

Everybody turns and looks in her direction. Tears are already streaming down her face. I think she knew. I think we all did. Several of us walk over and hug Bianca as the show winds down to a close, and we return to our regularly scheduled programming.

# CHAPTER 12

SAVANNAH

THAT WAS BRUTAL.

I slump over onto the couch in the courtyard area, trying to hold back tears that have been threatening to spill over for several minutes now.

The room is buzzing with activity as the other contestants talk about the challenge, but I can only think about how badly I did. I feel like an absolute failure. Zara notices and makes her way over, her presence immediately calming me a bit.

She's beautiful in that natural way, with her black hair and ringlet curls that perfectly shape her face. She sits down beside me, giving me a sympathetic smile.

"Hey there, Savannah. Tough day?" I laugh and nod,

unable to trust my voice. It's probably pretty shaky right now. It feels like there's a lump in my throat that's going to choke me. "Let me tell you something," Zara says, leaning in a little bit closer. "I've had my fair share of failures. More than I can count, but every single one of them taught me something valuable."

I look at her, trying to find comfort. "Oh yeah, like what?"

"Well, like how to pick myself up and keep going," she says. "You know, failure is just a stepping stone. It's not the end of the road unless you decide that it is. It's just part of the journey, and from what I've seen, you've got skills and determination that will keep you going no matter what."

I sigh, my shoulders sagging a bit. "This just all feels so overwhelming. I want to do well so badly, not just for me but for my sister, too."

She nods, her eyes filled with understanding. "I know, and that's exactly why you can't give up. You must show your sister and yourself that setbacks don't define you. What matters is how you bounce back from them."

I nod, trying to take her words to heart. "Thanks. I guess I needed to hear that."

She leans back, looking around the area. "You know, I've traveled all over the world. I've learned a lot from my experiences, and one thing that stands out is that people appreciate resilience no matter where you go. They respect someone who doesn't give up even when things get tough."

"You've been to a lot of places. I've barely been out of Georgia."

She smiles. "Traveling taught me that the world is full of possibilities. Every place has its challenges and rewards, but the most important journey is the one you take within yourself. What you learn about yourself through your travels. Finding your own strength and courage is what really matters."

I manage a small smile. "I wish I had your confidence. You make everything sound so easy."

She chuckles. "Trust me, it's not always easy. I've had my share of sleepless nights and moments of doubt, but I've learned to embrace those moments as part of my growth process, and you will, too."

At that moment, I notice that Rhett is nearby, his eyes on us. There's a flicker of something in his gaze. Concern. Could that be it? He quickly looks away and continues talking to someone else, but seeing that softer side of him is strange, even if just for a moment. I've seen it a few times now, like at the assisted living center and when he helped me with the blender, but then he turns right back into good old Rhett—competitive, silent, walls up all around him like some sort of fortress.

"Remember," Zara says, continuing, "we're all in this together, even if we're competing with each other. Everybody should be rooting for everybody else, even if it doesn't always feel like it."

I laugh. "Thanks, but I know some people here are definitely not rooting for me, including my ex-boyfriend."

She rolls her eyes. "Oh, yes, I heard about that. Gossip flies through here pretty quickly. To be honest, I don't really like that guy."

I look at her and smile. "Neither do I."

She squeezes my leg before she gets up and walks back inside. As the evening wears on, I try to join in conversation with others, but my mind just keeps drifting back to my failure of a challenge. I can't shake the feeling of inadequacy. The room finally starts to empty out, and everybody starts heading off to bed. I find myself sitting alone, lost in thought.

Rhett walks by, apparently heading to his own room, and pauses momentarily.

"You okay?" he asks, his tone surprisingly gentle. I force a smile.

"Yeah. Just processing, I guess."

He nods, not pressing further. "You'll bounce back, Sunny. We all have our off days."

I raise an eyebrow. "Even you?"

"Especially me", he says with a smirk. "Don't let it get to your head."

I chuckle softly as I watch him walk away, and I feel a strange sense of comfort, knowing that maybe, just maybe, I'm not as alone in this as I thought.

SAVANNAH

The next morning, the producers call us out into the courtyard for a surprise activity. I got a decent night's sleep, but I really didn't want to get up this early today.

The air buzzes with anticipation as everybody gathers around, wondering what they have in store for us. Dan, our tall and dorky host, steps forward with his trademark toothy grin.

"Good morning, contestants. Today, we have a fun little competition to lighten the mood. We're going to do a blindfolded taste test."

Some people murmur with excitement, others with apprehension, as we all exchange glances. A blindfolded taste test. This should be interesting. "We'll be pairing you up randomly," he continues, pulling a hat out from behind his back. Come draw a partner's name from the hat when I call your name."

The contestants are called up one by one. When it's my turn, I reach into the hat and pull out a slip of paper.

Unfolding it, I read the name Rhett. Great, just great. Rhett walks over, a smirk already on his face.

"Looks like we're partners, Sunny," he says. I roll my eyes at his nickname for me.

"Don't get too excited."

Dan claps his hands to get our attention again. "Okay, everybody. Let's get started. Each team will be blindfolded and have to guess the ingredients in five different desserts. The team with the lowest score will face a penalty."

Rhett and I look at each other. "A penalty?" I whisper.

"I guess we'll find out what it is later," he says with a shrug.

Dan grins like a Cheshire cat. "Savannah, you're going to be blindfolded first. Rhett, you'll feed her, and she has to guess the ingredients, and then we'll switch. You'll have thirty seconds for each dessert."

I put on a blindfold and take a deep breath, feeling excited but nervous. Rhett's proximity to me is a little bit unnerving. I can smell his cologne, and I like it more than I would ever care to admit out loud.

I can almost hear the smirk in his voice when he says, "Ready, Sunny?"

"Stop calling me that and just get on with it," I mutter, trying to focus. The first dessert is placed in front of us. I can hear the plate touch the counter. Rhett puts his hand on the back of my neck and then gently guides a spoonful into my mouth. I taste something rich and creamy with a strange aftertaste. "Is this chocolate mousse, and is that lavender?" I guess.

Rhett chuckles. "Nope. Try again."

"I don't know. White chocolate?"

"Wrong again."

Dan calls time. Rhett is barely containing his laughter.

"It was goat cheese."

"Seriously? Who puts goat cheese in a dessert?" I say, gagging.

"Next one," Dan announces.

Rhett feeds me another spoonful, and I'm hit with a confusing mixture of flavors. "Okay, is this apple, cinnamon, and blue cheese?"

"Close, but no cigar," Rhett says.

"I don't know. I give up."

Rhett corrects me. "It's Gorgonzola."

"Okay, disgusting," I mutter.

The next few rounds go similarly, with Rhett feeding me increasingly bizarre combinations that I can barely identify. By the end of my turn, I feel frustrated and a bit nauseous.

"Okay, switch," Dan calls out. Rhett puts on a blindfold, and I can't help but smile.

"Your turn," I say teasingly. I'm handed the first dessert, and I take a moment to appreciate the role reversal. I feed him a spoonful, and he chews thoughtfully. "Is that dark chocolate and cayenne pepper?"

"Wow, you got it," I say impressed.

He smiles a bit. "I told you I've got an educated palate."

The next dessert is a bit trickier, and I watch as he furrows his brow, trying to figure out the flavors. "Mango and something earthy. Is it turmeric?"

"Nope, it's ginger," I say.

"Close enough," he mutters under his breath.

We continue through the remaining desserts, and Rhett does slightly better than I did, but not by much.

When the taste test is finally over, and everybody else has finished, Dan announces the results. Some of the teams did very well, surprisingly well. Others, not so much, but I feel like none of them did quite as terribly as we did. I hate going first.

"The team with the lowest score is…" Dan says, pausing for dramatic effect. "Savannah and Rhett!"

I groan, "Seriously?"

Rhett smirks. "Well, I guess we need to brush up on our taste buds."

"Or not eat crazy combinations like that. I feel sick to my stomach."

Dan's grin widens. "And now for your penalty, Savannah and Rhett. For the next seventy-two hours, you two will be chained together."

There's a collective gasp from the group, and my jaw drops. I feel like it's about to hit my feet.

"What?" I say, staring at him like he's speaking a language I don't speak at all.

"Are they joking?" Rhett whispers in my direction.

Two producers step forward, holding a metal chain with cushioned cuffs at each end. They fasten one around my wrist and the other around Rhett's, securing us with what looks to be about a three-foot chain.

"You have got to be kidding me," I mutter. Is it too late to go home? I wonder to myself.

"We'd better get used to it," Rhett says, giving it a gentle tug. He thinks this is funny.

Dan claps his hands again. "Remember, you'll be chained together for seventy-two hours, including the reward challenge, which means you win or lose together. Good luck."

As the producers walk away, I turn to Rhett. "This is a nightmare."

RHETT

I'm chained to Savannah. What has my life become? I try to imagine my mother watching this at home, her face beet red and her blood pressure surging. It actually makes me smile a little.

Is she watching? Doubtful. My mother doesn't really watch television. She's one of those people who proudly announces that fact any chance she gets, as if it's one more thing that makes her better than other people.

"This is insane," Savannah says. We haven't moved a muscle yet. Everyone has left the courtyard, and here we stand like two injured animals afraid to move.

"Three whole days. Who thought this stupidity up?"

She sighs. "I have no idea."

"You know, if you were better at guessing, we wouldn't be standing here chained together. And I would be making my famous maple bacon waffles for myself."

"First of all, don't you dare try to blame this on me, Rhett Jennings! You didn't guess right either."

"I got a couple right. How many did you get? Um, I believe it was *zero*," I say, leaning in front of her face and forming my fingers into a zero like a toddler. Why is she so pretty? It's annoying on so many levels.

"Maple bacon waffles. That sounds pretty good right now."

We're still standing here like two morons.

"Since I'm right-handed and my right hand is currently chained to you, I will need help."

She smiles slightly. "I can do that."

We finally start walking toward the door.

"How are we going to sleep?" I suddenly blurt out.

"Well, I personally like to lie down and close my eyes," Savannah starts to say, laughing. I stop at the door, which jerks her back toward me a bit, causing her to fall backward. Again, I catch her.

"You know what I mean. We can't sleep… together." My heart speeds up a bit, and everything that happens to young men starts to happen. Launch sequence activated. I can't stand this woman. This shouldn't be happening. I need bolt cutters. My mind is racing. Cameras are all around, and the audience will get the wrong idea all over again.

"Relax, Rhett. We have twin beds. We'll just pull them close enough for our arms not to break off. Lainey can move to another room. I'm sure she'll gladly join Connor in your room anyway."

She seems unbothered. How can she be unfazed by all of this? Oh, that's right. She's Sunny. She bounces right back from stuff, even her loss last night.

We start walking again and walk inside the house to the communal kitchen. Thankfully, there aren't that many people there. They've made their food and either moved to their rooms or into the dining room.

Everybody chatters away, and only a few of them make fun of us as we finally get into the kitchen. This is not ideal, to say the least. We've already tripped over each other twice just since leaving the courtyard. I cannot imagine how we will face the reward challenge together, but for now, I'm starving. We just need to make these maple bacon waffles.

"This is the most ridiculous thing I've ever done," Savannah says.

I smirk. "Just think of it as a bonding experience."

"More like a punishment," she mutters under her breath.

"Can you just stand still for even a minute?" I ask her. She's the most fidgety person I've ever met.

"Do you really want to make the woman you're chained to mad right now?" she says, raising an eyebrow.

"This is going to be a long seventy-two hours," I mutter under my breath.

We get over to the kitchen counter, and I start trying to figure out exactly how I will gather all the ingredients with my right hand tied to Savannah. I'm definitely going to need her help. We're going to have to work on our communication skills.

"Okay, let's get this over with. So I take it you've never made maple bacon waffles?" I ask her.

She looks at me, raising an eyebrow. "I can't say that I have. Usually, I just make frozen waffles."

I roll my eyes. "You're a pastry chef, Sunny. You're supposed to make waffles from scratch."

"I make pancakes from scratch," she says as if that makes up for the fact that she's been eating frozen waffles all these years.

"It's basically the same kind of thing. I'm going to need your help getting everything because, obviously, I can't use my hand," I say, holding it up as if she doesn't remember that we are shackled together like two prisoners.

"First, we need flour, eggs, milk, maple syrup, bacon…"

She holds her hand up. "Can you slow down a little bit? We're going to have to really communicate to navigate this."

"Fine," I say with a sigh, repeating the ingredients more slowly.

The whole time, we hear the chain clinking between us. It's very distracting.

"We need to cook this bacon until it's crispy," I instruct, handing her the package of bacon. Only she can't open it without my help. I help her open the package of bacon, and then she starts laying the strips in the frying pan. "Now remember, don't burn that bacon," I repeat.

She gives me a mock salute. "Yes, sir."

Eventually, we start to get a rhythm to moving around the kitchen. We mix up the dry ingredients— flour, baking powder, some sugar, and a pinch of salt —and before we know it, we have the batter ready to put into the waffle iron.

"Now we crumble the bacon into the batter," I say as if that's not patently obvious. The smell of maple syrup and bacon fills the kitchen, making my stomach growl. "All right. Now, we need to pour them into the waffle iron. I've turned it on and preheated it. This is the easy part. Just pour in the batter, and we'll wait."

She looks at me, "Yes, I understand how a waffle iron works, Rhett. I'm not stupid."

I realize I'm not treating her like a trained pastry chef. I'm treating her like I'm teaching her something she doesn't already know. And as bad as the challenge went, I know Savannah has skills. I saw them when we were in school. She made some stunning desserts, and she was highly focused. So far in the competition, she seems scared. Distracted. Worried.

I'm sure part of it is worrying about her sister, but I think a lot of it is Connor. I try to imagine what it'd be like to have one of my ex-girlfriends in the house, and I shudder a bit.

"What was that?" she asks me when I shake.

"Just got a chill."

"Oh Lord, I hope you're not getting a fever or something. I don't want to get sick."

I look at her. "Thanks for your overwhelming concern, but I'm fine. I was just thinking about something."

"You literally shook. What were you thinking about?" she grins, obviously giddy with excitement to do a deep dive into my mind.

"None of your business." I continue staring at the waffle iron as if that will speed up time.

"Come on! We have to spend a lot of time together. Tell me your deep, dark secret, Rhett."

When she looks at me, I feel a wave of something. She's smiling. Her teeth are so perfect and white. Her lips are naturally full, and she wears the perfect shade to highlight her red hair. There's a smattering of freckles on her nose that some women would kill to have.

What is wrong with me?

This isn't good. She's my competition. My nemesis. My complete opposite. My body and mind are betraying me with these thoughts.

"Fine. I was thinking how awful it would be to have an ex in this house."

She pauses for a moment. "It *is* awful."

"Maybe he'll leave soon," I say, half wishing it for her and half wishing it for myself.

"Doubtful. As horrible as Connor is, he's a talented pastry chef. I've seen him create amazing things."

"Well, we can hope he'll leave."

"Agreed."

We finish making the waffles and carry them to the breakfast bar in the kitchen. Neither of us wants to join the table full of people in the other room and listen to jokes about the chain between us.

"These are delicious, Rhett," she says. Savannah is one of those people who can despise you and still compliment you. I don't understand it. I don't have a good poker face.

"Thanks. I've perfected them over years of being on my own, traveling all over the world."

"Oh, that's right. You work on celebrity yachts. Anyone I'd know?"

My mind scrambles. "Probably."

She grins. It's a nice grin. She could be on a toothpaste commercial. "Well, give me some names!"

"I really can't. Non-disclosure agreement and all." What a stupid excuse.

"You had to sign an NDA to make desserts on celebrity yachts?"

"Yep," I say, purposely filling my mouth with waffles so hopefully she won't press further.

"Huh. I never thought they'd make you do that. Still, you can trust me. Just tell me one big-name celebrity," she says, leaning closer.

I lean in, and I can smell her shampoo. It smells like strawberries and vanilla, and I have a sudden urge to press my nose into her thick, red hair. That ought to get me booted from this house right quick.

"I can't. We're currently on national television," I whisper before leaning back.

She laughs. "Wow. I forgot about that." She looks around at the cameras. "Amazing how quickly we forget everyone's watching us. Hi, everyone!" she says, waving at a camera in the corner of the kitchen.

It's true. Thousands, if not millions, of people are watching the show's livestream. That is amazing to me. I watch TV occasionally, but I can't imagine staring at my computer between shows and watching strangers live in a house. Reality TV really has been society's downfall.

"So," I say, trying to divert her attention away from asking me any more personal questions, "you work in a bakery?"

"I work in a bakery inside a grocery store."

"And how is that?"

She shrugs her shoulders. "It's not working on celebrity yachts, I'll tell you that much."

"What's your end goal with all this?" I ask, waving my hand around.

"Help my sister go to college and hopefully have enough left over to rent a space and open my own bakery. Long term, I'd love to own a chain of bakeries."

I can see her doing that. She'd be perfect in some

little small-town bakery, like in one of those cheesy Christmas movies I swear I haven't watched on TV.

"What about you? What's your big goal?"

"Work in a Michelin star-rated restaurant, and then own one someday."

She nods. "I can see that."

I cock my head to the side. "Oh yeah? Why?"

"You're kind of... fancy."

Fancy? That wasn't what I expected her to say.

"What is that supposed to mean?"

"Relax, Rhett. It wasn't a putdown. It's just that what I know of you from school is that you're buttoned up. You're white dress shirts, and I'm vintage aprons. You're drawing your designs, and I'm flying by the seat of my pants."

"I'm a winner, and you're a loser," I blurt out before I can stop myself. Geez, why did I say that? I'm going to be chained to this woman for days, and I decide to be a jerk right out of the gate.

She stares at me with her big blue eyes and swallows hard. I expect to see her eyes well up, but her face turns red instead. I can barely make out her face from her fiery hair within moments.

"That was rude, even for you, Rhett."

"But he's not wrong." We both hear his voice at the same time.

Connor.

"Go away, Connor," I say, wishing I could put my words to Savannah back into my stupid mouth.

"Um, it's a free house, dude. I can roam around as I please." He leans against the doorframe leading to the foyer. "Don't feel bad for pointing out the truth."

"You haven't won anything either, Connor," Savannah says, pushing her plate away from her like she's lost her appetite.

"Well, I've come a lot closer than you. The judges eviscerated you, Sav. If Bianca hadn't royally screwed up, you'd already be back in your crappy little apartment with your annoying sister."

I stand up without thinking and face Connor, pulling Savannah up from her chair. My nose is inches from his nose.

"Watch it, Connor," I say, a warning woven into my voice. He looks surprised.

"Wait. Is something going on between you two? Was the audience right? Are you and Savannah here… what's the polite way to say '*having relations*' on TV?"

Without thinking, I grab his shirt in my left hand. It's not my best hand, but I could do some damage if I wanted. That's the perk of being the biggest guy here… or in most places, really.

"Shut your stupid mouth, Connor," I say through gritted teeth.

"Rhett, don't! You'll get yourself kicked out of the competition, and that's what he wants because he's afraid he can't win with you here."

What did she just say? Did Savannah just compliment me? Or is she just trying to keep me from ripping this guy apart and getting blood on her vintage apron?

I slowly release him so that his feet are fully touching the ground again, and I see the color come back into his face. If nothing else, Connor has received a warning he needed.

"Savannah, your boyfriend seems to have anger problems," he says with a sneer. "Enjoy your waffles, lovebirds."

Savannah and I just sit there in silence. What else is there to say?

# CHAPTER 13

AFTERNOON CONFESSIONAL

*PRODUCER: So, Connor, what's the history with you and Savannah?*

*Connor: We dated for a couple of years, but she's obsessed with her sister.*

*Producer: And you didn't like that?*

*Connor: Who would? Her sister is annoying, and she's twenty years old. Like, move on with your life.*

*Producer: Savannah broke up with you then?*

*Connor, after a pause: It was mutual.*

## SAVANNAH

I don't know what to make of Rhett at this point. The way he stood up for me to Connor was shocking. It was fun to watch Connor squirm, quite literally, under Rhett's hand. But why did Rhett do that? Why didn't he join in the fun of criticizing me?

Normally, I'd talk to Maggie about it and get her well-earned wisdom, but I can't because Rhett is attached to me. This is going to be tough.

I asked a producer what we do when we have to change clothes. She said they will release us, and someone will come stand outside the bathroom door while we change. We have five minutes. As for showering, they will do the same. Release us and give us ten minutes each to shower.

"Um, I have a little problem," I say as we walk toward the courtyard.

"What?" Rhett says, exasperated.

"I need to use the bathroom."

He pauses for a moment. "What do you mean by 'use the bathroom'?"

I stare at him. "Do I have to go into details?"

"Ew."

"No! I just have to pee, but what are we supposed to do?"

He nods toward the bathroom where he hid on that first night. "You go in, and I'll stand outside."

I walk into the bathroom, but the toilet is too far. The chain won't stretch nearly enough.

"Not going to work," I call out. Our camera guy stands in the hallway with Rhett, obviously waiting for us.

"We can go upstairs," Rhett says. The bathroom up there is even bigger than this one. There's no way he's going to be able to stand outside there either. I yank the chain, pulling him into the room. "What are you doing, crazy woman?"

I shut the door. "I need to go, so you're going with me."

"Again? Is this some kind of fetish you have?"

"Shut up. My bladder is about to explode!"

"So glad I'm going to be here for that," he says sarcastically.

I flip the switch on my mic and point for him to do the same. I don't need to whole world to hear me pee. Everything gets judged on social media, so I'm certain trolls would discuss the rhythm or flow of my urinary tract.

"Turn around," I say, pointing to the corner.

"Better hurry. They're not going to like that you turned off…"

Just then, someone bangs on the door.

"Savannah and Rhett, you need to have your mics on!" one of the producers yells through the thick wood.

"I deserve urinary privacy!" I yell back.

"No more than five minutes!"

"Geez, wonder what happens when you need to… well, you know," Rhett says. "Five minutes? What if you want to do a little light reading?"

I stifle a laugh and finish my business before flushing the toilet and dragging him to the sink with me. Well, as much as a petite woman can drag a giant with her. Rhett is built like a superhero. He's definitely been lifting weights since our time in school together.

"Okay, I guess we can go," I say, turning toward the door. Rhett doesn't move. "What's wrong? Do you need to go?"

"No," he says. "And when I do, you won't be attached to me."

"Why? Embarrassed?" I tease, poking him in the chest.

"Savannah, have you ever seen *how* a man goes to the bathroom? We sort of need both hands."

"Ew. Yuck. Say no more."

"We'll work this out with the producers so they can let us loose for bathroom time. But before we leave, I need to say something while we're not miked." He pulls the chain so we're in the corner, as far away from the door as possible.

For some reason, my heart starts to pound. What is that about? I have no feelings for this man. Well, no good ones. He's arrogant and cocky and rude. He's also talented and handsome and hot.

Maybe I need hormone cream.

"What's going on, Rhett?"

His voice is barely above a whisper. "Have they been asking you questions about us?"

"Who? Production?"

"Yes. In your confessionals?"

"All the time. Why?"

"One of them let it slip to me that the audience is asking these questions."

"So?"

"The audience votes, Sunny."

"And?"

He smiles slightly. "You really are naive, aren't you?"

"I guess I am because I don't know what you're trying to say."

"The object of this game is to get to the end, right?"

"Of course."

"And how do we get to the end?"

"By winning the challenges. I want to take a nap. Can we wrap this up?"

"A nap? What are you? Three years old?"

"No, I'm thirty years old and chained to a big goober who won't let me take a nap."

"Listen, I think there's a way to greatly improve our odds of getting to the end."

"How?"

"Come on out of there, guys!" the producer yells again. "I heard you flush two minutes ago!"

"Coming!" I yell back.

"She's going for a second seating!" Rhett yells back. "Extra-long intestines, it seems!"

I slap him. "Stop it!"

"Anyway, as I was saying, I think I have a plan to get us to the end so we can battle it out."

"Oooh, so conniving. I love it. What's the idea?"

"We pretend to be in love."

My heart starts pounding against my chest bone again. I feel like it will pop out and smack Rhett right in his chiseled chest. "Excuse me, what?"

He holds up his free hand. "Look, I know it sounds crazy…"

"Crazy? Um, yeah. It does sound crazy that I would pretend to be in love with my rival. The man who picks on me and annoys me more than most other humans. Well, maybe except Big Thelma…" I say, my voice trailing off as I pit the two of them against each other in my mind.

"Who in the heck is Big Thelma?"

"Never mind. I'll tell you later while you're chained to me, and we have nothing else to talk about. Explain yourself, Rhett. This is a crazy, insane, idiotic idea. Are you well?" I reach up and put my hand on his forehead.

"Haha. Very funny. Do you want to win? And open your bakery? And help your sister?"

"Of course I do," I say softly.

"Then think about it. If we pretend to be in love, or at least heading that way, viewers will eat that up. They'll vote us through to keep watching."

"Their votes only count for thirty percent, though."

"That's a lot, Sunny. At least it gives us an edge."

I think for a moment. "No. I can't. There's no way anyone would believe us. We can't stand each other."

"Agreed. But couldn't we fake it enough to get to week six?"

"So you want me to act like I love you for five more weeks?"

"A little over four now. It's not that long. How long did you pretend to love Connor?"

I giggle. "No comment."

"And you didn't even get paid for that."

"Rhett, this isn't going to work. What if it back-fires? What if people hate us as a couple and send us home?"

He shakes his head. "I don't think they will. I've put a lot of thought into this. It's our best chance."

"I need time to think about it."

"I'll tell you what. You think, and you give me some kind of signal one way or the other."

"What kind of signal?"

"I don't know. Just something I can't miss."

"Well, that's totally helpful," I say, rolling my eyes.

"Okay, fine. If you want to move forward, say the word '*hippopotamus*.'"

"Are you serious right now?"

"I'm picking this lock in ten seconds," we hear a producer say from the other side of the door. We both turn our mics back on and walk out.

"Don't forget the code word," Rhett whispers before turning our mics back on.

What in the world am I going to do?

RHETT

I just asked Savannah to pretend to love me.

I've obviously lost my mind.

It's an insane plan. It's not something I would normally do. I don't know what came over me.

I can't put the genie back in the bottle now. It's out there, and she thinks I've lost my marbles.

I know it will work. If we can seem believable, the audience of these shows will devour a love story.

But Savannah hates me. She's right. There's no way people will believe we care about each other. That we *love* each other.

"Are you actually going to take a nap?" I ask as she drags me along behind her. For a tiny woman, she sure is strong.

"Yep," she says as we enter her room. Lainey has already moved to Connor's room until our chains are removed, so her bed is empty. "Let's push these closer together."

I can imagine what viewers are thinking right now. This is TV gold.

I do as she says and move Lainey's bed closer to hers. She kicks off her white tennis shoes and lays down, pulling the fuzzy blanket she brought up to her waist. I just stand there looking down at her.

"How long do your naps typically last?"

"Just an hour or so."

"An hour? Seriously?"

"What's wrong with that? There's nothing else to do here anyway."

"Oh, Sunny, life is passing you by. You could be exercising or playing a game of pool or practicing a skill…"

"No thanks," she sings back at me. "Are you just gonna stand there while I sleep like some kind of creeper?"

I sigh, knowing I'm not going to win this fight. I sit on the bed and swing my sock feet around before lying down and staring at the ceiling, our arms dangling between the twin beds. This is like some weird summer camp for convicts.

I look over at her, and her eyes are closed, her long red hair trailing behind her head on the pillow. "So, this is it? You just lie here and fall asleep? Just like that?"

She turns and looks at me, obviously amused. "That's how naps work, Rhett. And here's the crazy thing—I do it all over again when it gets dark!" She gasps and puts her hand over her mouth to mock me.

"I don't think I've taken a nap since I was a toddler," I say, looking back at the ceiling and wondering why no one has painted over the stains on the ceiling where rain leaked through at some point. I notice these sorts of things.

"I love to nap. My favorite is on a rainy day when it's gloomy and gray outside. I love to hear the raindrops hitting the roof. I live on the top floor of my apartment building, and I wish it were a metal roof. I dream of having a metal roof one day."

"So it can sound like you're being shot in a war zone every time it rains?"

She pokes out her ample lips. "Are you always this much fun?"

"Always," I say, winking. Why did I just wink? I never wink.

"I'm closing my eyes now, Rhett," she says. Within moments, I can tell she's actually asleep. People really do this? They just decide to sleep? In the middle of the day? How magical to be able to lie down, close your eyes, and drift off like the world isn't this crazy place you need to think about all the time.

I roll onto my right shoulder and watch her like a lunatic. I can't help it. She looks so peaceful. I would think she was dead if her cheeks weren't so rosy. Is that makeup? I don't think it's makeup. She doesn't seem to wear anything but a light shade of lip gloss. Savannah is what one would call a girl next door. She's pretty without knowing it.

What is going on with me? Why am I romanticizing this woman who isn't anything like the women I date? Who honestly can't stand me? Who annoyed me by her mere existence during school?

She sighs in her sleep, and I want to scoop her up like a lost kitten.

Oh no. This isn't good. Is that why I suggested we pretend to be in love? Do I have some completely wrong feelings stirring around inside my cold heart for this woman?

Certainly not. Impossible.

SAVANNAH

It's startling to open your eyes from a nap and see someone staring at you, but here I am. Rhett is lying on his side, his piercing blue eyes staring back at mine.

"Hello," he says dryly. "I was wondering if you were ever going to wake up. I considered checking your pulse."

"Whatever," I mumble, really wanting to continue my nap a bit longer. "How long was I asleep?"

He looks at his watch. "Five weeks. Everyone has gone home, and we both lost."

"Very funny."

"We need to go downstairs. We have kitchen duty, remember?"

I totally forgot it was our turn to do the dishes

after lunch. There was probably a sink full of dirty dishes waiting for us. "Right."

We make our way to our feet and maneuver down the curved staircase. This whole show has been one uncomfortable thing after another. Cameras are watching me 24/7. Ex-boyfriend right down the hall. Rival literally attached to me by a chain.

I must be insane to continue this competition.

"Do you want to wash or dry?" Rhett asks.

"Isn't there a dishwasher?"

"I'm sure there is, but if we do that, we'll have five loads to clean all the dishes. I think we should put in a load and wash the rest by hand."

I sigh. "I'll dry."

He chuckles. "How did I know you'd pick that?"

"Then why give me a choice? Of course, I'm going to pick the one that doesn't involve me sticking my hands in dirty water where other people's food is floating."

"They have these things called gloves, you know?"

We walk into the kitchen, and everyone is gone. They're all out in the courtyard playing pool, chatting, or sitting in the hot tub. I wish I was with them.

Rhett plugs the sink and turns on the water to

allow it to fill up. He squirts some blue dish soap into the water and then hands me a dish towel.

"I need a snack," I say, looking up and down the countertops. Maybe I'm procrastinating a bit but doing dishes has always been something I abhor. It's Sadie's job in our apartment.

"You'll do anything to avoid these dishes, won't you?"

I bump my shoulder into his side. "I'm hungry. Open that cabinet and see if there are any chips."

He rolls his eyes. "For such a tiny woman, you sure like junk food. You've risked your life for it once already."

"What can I say? It's my only vice."

Begrudgingly, Rhett walks away from the sink and opens the corner cabinet, reaching high up and feeling around for my prized snack selection.

"There's nothing here but a box of raisins and a package of stale cookies," he says, pulling each of them out of the cabinet and examining them. I rise onto my tiptoes and look around his hulking body for proof.

"So, no chips?"

"You need to see a nutritionist."

Just as I'm thinking of a witty retort, I feel something under my bare foot. Water?

As if in slow motion, we both turn around and

see a mountain of bubbles in the sink that almost covers the window, looking out over the courtyard. There's water pouring over the side of the sink and onto the floor.

"Oh no!" I screech as Rhett immediately rushes toward the faucet to turn it off. But we're attached by a chain, and he yanks me along with him. My bare feet slip from under me, and I fall toward the floor. Rhett manages to hit the faucet handle with his hand, turning it off, before he topples to the floor with me, landing right on top of me.

Having the wind knocked out of you by a giant man isn't something I'd recommend.

"Ouch!" I yell. He looks down at me, shock written all over his face, and then pushes up onto his forearms.

"Are you okay?"

"I'm fine," I say, breathless. That's when I realize Rhett is on top of me. All of him. I can feel his chest heaving, his heart pounding. I can feel his warmth and taut muscles. All of it is good. My face flushes, giving my thoughts away.

"I guess we should get up," he says. Well, it was more of a whisper. Like one of those hot, sexy whispers in a movie.

"I guess we should."

Neither of us moves. How have I never noticed

those little flecks of green around his blue eyes? Or how naturally pink his lips are? Or how he has this little scar just over his right eyebrow that I want to know the story of?

Finally, Rhett adjusts his body and makes it up onto his hip. All of this is harder due to the stupid chain that connects us. I feel like I need to escape. Get away from whatever these feelings are. Maybe I just need to get on one of those dating apps and have more male interaction, so when a good-looking guy falls on top of me, I don't go to places I shouldn't in my mind.

I don't like Rhett. In fact, he annoys me in ways I can't imagine anyone else would. He gets under my skin like pieces of fiberglass.

*I don't like Rhett.*

"I'm going to try to get up. You stay here until I get my footing," he says.

I can't believe no one came inside when they heard us yelling. They're all too focused on hanging out, so we're on our own.

Rhett slowly pushes off with one hand and knee until he's almost standing, but then the soapy water on the floor takes him down again. This time, he manages to land beside me, both of us on our backs staring at each other. Within seconds, I'm in hysterics laughing.

He eyes me closely for a few moments before I see it. A smile. An actual smile. The smile turns into a chuckle. Then, a full-blown laugh. Before we know it, we're both laughing so hard that we're sobbing. Just me and Rhett, lying on the floor laughing our heads off.

I finally catch my breath enough to speak. "I'm soaked from head to toe!"

"You look like a wet dog!" he says, cackling. I've never seen this side of him before. He has little laugh lines at the corners of his eyes. He has an actual dimple. If I had a dimple, I'd smile all the time just to show it off.

"Oh yeah? Well, you look like a…"

"What on earth is going on here?"

We turn our heads and see Maggie standing by the stove, staring at us with her mouth hanging open. I feel like I just got caught by the principal.

"We had a little… incident," Rhett says. His nonchalant explanation sends us both into hysterics again. By the time we finally calm down, Maggie has gone to get help. Nate and Hank help both of us up to our feet and away from the water while Zara and Tanya start wiping the floor.

"I'm so sorry, y'all. Thanks for helping us," I say, feeling embarrassed by what they just witnessed. They have to wonder how I got on this show. So far, my reputation as a professional pastry chef hasn't been great. And now I look like I can't even wash dishes without creating an international incident.

"We're going to go get changed, and then we'll do the dishes," Rhett says to the group that has now formed in the kitchen.

Maggie waves her hand. "We'll take care of the dishes. Just go get dried up." She rolls her eyes like a scolding mother as we slink away up the stairs, still laughing.

# CHAPTER 14

RHETT

AFTER OUR LITTLE incident of slip-and-slide in the kitchen, Savannah and I went upstairs to get changed since we were both soaked all the way to the bone. Thankfully, they unchained us for a few minutes so that we could change our clothes and get a moment to ourselves. I don't know about her, but that was not only an embarrassing, but highly funny episode in the kitchen. Nothing like that has ever happened to me in my life.

I don't tend to live a very humorous life. I'm a pretty serious guy. I think most people would agree, but I just couldn't stop laughing for some reason. I don't remember laughing that hard in my entire life. And then there was the falling on top of the beautiful woman who's supposed to be my archrival. That was unexpected. I want to say that I didn't enjoy it immensely, but I can't.

Thankfully, I got off her as quickly as I landed there, just so there was no miscommunication. Although I'm sure the viewers at home had a good time with it. I still hold to the fact that if we pretend to be in a relationship, we'll get further in this game, but I'm not going to press the issue with Savannah.

Maybe it was a crazy idea. Maybe I secretly have some feelings I don't want to admit. Either way, she hasn't said anything else about it, and I'm sure falling on top of her on the kitchen floor probably did not endear her to me enough to want to pretend to be in a fake relationship. Oh, well, it's a good memory anyway.

We have to get ready and go to the reward challenge now. So the producers chain us back together like a couple of prisoners as we head off to the industrial kitchen. Everybody is chatting away. I can tell they are making friendships that I'm not. Of course, I have to be friendly with Savannah since I'm chained to her, but I'm sure that after she gets disconnected from me, it will go right back to what it was before—her hanging out with Maggie and me hanging out by myself looking sullen, as usual.

There have been times in my life when I've

wanted to be more interactive and social, but I'm always in my head. I can't seem to get out of there. I don't know if I ever will, but it is useful when we're doing challenges like this.

Today, Savannah and I have to work together in the same kitchen area. So far, that hasn't gone well, but we'll see how it pans out. As long as I don't turn on the faucet, we should be fine. Only a few nights sleeping next to each other, and this will be over. Of course, there could be some crazy twist where we're chained together for life.

We walk into the kitchen, and everybody goes to their stations, waiting for Dan to come out and give us instructions. The three judges file in and sit behind their little table at the head of the room. The cameras and lights get ready, and taping begins. Today, Dan is wearing one of the tackiest suits I've seen so far. It's pink, which isn't a problem in and of itself, but on him, he looks like a giant bottle of Pepto Bismol.

"Welcome to this week's reward challenge," he says so excitedly that I can barely listen to him without covering my ears. "Today's challenge is that you're going to create a dessert that looks like a breakfast item. When we look at it, it should look like something we're about to eat for breakfast, but when we bite into it, it should be a sweet and tasty dessert. You will have just two hours to complete this task. Ready, set, go!"

He throws his arm up in the air like we're about to take off in a foot race, and everybody starts running around the kitchen. But we can't run around the kitchen because we're chained together, so we just stand there like two animals with their legs caught in a trap.

"So what should we do?" Savannah says, looking at me with those big doe eyes of hers. Why do they make me feel tingly?

"Where's my sketchbook?" I say, looking around.

"I don't know where your sketchbook is," she says.

Oh, no. I've left it in the room. I wasn't even thinking straight after the whole kitchen floor incident. I can't do this without my sketchbook.

"Are you okay?" she asks, looking at me concerned.

"Yeah, I'm fine," I say quietly. "I just didn't know I didn't have my sketchbook, and it's too late to get it now."

"Oh. It's okay, Rhett. We can do fine without it," she says, trying to ease my nerves.

My sketchbook is like a child's teddy bear. If I'm cooking, I take it with me. It's the one thing I can count on. I know if I can draw it, then I can make it.

229

Otherwise, I don't have nearly as much confidence in myself.

"Yeah, I guess so," I say under my breath.

She looks at me as if she realizes my confidence is fragile. "You know what? I have a great idea. Why don't we make a stack of pancakes out of sponge cake with mascarpone cream filling between the layers, and we'll top it with a caramel sauce that looks like maple syrup? And then we can add some macerated strawberries on top."

I just stare at her like she's a genius. Like Einstein himself is standing in front of me. How did she come up with that so quickly?

"That sounds like a great idea, actually," I say, slightly smiling. I'm kind of impressed with her right now. "I'll let you lead then because it's your idea, and I don't have my sketchbook."

She looks over at me before she starts making the recipe. "You're more than just a sketchbook, Rhett. You need to remember that."

I nod imperceptibly, and then we start moving together around the kitchen. It's like we're perfectly in sync all of a sudden. We haven't been chained together all that long, but it seems like if we had to do this for a lifetime, we would be okay. Not that I would want to be chained to anybody for a lifetime. It's incredibly hard to change your clothes or go to the bathroom with another person chained to you, even if she's pretty. Even if you need your hormones to be medically turned off.

We continue moving around the kitchen and then we stop to start assembling the ingredients. I reach over to grab the powdered sugar that we've set on the counter in front of us, and Savannah reaches for it at the same time I do. Without warning, our hands are touching, mine over the top of hers. Her hand is so small and warm. Her skin is very smooth and soft. I feel like I have a giant mitt covering up her tiny, dainty hand.

Both of us just freeze in place and stand there for a moment, looking at each other. It's like one of those silly scenes out of a romance movie. I don't know what's happening here. Is she feeling something, or is she just concerned I'm about to break her hand?

"Sorry," she says, pulling her hand back like she's touched a hot stovetop.

Yeah, she's not interested. I'm just making all of this up in my mind. I really need to go out on some more dates. Obviously, I'm not getting enough female attention, and now I'm assuming that every woman who accidentally brushes her hand against mine is suddenly in love with me.

"It's okay," I say, brushing it off.

But is it okay? It doesn't feel okay. When the competition is finally over, which includes a reward of finding out what the main competition is ahead of time and getting fifteen minutes of extra practice, Connor wins.

Connor, that idiot, somehow wins even though our pancake stack looks just like real pancakes. If I saw it sitting on a counter, I would walk over and think I was eating pancakes. The judges seemed to like it, but they liked a lot of people's creations today. I think we were at the very bottom, in fact. I needed my sketchbook.

It's not that Savannah's idea wasn't great—it was. It looked good. It just wasn't intricate or complicated enough to win. It's my fault for not bringing my sketchbook so we could design something more elaborate together.

Connor made a stack of waffles that looked like real waffles with crumbled, candied bacon on the top. He also made a side yogurt parfait with crumbled pieces of toffee. He went over the top, and he won. That's a note for next time. Go over the top, be intricate. Be "extra", as the young kids say. That's the only way to win here.

SAVANNAH

"Sorry again that we didn't win," I say as we leave the industrial kitchen. I don't know how many times I've said it so far, but it seems excessive, even to me. Rhett shakes his head.

"Again, it's not your fault. We were a team."

"I know, but I came up with the idea…" I start to say.

He holds up his free hand. "It's not your fault, Savannah. Connor won fair and square, as much as I hate to say it. It actually makes a little bile come up in my throat."

I laugh. *Rhett* is making me laugh. That's weird.

"He's talented, I'll give him that. He's just a horrible person."

"Yes, that's very true from what I've seen."

"Excuse me, Rhett and Savannah?" One of the producers walks up to us. She's the one with the perky bosom and blonde hair. I glance over to see if Rhett notices the perky bosom. If he does, he doesn't show it.

"What's up?" he says in his normal deadpan-sounding voice.

"We would like to get you both in for a confessional." The confessional is where the producers pull you into a soundproof room and ask you questions.

We've realized that the questions they ask often come in from social media. This is how they add drama to the show, but it's something that we have to do multiple times a week, if not daily.

"We'll follow you," Rhett says, pulling me along by our chain.

We enter the room and sit on the small, sleek, modern sofa they have set up with a green screen behind it. I don't know what they put behind us on the TV, but it doesn't really matter.

"Okay, let's get started," the producer says. They never waste any time because this is a reality show, and it's supposed to seem real. They can't interact with us or ask us how things are going unless cameras are rolling to catch it. They can't have normal conversations with us. It's all about the show. "So, Savannah, how do you feel after another loss today?"

"Well, that makes me feel good to hear you say," I say, rolling my eyes. "Connor won fair and square. His dessert was better than ours. Plain and simple." I try to brush it off, but what I really want to say is that *Connor is a jerk, and he should win nothing and be kicked off the show and kicked out of the United States and maybe kicked off the planet.* But I just smile.

"What about you, Rhett? Do you feel like working with Savannah caused you to lose the challenge?" I can see Rhett's face turning a shade of red I haven't seen before. I feel his pinky nail dig into the side of my leg. I don't even know if he realizes he's doing that. I mean, we're sitting close together.

"No, absolutely not. Savannah had a great idea, but we were just beaten by a better idea. It's really as simple as that."

"So we saw something interesting from the two of you earlier today." Here it comes. The dishes, the water on the floor, the giggling like two children.

"Oh, yeah. What's that?" Rhett says.

"It seems that you overflowed the kitchen sink and ended up in quite a predicament on the floor." She smiles like she's got inside information. It's not inside information. It was broadcast online in real-time and will likely be on tonight's taped show for TV viewers to enjoy.

"Accidents happen," Rhett says, crossing his arms and pulling my arm straight up in the air. When he realizes what he is doing, he drops his arms back down by his sides, the edge of his hand brushing against my bare leg. It gives me a shiver that I hope people can't see through their screens.

"Would you call it an accident, Savannah, or do you think maybe Rhett purposefully overflowed the sink so you two could roll around together on the floor?"

I stare at her with my mouth hanging open. "What? Why would anyone do something like that?"

"Our audience seems to think there's something romantic going on between the two of you. They're quite mesmerized by it, to be honest." This is interesting. The producers aren't supposed to tell us stuff like that; at least, I didn't think so.

"Again, there is no romance going on between me and Rhett," I say, looking over at him. He doesn't make eye contact. He wants there to be a fake romance, but I don't see the point.

"Are you sure? You two seem to have some great chemistry."

"I don't know how anyone is seeing that. It was just funny that we slipped and fell in the water. It was pretty soapy."

"Still, it seems like something might be going on between you two. Why don't you want to admit it?"

Rhett has finally had enough. "Look, Savannah says nothing is going on, which means nothing is going on." He stares at the camera. There's a long, awkward silence.

"Okay, then, well, I guess we're finished here," the producer says, looking down at her notes. We both stand up, walk out of the room, and head straight up the stairs. I can tell Rhett is bothered but can't say anything. The confessional is private. Only the audience at home sees it. We can't talk about what we said in the confessional on camera. We can't talk about much of anything on camera.

Suddenly, he takes a detour into one of the hallway bathrooms.

"Do you need to go?" I ask.

"Yeah, come on," he says, pulling me into the bathroom with him before the cameraman down the hallway can spot us. Sometimes, we're being filmed just by moving cameras on the walls. Other times, there are actual camera people following us around, depending on what shots they need to get. Somehow, he managed to get us into the bathroom without us being seen by one of those people, but I'm sure the cameras on the wall just caught that.

Usually, we get one of the producers to unchain us before going to the bathroom. But this time, he pulls me in with him and shuts the door.

"What are you doing? We can get unchained. Wait, is this like an… emergency?" I say, scrunching up my nose.

"No, I don't have to go to the bathroom," he says after taking his mic off and reaching around to take mine from my lower back. My skin prickles.

"Then why are we in here?"

"Because I need to talk to you," he says, pulling us

closer to the corner. Now we're standing face to face, just an inch or so between our noses.

"Did you hear what they were asking us?"

"Of course I did. I was sitting right beside you."

"Do you see how they're focused on thinking we're in some sort of a relationship?"

"Yes, I know. The audience has a vivid imagination, apparently."

"Well, I still think that you need to consider us playing into that. We will definitely get further in this competition if we do."

I stare up at him. "You're very talented. We don't have to play games to get further. We don't have to pretend something that's not real."

"This isn't just about talent, Savannah. This is about popularity."

"What do you mean?"

"The audience at home is voting on these main challenges. We can already see that the judges are not a huge fan of yours."

"Gee, thanks."

"You haven't won any of the challenges yet. This is a chance for you to get further."

"Well, maybe I don't want to get further unless it's on my own merit."

"Savannah, you've got to get in the real world with me."

"Excuse me?"

"Again, this is a mixture of talent and popularity. And maybe I'm a little bit worried about myself."

"How so?"

"I'm not exactly the most likable guy. On my own, I'm not going to make it far in this competition. I'm going to say something snarky, and the audience will vote me off."

"Oh, so you want to use me to your own benefit?

"In a word? Yes. And I want you to use me."

My face heats up. "What does that mean exactly?"

"Not what you think. Get your mind out of the gutter. What I mean is that with your personality and my talent..."

"And *my* talent," I interrupt.

"Of course, you have great talent. I thought that was a given."

"Well, it wasn't."

"Okay. Anyway, with your personality and both of our talents, I think we can get to the end. But alone, I'm not so sure."

"So you're saying that people will keep voting me through even if I don't win the challenges just because they want to continue watching our supposed romance?"

"That's exactly what I'm saying. And they'll keep

me here despite my terrible personality because they like you and want to see this romance."

"Why would they want to see this?" I'm completely baffled by all of this.

"Because there's nothing better than a romance trope where the woman is sunshine, and the man is dark clouds, and she changes him."

"I think that's a very stereotypical way of looking at romance readers."

"Well, I'm sure if you looked at the sales of those kinds of books, you would see what I mean."

"Either way, Rhett, I don't think we need to do this. Deceive the audience? It just doesn't seem right."

He laughs. "And this is why you're all sunshine. You see everything as the glass half full."

"And you don't?"

"I don't even see the glass."

# CHAPTER 15

RHETT

I TRIED my best to talk her into it. We stayed in the bathroom far too long, and then Lainey knocked on the door because she needed to touch up her makeup. She should be finished by sometime tomorrow.

We went through dinner with everyone, sat at the table, and listened to lots of small talk, but all I could think about was my plan; if we could just convince the viewers that we were falling in love, they would keep us around for longer.

Sure, I should want to win based on my own talents, but I know myself, and I know how other people react to me. I'm a nice guy, but sometimes you can't see it. I seem like a grump, a grouch, a pessimist. Sometimes I feel that those things are true, but I know there's a different man inside of me somewhere. He's just a little too scared to come out and show his face.

Either way, I can't think about that right now. All I can think about is how this plan would work if Savannah would just agree to it. Sure, I could make some kind of bold move for the cameras, but she's liable to punch me right in the nose if I try to hold her hand or sneak a kiss on her cheek. She's having none of it.

I get the feeling that Savannah is a romantic at heart. She wants that big grand love and doesn't want to pretend with me on national television. I can see her point, but I know that $200,000 would be a nice amount to see in my bank account. In the end, only one of us can win, so maybe she doesn't want to give me a leg up by participating in this charade.

"I'm exhausted," she says, which makes me laugh. "What are you laughing at?"

"You're always tired. Maybe you should get your blood checked."

We're walking upstairs to the bedroom. Maggie is already lying down and snoring by the time we get there. I think she's narcoleptic, but I would never say anything. She's a sweet woman, but she sleeps like a rock, and she snores like a freight train.

"Let's not wake her," Savannah whispers.

"I don't think that's possible," I whisper back.

The producers disconnect us for five minutes so we can change into our sleep clothes. I am in a pair of shorts and a white T-shirt, and Savannah is in a pajama set with shorts and a little top. I try not to glance at her legs. They're very nice, but she's made it supremely clear that she does not want to be my fake girlfriend. We both slide into our beds, pulling the covers up, and she turns out the lamp, and then it's just darkness. I've never understood how people can go to sleep like this.

When I go to bed, it's a whole routine. First, I stay up as late as possible until I'm about to fall over. Then I turn on the TV and lie down in my bed. And at some point, I pass out. When I wake up in the morning, the TV is still running. I turn it off and go on about my day.

But apparently, there are people just like this who turn off the light, lie down, and go to sleep. It seems like magic. But Savannah's not falling asleep for some reason, even though she said she was tired. The moonlight is shining into the room, casting a long line across our beds and the hardwood floor. I can see her staring at the ceiling.

"You okay?"

"Yeah. I guess I wasn't as tired as I thought." Her voice sounds different. Sad. Is she crying?

"What's going on?"

"I don't know. I guess I'm thinking about my sister and what she's doing. We've never been apart this long."

"It's great that you have such a wonderful relationship with her. I wish I had that with my siblings."

"You don't?" she says, turning her head. "I didn't even know you had siblings."

"Yeah, I've got two brothers. We're not close."

"Why not?"

"I guess because I'm the black sheep of the family," I say, staring back up at the ceiling. "They're all attorneys and doctors in my family. They wanted me to follow suit, and I didn't, so here we are."

"Surely they're still very proud of you. I mean, you're working with celebrities on yachts."

"Yeah, my mom thinks I should *own* the yacht, not cook for people on it."

"Oh, I'm sorry. It's hard not to have a supportive family."

"It's definitely difficult."

I realize I'm on national television, so I don't want to say much more, but I'm glad I got to share at least that much with her. I don't share much with anybody.

"I know how hard it can be not to have people cheering you on. The only person that cheers me on is Sadie. My mom never could do that in my life, really. She was a mess."

"How long ago did she pass away?"

"Oh, it's been a while now. She died when Sadie was twelve, so about eight years ago. But even before that, she wasn't a great mom. She had her own demons."

"That's hard to imagine."

"Why?"

"Well, I mean, you seem so put together. Nice and proper and modest."

"I do?" Savannah says, laughing. "I never realized that about myself, but yeah, my mom was pretty screwed up. Addiction will do that to a person. She had mental health issues that made it more complicated. She never should have had children."

"I'm sorry you had to grow up that way."

"Well, it made me who I am, and I guess I like myself pretty well. I just wish I was richer."

I laugh. "Well, for what it's worth, I think you're doing really well in the competition. Getting to work with you, I can see how hard you work at this, and I think you'll start winning some competitions."

"Yeah? I don't know. I'm not sure that I will. I'm not really much for competition. I kind of like everybody to just work together and get along."

"Well, it's not exactly interesting television," I say.

We lay there for a few more minutes, just staring up. Finally, Savannah sighs.

"This is pretty boring. Want to go for a run?"

She laughs. "How in the world are we going to run while we're wearing these chains?"

"We'll figure it out."

We quietly make our way down into the courtyard. The lights are dimmed at night, so it doesn't keep everyone in the neighborhood awake to see the lights that normally illuminate it. That's fine with me. I like running in the dark.

Of course, I've never taken a run with another person chained to me. Surprisingly, Savannah couldn't sleep either. There's just something about being chained to another person and worrying about the upcoming main challenge later this week that keeps you from getting a restful night of slumber.

"So how are we going to do this?" Savannah asks,

breaking me out of my chain of thought as we enter the courtyard grassy area. It's fake grass, bright and green. Perhaps if you saw it in somebody's yard, you would think it was real, but out here, you can tell. It's not a big area. I just usually run back and forth until I tire myself out.

"I'm not sure. Obviously, we're not going to be able to swing both of our arms very well," I say, laughing.

"I'm not much of a runner, so I hope we don't have to go fast," Savannah says. She's wearing a short-sleeved pajama shirt and shorts. It's kind of cute. I'm trying not to notice. I'm also wearing a T-shirt and shorts, but I've also put on my running jacket after catching a producer in the hallway and asking to be unchained for a moment so I could slide it on. It's not cold outside, but sometimes, these early summer nights can have a little bit of a cold snap, which seems to be what's happening tonight. Plus, I like to sweat a little extra to burn calories.

I don't really need to lose weight, but on a frame as big as mine, putting on weight would be very easy.

"We'll just take it slow," I say. I start stretching my quads and my calves. Savannah notices what I'm doing and does the same. She bends over and touches her toes like we're in an aerobics class, and I try not to steal a look. But still, I'm a guy. I can't help it.

"Were you just looking at my butt?" she says, catching me in the act.

"Absolutely not. I was making sure that you were doing proper stretching form," I lie. I can't really see her rear end very well anyway, given that we're chained together, but I got a good enough look that I know it's not a bad visual.

"Yeah, sure you were," she says, eyeing me carefully and stifling a smile. "It's a little bit cooler out here than I thought it would be."

"I suppose it is. I wish the days were as cool."

"Me too. It's pretty hot. I don't come out here much during the day because of being a redhead and fair-skinned. We're not exactly known for our tanning capabilities."

"Well, you can't have everything," I say, wishing I could put the words back into my mouth. Telling her that she has everything else except for the ability to tan is why the viewers at home think that we have some sort of romance going on, or perhaps they think that I'm just some love-struck fool and Savannah has no interest in me. Maybe that's true, but I don't think too hard about it.

"I guess we should get started," I say. We start with a light jog, trying to get the right rhythm between us, a chain hanging between us.

We can swing our arms just a bit, but not as much as one would during a normal jog. We go back and forth a few times before Savannah says she needs to take a break.

"I guess my lungs aren't as healthy as I thought they were. I've got a touch of asthma."

"Oh, I didn't know that," I say. "I'm sorry. Do you not want to do any more of this? It's totally fine if you can't do this."

"No, it's okay. I exercise regularly. Well, at least when I have time, but I don't do a lot of cardio, and I can certainly tell," she says, holding a hand to her chest. "Maybe we could just take a little break?"

"Of course." I see her rubbing her arms, and I can visibly see the goosebumps. "Are you cold?" I ask her as we walk over to sit on the outdoor sofa in the corner of the courtyard.

It's a big sectional piece that fits many people, and most of the contestants sit out there all day chatting, some of them smoking.

"Just a bit. It's fine."

"No, it's not," I say, stopping. I turn my jacket inside out and slide one sleeve across the chain and onto her shoulders. "Here, let me help you," I say, pulling her arm into the other sleeve. She looks at me and smiles.

"Wow, that was quite a smooth move, Rhett Jennings," she says, laughing. "Have you been chained to women before?"

"Listen, I might be a jerk a lot of the time, but I'm never going to let a woman feel cold while I wear a jacket."

"Careful. You might just ruin my image of you as the evil villain."

I stifle a smile. Why do I feel like this woman *sees* me? I can't put my finger on it, but I feel more myself when she's around.

We sit down on the sofa and lean back, our arms pulled apart by the chain. "I like it out here when it's a little bit darker. During the day, you've got the bright sunshine, and in the evening, they've got these lights on that are like being on a baseball diamond for a night game."

"Yeah, it is kind of nice out here without such bright lights, and you can see the stars," she says, looking up. Even though some light obscures our view, we can still see the black night sky overhead. It's a clear night, and there's a smattering of twinkling stars above us.

"Do you like to stargaze?" I ask.

"I don't ever really get much of a chance to do that. I go to work so early in the morning that I'm exhausted by early evening. So, there's not much reason to go out and stare at the stars. Besides, I think that's kind of a thing couples do, and I didn't have the type of boyfriend who would've been interested in stargazing."

"Yeah, I can see that," I say, grunting. "Connor doesn't seem like the type to do anything overly romantic."

"Believe it or not, he was pretty romantic initially, but I think it was just a fake-out to get me to date him. I turned him down the first few times he asked me out, and he didn't like that at all."

I laugh. "I wish I could have been there for that. I would love to see you turn Connor down."

She giggles and then looks back up at the stars. "It really is beautiful tonight. I remember once in high school, I went out with this guy, and he wanted to impress me on our first date. So we went out to a fancy dinner, and then he took me out to the golf course in the neighborhood where he lived. I certainly had never even been on a golf course. I didn't grow up that way. My mom barely could afford a one-bedroom apartment in the seediest part of town. Anyway, he had a blanket, and we went out on the golf course, laid down, and looked up at the stars."

"And did you enjoy that?" I ask, smiling over at her.

"I did. He was the biggest nerd in our high school, and nobody else would go out with him, but his parents were rich, so he had everything at his disposal. I only went out with him one time. He talked the entire time about mathematical equations and explained every star in the sky and all of the constellations."

I chuckle. "That sounds super romantic."

"Yeah, it really wasn't," she says, looking over at me. "But I learned a lot about stars that night. Like, I know that one over there is the Big Dipper. I'm sure everybody knows that. And I think that up there isn't really a star. I think that's actually Jupiter or Saturn, or… maybe I don't remember as much as I thought I did."

I laugh out loud. Savannah is actually pretty funny if you give her a chance. "Yeah, I don't think you should teach astronomy classes anytime soon."

"Oh, yeah? Well, maybe you should teach me something about stars. What do you know?"

"They're twinkly," I say. Savannah laughs loudly.

"You know, this hasn't been so bad."

"What hasn't?" I ask.

"Being chained to you. Honestly, I thought it would be a nightmare of epic proportions."

"Yeah, I thought the same thing about you, but I think we've done very well in not murdering each other… yet."

"I think so. I'm going to consider that a win."

Honestly, I can't tell her how much I've enjoyed this. I'm not exactly a people person. I don't open up well to others. I don't have a large circle of friends. I've always been a loner, all about business.

And being forced to have these small talk chats with someone seemed like it would be horrible. But with Savannah, it's been easy. I see why people like her, and I feel kind of bad about being such a jerk during our days at pastry chef school.

"Can I say something?"

"Well, I really can't get away from you, given that I'm chained to you right now," she says.

"I want to apologize."

"Rhett Jennings is about to apologize to me for something. Hang on, let me get settled." She sits up straight and turns her body toward mine, looking very interested in whatever it is I'm about to say.

Honestly, I don't know what I'm about to say, but for some reason, I love it when she says my full name. I sit up and face her. "I was horrible to you during school, and I just want to apologize for that. I didn't know you well, and I didn't make any kind of effort to get to know you better. I just judged you on surface-level stuff, so I just wanted to apologize."

She smiles slightly and nods her head. "Thank you. You actually don't know how much I appreciate that. I never understood why you didn't like me, and unfortunately, I'm one of those people who cares if other people like me."

"Yeah, well, I'm one of those people who doesn't care if other people like me, as you can probably tell."

She reaches over and touches my knee, which shocks me and sends a bolt of electricity up my body. "Well, for what it's worth, I think you're actually a pretty nice guy sometimes."

She pulls her hand back, and I instantly feel a void. Should I ask her to put it back on my knee? Would that be weird? Would that get me arrested? I decide not to say anything. "Don't tell anybody I'm a nice guy. It'll ruin my reputation."

She laughs, and then I feel this moment of chemistry between us. The smile goes away on her face, and suddenly, I can feel us leaning toward each other. What's happening? It's like some sort of magnetic attraction. Are we about to kiss? I don't understand. Just as I'm about to find out, the light flips on in the courtyard without warning.

"What's going on out here?"

*Connor.*

Connor is standing there ruining the moment, as usual.

"Are you trying to blind us?" I yell out.

"I was coming out here to play some pool. I can't sleep. I'm too excited about the upcoming challenge, but it seems like I may have interrupted a romantic interlude."

Savannah's face turns red, but I can't tell if it's due to embarrassment or anger.

"You're not interrupting anything, man. Except for us relaxing out here after a run. We're not exactly able to get away from each other."

"Yeah, I bet you'd love to get away from her. I remember that feeling all too well," he says, walking over to the pool table, oblivious to the fact that he actually did just interrupt something. What it was, I have no idea.

"Maybe we should head back upstairs," Savannah says.

"Yeah. Suddenly, the air down here has gotten very limited," I say, standing up.

"Good night, lovebirds," Connor says under his breath as we pass him. I've never wanted to punch somebody square in the nose as much as I want to punch him right now. He has the most punchable face I've ever seen. Instead, I follow Savannah through the kitchen and the foyer and up the stairs, wondering what that moment between us was. We're going to go lay in beds now, right next to each other, chained together, and I don't know if I just missed out on a kiss or if she was about to headbutt me or what was going on. I guess I'll never know.

# CHAPTER 16

SAVANNAH

WHAT IN THE heck just happened? I think I almost kissed Rhett. Was he leaning forward toward me, too? Why did I touch his knee? That was a strange thing to do. He probably thinks I'm some kind of a weirdo.

These are all the thoughts that I'm thinking as we walk back upstairs to go to bed. Now I have to lay next to him all night, him in his little twin bed and me in mine, with a chain draped between us. I'll be so glad when we can disconnect, and I can go back to my normal life of talking to Maggie about my problems and missing my sister. I don't know what's going on in my head. Maybe it's just because I need some companionship, and it feels good to have somebody talking to me and paying attention to me. Connor never really did very well at that. Maybe that's all it is.

Surely I'm not attracted to Rhett Jennings, of all people. He's my rival, isn't he? Is he still my rival? Have we become friends? I'm completely confused. My brain is just going round and round in circles, and I can't get the chatter to turn off.

We get back to the room, and Rhett asks one of the producers to disconnect us for a moment so he can remove the jacket that he's given me. Neither one of us wants to sleep with a jacket on. I go to the bathroom, wash my face, use the restroom, and come back out. The producer chains us back up again. Thank goodness this will be over soon.

Rhett will go back to his side of the house. I'll go back to mine. We'll continue our snarky comments at each other. And then, hopefully, I'll beat him in the sixth week. He'll go home to wherever he lives, on a yacht somewhere with celebrities, and I'll go back to my little apartment, hopefully with a $200,000 check in my hand. This is what I'm planning, anyway.

Right now, I feel very out of control. I don't know what's happening in my mind, in my heart, and why are there butterflies in my stomach all of a sudden?

We both lie down in the beds. Maggie is over in

her bed, still snoring away happily, occasionally kicking a leg or punching something on her side table. I really think she needs to get checked out for some sort of REM sleep disorder. We both lay there staring at the ceiling again, just like we were before we went downstairs to take our little run.

I'm not getting out of this bed again. If I have to pretend to sleep, just so we don't have to talk about anything, I definitely will.

"Should we talk?" Rhett suddenly says.

"About?"

"About whatever that was that just happened."

"You mean the one where my ex-boyfriend flipped on the lights in the courtyard and then acted like a jerk? Is that what you mean?"

I'm hoping that's what he wants to talk about.

"No, I mean, what happened before the jerk came down there."

"We were talking. What are you referring to?"

He turns and looks at me.

"Savannah, come on."

"I really don't understand, Rhett." I can't make eye contact with him. There's no way. If I make eye contact, I will completely give away the thoughts popping through my little redheaded brain. I have a terrible poker face.

"You know exactly what I'm talking about. We were leaning."

I turn onto my left shoulder.

"We were leaning? You want to talk about us *leaning*?"

"You know what I mean."

He's trying to whisper as if the microphones attached to our bodies and all over the room will not pick up what we're saying. Right now, people are sitting in their homes staring at their computers, watching the livestream because they don't have anything better to do with their lives. They want to see what we're doing. And maybe Rhett is right. Maybe they're sitting there hoping there's some sort of romance happening between us, and we just gave them exactly what they wanted. Or maybe I'm just making it all up.

"Fine. It was just a moment. Nothing happened. Nothing's going to happen. Nothing has to happen."

Now, I'm just blabbering away.

"What if it's something that *should* happen?" he says.

"What do you mean?"

"I mean, what if we had continued leaning?"

"Then maybe we would've fallen over," I say dryly. "Look, nothing happened, and we don't need to discuss it. It was just a silly little moment where we both felt a little vulnerable. And thankfully, my idiot ex-boyfriend flipped on the light and ruined everything."

"See? You said *ruined* everything. You wanted it to happen, too," he says, sitting up on one of his elbows. "I'm just trying to figure out what this is all about."

"What do you mean, what it's all about? We're probably just lonely," I finally say.

"I'm lonely all the time, Savannah. All the time, even when I'm around people. But why don't I feel lonely when I'm around you?"

He looks like he would rather have said anything else but that. His mouth clamps shut as if his brain doesn't want any other words to escape.

"What did you say?"

"You heard what I said. I don't want to say it again."

"I don't even know who this person is. You're nothing like you were when we were in school together. You're nothing like you were when we first got in this house together a couple of weeks ago."

"I know, it's very frustrating," he says, using his other hand to massage his brow line. "I don't talk about things like this. I don't get vulnerable."

"Wait a minute," I say in a whisper. Again, thinking that microphones can't catch me. I reach around and flip mine off for a moment, hoping that nobody can make out what I'm about to say. I nod at him, and he flips his off.

"What are you doing? We're not supposed to turn these off."

"I need to ask you a question."

"Okay, what?"

"Is this a part of the whole act?" I ask, using air quotes with one hand.

"What?

"The act that you want me to participate in."

Suddenly, over the loudspeaker, we hear the producers call out, probably waking everyone up in the house, and say, "Savannah and Rhett, put your microphones back on."

Turning your microphones off in a reality TV show house is a big no-no. We were told this over and over.

"Is it part of the act?" I ask before reaching around to turn mine back on.

He looks at me. "Goodnight, Savannah," he says, flipping onto his back.

He then closes his eyes and looks like a corpse. No other words are uttered for the rest of the night. I close my eyes, still staying on my left shoulder because I usually sleep on my side, and look at him, waiting for him to open his eyes. Waiting for him to nod his head and tell me that, yes, this is just part of the act that he wants us to do. The one where we pretend to be in a relationship.

But he never does. He never makes a move. He never says a word. And now I'm wondering: Does Rhett Jennings actually have feelings for me, or is he trying to do something so that we can get to the end of the competition?

If there's one thing I know about him, it's that he will do anything to win this. I can't trust what he's saying or what he's doing, and I have to remember that. Rhett Jennings was my rival and will always be my rival.

RHETT

I wake up earlier than Savannah and turn onto my shoulder to look at her. She is a beautiful woman, so delicate looking with her features, her little upturned nose, full lips, and freckles across the bridge of her nose. She also has them on her arms, but they're not dark. They're just noticeable enough to be adorable.

Her red hair is splayed over her white pillowcase, and she's breathing quietly, unlike Maggie, who sounds like a chainsaw beside me. There's one thing for certain. This woman has no problems sleeping and letting everyone in the world know about it. But still, it doesn't break my concentration as I look at the sunlight starting to pour into the blinds on the window next to us and go right across Savannah's cheek.

I don't know what happened last night. The whole thing is a blur. I felt like I was about to kiss her. Connor interrupted us. I asked her about it and then was accused of faking it for the show.

Of course, there's no reason for her to believe otherwise. I told her I wanted to fake a relationship so we could get further in the game. Of course, she would think that's what I was doing, but unfortunately, that's not what I was doing.

I'm falling for Savannah, which is something I never thought I would hear myself say. If I had said it before, I probably would've checked myself in for a mental evaluation.

Savannah, the goody-two-shoes, always sunshine, always positive Savannah. Not my type at all.

I've never dated anyone like her, and I never planned to. I'm Rhett Jennings. I'm a curmudgeon. I'm a 31-year-old grouch. How in the world could I be interested in her, or she interested in me? Is she? Has she started playing the part without telling me? I don't know what's going on. The lines of reality and make-believe have gotten muddied together.

Everything's a blur. I don't know what to think, and I wish I could wipe away everything that happened in the last twelve hours, but right now, she's asleep, and I'm watching her like a stalker. It's not like I can go anywhere. I'm chained to the woman. If I were standing in her doorway and we weren't chained together, that would be stalking, I tell myself. That would be weird, but this isn't weird at all.

As I'm thinking through all these things, she suddenly opens her eyes and looks at me, startled, like she forgot we were chained together.

"Good morning," I say, trying not to have any emotion in my voice whatsoever. Trying not to tell her that I can smell her shampoo. It smells like strawberries to match her hair color. I remember when I was younger, my friend's older sister had a Strawberry Shortcake doll from the '80s. You could still smell that strawberry smell in its hair. That's what Savannah smells like. She's like a grown-up human Strawberry Shortcake doll.

I probably shouldn't tell her that, but she does wear those cute little vintage aprons that she brought from home with things embroidered on them, including strawberries, so there is precedence for it.

"Good morning," she says, her voice groggy. It sounds about two octaves deeper. She clears her throat. "How long have you been watching me?"

"Not very long," I say. "I just woke up. It's hard to sleep with chainsaw Maggie over there."

She laughs. At least she's laughing. At least maybe she's not so mad at me about last night. I think I was definitely the one leaning in, but she was leaning too, and there's been far too much talk of leaning. It's ridiculous. We're grown-ups. Why can't we just say we were about to kiss? I'm not saying it, but maybe she will.

"Yeah, she's kind of loud. Imagine sleeping in here with her every night, and Lainey, who talks in her sleep, always about herself."

I smile. "I can see that. I hate to have to move back to my room and leave you with that."

"Yeah. It's super fun to hear her give makeup tips in the middle of the night."

"Well, she shouldn't be giving makeup tips unless it's how to wear too much makeup. I swear, some-times I think her face will crack, and everything will fall straight to the ground. The only thing holding it on her face are those giant fake eyelashes that she wears. How many pairs is she wearing at one time?"

"I don't know. I guess I'm just more natural, for better or for worse."

"It's for better," I say without thinking.

"I guess we should get up and start our day," she laughs nervously.

"Yeah, definitely. I'll call the producer to disconnect us so we can get ready. I think we have some kind of an outing we're doing today."

"Yeah, something to distract us from the main challenge coming up."

"Are you nervous?" I ask as we both sit up and face each other.

"I'm always nervous, Rhett."

"You shouldn't be. You're very talented if I've never told you."

"Yeah, I don't think you've ever told me," she says.

"Well, you are, but sometimes I think you psych yourself out. You don't need to do that. You have the skills, Sunny. You just need to use them and be confident in yourself."

"Maybe some of your confidence can wear off on me."

"You don't want this kind of confidence."

"Why not?"

"It's fake confidence, I guess you'd say. I have to really wind myself up to feel like I can do hard things."

"Well, you seem confident. Let's at least say that."

"I'm sure I do."

"I guess we should call the producer then."

"Yes, of course."

## SAVANNAH

We get dressed and head downstairs, where the producers have again called us together. I assume we have another public service day, although I'm unsure what it would be.

Things between Rhett and I seem a little bit strange. I'm not sure exactly what to make of it. I still don't know if he's playing the game of fake relationships or if he's trying to express his real feelings for me; that would seem very out of character for Rhett. I don't think he has true feelings for me.

Maybe he's just bored in the house or trying to convince the audience that we're falling in love so he can get further in the game. Whatever it is, I'm not falling for it. I have to stay focused. It's very important that I get to the end and at least give myself a chance to win that money for me and my sister.

I've allowed myself to start dreaming about opening a bakery, about all the things that could happen if I got my hands on that kind of cash. I found in my life that dreaming is dangerous. Allowing myself to think that things can get so much better can be heartbreaking in the end. But for some reason, I have nothing else to do in this house but think about it.

Maybe I could try manifesting it. I've never tried anything like that before, but I've read and heard about the law of attraction. Maybe it works. If I think about it and pretend I already have it, I'll win it. I don't know. At this point, I would do just about anything to win this competition.

I feel like maybe it's possible. Maybe I'm more talented than I think. After all, Rhett told me so this morning. I never thought I would hear him say that. He was pretty horrible during pastry chef school. Not usually directly at me, but he was still ornery or a curmudgeon, as my grandmother would've called him. He was not friendly. He was not nice. He didn't want to befriend anyone, so he put off that vibe. But here, he seems so different, almost like a nice guy, like a sheep in wolf's clothing instead of the other way around.

"Good morning, everyone," Dan says. His voice is far too loud for the hour. Actually, it's far too loud for most hours. I think Dan needs a volume adjustment. As I listen to him, I realize he reminds me of those cheesy game show hosts from the 70s that I've seen in old clips.

It's just after 8:00 AM and I'm wondering what they've got up their sleeves that we have to do at this ungodly hour. I like to ease into my mornings, have a cup of coffee, make a nice breakfast, and maybe read a little bit before I get on with my day. Of course, when I'm back at home, that doesn't happen. I'm standing in the bakery at 4:00 AM, wishing that I was a self-made millionaire, but instead, I'm making birthday cakes for annoying six-year-olds.

But here, I can kind of do what I want most of the time, except until yesterday when I became chained to Rhett. He goes along with what I want to do for the most part.

"As you probably imagined, today is another public service day. We will be going to a local beach and cleaning it up."

Oh, great. Cleaning? I hate cleaning. If I could buy one thing with money, it would be a housekeeper or a cleaning crew that could come in just once a week. I would even take it once every two weeks. I hate cleaning. Sadie does most of it.

"Yay, that sounds fun," I say dryly under my breath.

Rhett chuckles. "I'm sure it'll be nice to leave this house. Don't you like the beach?"

"I have no idea. I've never been."

"You've never been on the beach?" Rhett says to me, staring like I've just landed from some other planet.

"No, not everyone has been to the beach, Rhett."

"I guess I just thought..." He stops himself and says nothing else.

"It's okay. I just didn't have the kind of upbringing where my mom would take me to the beach."

"I'm sorry," he says. I'm not sure if he's sorry that I've never been to the beach or that he said anything at all. "Well, I'm glad I get to be there when you see it for the first time."

The way he says it is very intimate. Strange. Is this part of the hippopotamus plan? That's what I've decided to call it. *The hippopotamus plan*. It sounds like a great book title. It would be confusing but cool.

They usher us into the van, and off we go. I don't know this area at all, so I have no idea what beach we're heading to or how far away it is. But we're pulling into a nondescript parking lot within about thirty minutes.

Palm trees and dunes are right by the parking lot, so I can't see the ocean yet. We get out, and I can immediately hear it. The sound is so soothing. Of

course, I've heard ocean sounds on YouTube or
meditation audio, but it's different in person. I can
taste the salty air. I can feel a different breeze on my
face than I've ever felt before. It's already warm even
at this early hour.

"Ready?" he asks.

"Yep."

We walk down a pathway, which turns into a
small wooden bridge at the end. As I get to the top of
the bridge, I stop in my tracks. Thankfully, we're at
the end of the line of contestants, and they're all
walking further out onto the sand. But I can't move.
I've never seen anything like this.

The ocean.

It's beautiful.

It's massive.

There's nothing on the other side for as far as the
eye can see. I think I see a little shrimp boat, or
maybe that's a barge of some kind. I can't tell
because it's so far away.

I hear children laughing at one end of the beach. I
see houses dotting the sand all the way down.

"Wow," I breathe out. I can't form any other
words. Seeing the ocean on video just didn't do it
justice.

"It's pretty amazing, huh?"

"I'm sure you see it all the time. You're on yachts."

He smiles slightly and nods his head. "Yeah. I've seen a lot of beaches and beautiful places. But I must say, witnessing you seeing it for the first time is one of my favorites."

Who is this man? Why is he acting this way? It has to be part of the plan. This can't be the real Rhett. I didn't miss this the whole time I knew him.

"It is something I will never forget."

"I need all the contestants over here!" Dan yells out, holding his hand up and looking directly at us. He doesn't care that I'm having a moment over here.

Dan isn't dressed in his normal suit today. Instead, he's wearing a pair of khaki pants and a pink golf shirt, as if heading straight to the golf course after leaving us. Maybe he is. I don't know Dan. I don't know what he does in his off time.

"This area of the beach tends to accumulate a lot of trash," he says when we walk closer. "Today, you're just going to walk up and down the beach, using this stick and putting trash into these big bags."

"Well, I feel like I'm literally on community service now," Rhett says, holding up the stick with one hand and the chain with the other. I laugh, but nobody else does. I guess they don't get our humor.

"We will be here for a couple of hours, so feel free to take your time walking around and picking up trash. I'll be over here looking at my phone," Dan says, sitting on a folding chair. I guess he's not going to participate.

"Well, I guess we should get started," I say.

We start walking around, and I can't help but continue looking at the ocean repeatedly. I kick off my shoes because they are way too hard to walk in on the sand, and Rhett does the same.

"People are so dirty," Zara complains as she walks by with her stick. "Who leaves trash on the beach..." Her voice trails off as she passes us.

I use my stick to spear a plastic water bottle, and Rhett pulls it into the bag. We do this over and over for what seems like the whole day, but I know it's probably only been an hour.

Finally, I need a break. "This is exhausting work. Zara's right. Why are people so dirty?"

"People are lazy, generally speaking. That's what I've found."

"Oh, yeah?"

"You know I am the lead pastry chef on the yachts?" He adds the word yachts as an afterthought, as if I've forgotten where he works.

I want to say, *Yes, Rhett. We all know that you work on yachts*, but I refrain. "I know."

"I have to hire people occasionally, or the boat captain does, and people are generally lazy. They don't want to do the work."

"Well, that's not been me. I've never had the luxury of being lazy." He nods his head.

"We have two totally different situations, but I've never had the luxury of being lazy either. Nobody in my family supports me in what I do."

"So why did you decide not to go be a lawyer or a doctor?"

"I didn't love it. I tried. I worked at my mother's medical office in high school. I went with my dad on legal cases when I was off for summer breaks from prep school. It just wasn't for me."

"How did you tell them?"

"Oh, that was a big argument. During one Sunday dinner, I sat down with my parents and brothers and explained that I wasn't going to medical school even though I had a scholarship, and I wasn't going to law school either. I was going to go to night school to be a pastry chef. I thought my mother was going to pass out."

I chuckle under my breath. "That must've been great to have those options in the first place."

"I'm sorry that you didn't, Sunny. I don't want you to feel bad for me. I would've made a terrible doctor. I'm a hypochondriac. I would've thought I had every single illness somebody came in with." He laughs. "Hey, do you want to walk down by the water a little more?" He points toward the waves, breaking against the shore as they come in.

"Sure." We put down our spears and bags and walk over to the water's edge. I allow the warm liquid to wash over my feet for the first time. I'm so glad I got a pedicure before I came here. My red toenails are visible through the water as it washes over my feet. "This is amazing," I say, smiling like a child. It's probably weird to him that I'm so excited about water on my feet. Instead, he just smiles back.

"I'm glad you got to experience this today."

"Me too." Just then, he looks down and sees something. "Oh, look, there's a crab…"

Before he can finish saying the word crab, the creature runs across my foot. I scream like I've been attacked by a bear and instinctively jump in the air, Rhett catching me. My legs are around his waist, and I have nestled my face in the crook of his neck. I didn't know I was scared of crabs until this very moment.

"It's okay, Sunny," he says, sounding like he's trying to draw a breath and someone's choking him. Oh, it's me. I'm the one choking him. His hands splay across my back, moving in circular motions.

"Oh my gosh. I'm so sorry," I say, suddenly sliding down back to my feet again. But I'm still against him. He still has his arms around me, and I still have my arms around his shoulders. "What happened?" I say as if I forgot what I just did.

"A crab crawled over your foot, and then you mauled me."

I laugh and finally let go. His hands slowly fall from my waist. Why does that make me feel sad? We turn around and notice that the other contestants are staring at us from different areas of the beach. Some of them smile as if they know a secret I don't know. And then there's Connor, who is looking at me like he's sending waves of fire in my direction. The last person I want to look at is Rhett, but I do. And the look on his face is nothing I've seen before. I don't know what he's thinking, but I know what I'm thinking.

*That was nice.*

# CHAPTER 17

RHETT

WE HAD a good day at the beach despite the fact that we were having to pick up trash. I have to say that was something I had never done before in my life. Coming from a family of wealth, we didn't even handle our own trash. We had "people" for that.

My parents had people for everything. They had people to cook for us. They had people to watch over us while they were at work or on one of their vacations. They had people for the yard and people for the cars. I'm glad that they could employ people, but at the same time, it left me with an unrealistic view of the world.

Watching Savannah pick up trash like it was nothing was interesting. She enjoyed the day and her first time at the beach. I have to say that it was inspirational to watch her at the beach. She was so awestruck. It was like watching a little child experience something for the first time.

That was something I had never witnessed in anybody. I've been all over the world. I've seen all kinds of things, but I don't think I've enjoyed seeing something as much as the look on Savannah's face when we came over that bridge onto the beach and she saw the ocean for the first time.

The rest of the day was spent as free time. Because Savannah is so social, we talked to just about every one of the other contestants, which is not something I would normally do. I can be friendly when I need to be, but I'm not a person who enjoys meeting others or small talk. I'm not sure why that is.

Still, we talked to Zara about her travels around the world. We talked to Maggie about losing her husband and how she had started her life over again. We talked to Nate about his family tradition of baking. We also talked to Tanya about her kids and her catering business.

Getting to know all these people wasn't as bad as I thought it would be. Of course, we avoided Connor and Lainey like the plague. We all had lunch and dinner together, so there was plenty of small talk. It wasn't as bad as I thought, either. We learned a lot about each other.

Of course, I didn't say much. I didn't talk about my job, even though I got asked a million questions about it. Connor kept eyeing me during these conversations as if he wanted to say something. I'm sure he did. He always wants to say something stupid. Thankfully, he refrained.

Now, it's our second night chained together. We have to go to sleep. Everybody's in bed, and Maggie, as usual, is already snoring. We asked the producer to unchain us so we could get into our nighttime attire before they chained us back together. Tomorrow is the last day of this.

I'm not sure whether to be happy or sad about that. I never thought I would enjoy being chained to another person for days at a time. We both lie down and turn off the light.

"Goodnight," Savannah says softly. She sounds tired. It's been a long day. We did a lot of physical work this morning.

"Goodnight," I say, knowing I won't fall asleep.

We lay there for a while before Savannah sighs, the same thing she did last night.

"I can't sleep."

"Why?"

"I don't know. I guess I'm thinking about the

competition. I'm thinking about my sister. I'm thinking about the ocean," she says, looking over and smiling. She has the best smile.

"I have an idea if you're up for it," I say, smiling back at her.

"Okay. What is it?"

"Well, why don't we go downstairs and do a little late-night baking?"

"Late-night baking?" she asks, laughing. "Is that a thing?"

"Yeah. We'll have the kitchen all to ourselves, and we can bake up some goodies to share with the others tomorrow."

"Rhett Jennings wants to share with others?" she says, rolling over onto her shoulder.

"Okay, well, maybe it's not really for them. I just like to bake, as you can probably determine."

She laughs and sits up, pulling my arm along with her. "In our pajamas?"

"Well, I'm not going to get dressed in formal wear for it," I say.

"Okay, let's go."

We get up and jog downstairs. I'm surprised we don't trip on the staircase as we go. Is this what giddiness feels like? Maybe I'm just overly exhausted.

We get down into the kitchen and start looking around for ingredients. For some reason, they always lock up the pantry at night, making it much harder to find what we need. But we do find enough to bake a batch of cookies. Maybe two.

"Okay. I want to make pecan praline cookies," I say, starting to look around on the counters.

"You think we're going to be able to find all of the ingredients for pecan praline cookies?" she asks, with her free hand on her hip.

"Okay, maybe you're right. Chocolate chip it is," I say, reaching over and grabbing the large canister of chocolate chips from the counter.

We move around the kitchen in perfect sync. We're getting used to this thing, this being chained together. This must be what married people feel like, the old ball and chain and all that.

Once we put the cookies in the oven, I pull myself up onto the counter and sit there, Savannah leaning against it below me.

"So, do you do a lot of late-night baking regularly?"

"Not really. Since I work at this all day, I'm not in the mood to bake at night. Plus, it's not a lot of fun to do something like this all by yourself."

"Well, you're not all by yourself on a yacht. Tell me some of the celebrities you've worked for," she says, looking up at me, her eyes bright.

I can't tell her the truth. There's no way I can tell her the truth because I wouldn't just be telling her. I'd be telling the entire world, and I'm not ready for that yet.

"I told you I have to sign non-disclosure agreements. Sorry, I can't say it, especially not on television."

She nods and shrugs her shoulders. "Yeah, I guess I understand. So what will we do while we wait for these cookies to finish?"

"We could go sit outside."

"No, I don't like leaving them in here unattended. It would just be like us to burn the whole place down. We couldn't even use the kitchen sink without an entire fiasco."

I laugh, thinking back to that moment.

"Okay, well, we could ask each other some questions."

"Wow. I like this side of Rhett, who wants to talk and ask questions. You go first." She pulls herself up beside me on the counter.

"What's your favorite color?"

"Ocean blue," she says, smiling. "Yours?"

"Emerald green."

"Interesting. My turn. What's your biggest fear?"

"Oooh, a deep one." I think for a moment. "Not being good enough."

She looks at me for a moment. "Good enough for who?"

I shrug my shoulders. "Honestly, I don't know. What's your biggest fear?"

"Spiders."

I laugh. "You must not love Halloween."

"I hate Halloween."

"Me too," I say, struggling to think of another question to ask her. "Do you like to dance?"

"It depends. Fast dance or slow dance?"

My heart speeds up a bit. "Either."

"I'm not so good at fast dancing. I don't think I was given the gift of rhythm, but I love to slow dance. It's been a long time since I've gotten to do it, of course. What about you? Do you like to dance?"

"I have to say I'm pretty good at fast dancing."

"Really? Rhett Jennings is good at fast dancing? I feel like I need to see proof of this."

Am I brave enough? Apparently so, because I jump down off the counter and walk over to the small radio in the corner of the kitchen. I don't know why it's here. I guess it gives us something to listen to without our phones, although it only goes to music channels. Somehow, they've managed to make it so that you can't access any of the news channels because they want us sequestered from the outside world.

I turn it on an 80s station until I find a song that meets my need for dancing. Ironically, the song is Whitney Houston's "I Wanna Dance With Somebody".

"Come on, you have to try it with me," I say.

She shakes her head. "Absolutely not."

"I'm not going to dance alone."

"Fine," she says, jumping down. "But, I warned you, I'm not a good dancer."

"It doesn't matter. If I'm doing it, you have to do it."

Finally, she relents, and we start dancing around the kitchen. The more I dance, the more she dances, and the more we laugh. Every time I'm around her, I laugh.

I wonder how I went through culinary school without realizing that Savannah is very fun and nice. Maybe I was just too focused on myself. Maybe I was just too focused on school. But for some reason, being chained to her has been the most fun I've had in years. I'm kind of dreading them taking us apart. I know she doesn't want to hang out with me twenty-four hours a day. Who would? So she will go back to talking to everybody else, and I will be by myself yet again, trying to fit in a world where I don't think I really fit in.

I try not to think about any of it while we

continue dancing and laughing. She's really not a bad dancer. She might think that she is, but I think it's cute.

Lord, I have got to stop saying things like this to myself. Am I really convincing myself that I'm falling for Savannah? I'm trying to have a fake relationship with her, even though she hasn't agreed to that yet.

*It's not real. It's not real. It's not real.*

I keep telling myself that over and over. This is all pretend on my end, and she's just being nice. I can't think of it as anything else. In a few weeks, if we're lucky, when we leave this house, I probably won't ever even talk to her again. We don't live in the same area. We don't do the same kinds of things. We don't hang around with the same kinds of people. Well, I don't really hang around with any people. I can't convince myself that this is going somewhere.

Maybe it's better that we don't have a fake relationship. Maybe she's right about that, but I can't tell if she's pretending or just being nice. It's definitely not that she has real feelings. She's told everybody who will listen that I'm her rival, that we hate each other, but do we? Maybe I'm overly tired, but the lines are becoming blurred. Finally, the song ends, and we're both breathless and laughing.

"I told you I couldn't dance!"

"I thought you did a pretty good job. I mean, I

don't think you'd win any competitions for that, so it's probably a good idea that you can bake well."

As soon as the song ends, "Careless Whisper" by Wham comes on the radio. A slow song. I don't know what to do. Before I can decide, she reaches her hand out.

"Let's see if you can slow dance."

SAVANNAH

I don't know what I was thinking. My heart races as I look at Rhett, this ridiculous man I'm chained to for a reality show. I keep telling myself that he's just acting, playing a game to win over the audience back home.

But he took my invitation to slow dance seriously. I don't know why I said it. I just suddenly blurted it out. I think I'm getting way too comfortable here. He slowly pulls me toward him, and I can feel the lines between reality and make-believe starting to blur.

"So you think you can slow dance better than me, huh?" Rhett says with a teasing smile. His warm breath tickles my cheek.

I can't help but notice how his eyes crinkle at the

corners when he smiles. I have the urge to reach up and smooth away the laugh lines. There's something so disarming about his expression right now, and I can feel my stomach fluttering.

"I know I can," I say, trying to keep my voice light and playful, hyper-aware that people at home are watching us right now. Deep down, I want nothing more than to get lost in his embrace, to feel his strong and steady presence. But there's something different about him at this moment that I've never seen before: a softness, a vulnerability. I wonder if he knows it's visible.

As the music fills the kitchen, he begins to sway gently, his hand resting on the small of my back. Electricity shoots through me as I feel him touch me, and I resist the urge to lean in closer and closer to press my body against his.

I can feel the warmth of his skin through the thin fabric of my pajama top. I wonder if he can feel my heart jackhammering against my breastbone. We move together in perfect sync. Our bodies fit together like puzzle pieces even though he's twice my size.

He looks down at me, his eyes warm but intense. I feel myself drowning. All the thoughts of the competition and the cameras are fading away. I needed them to keep me in reality, but they're gone.

In this moment, it's just the two of us lost in a private world we created.

I'm playing a dangerous game. I know it, but I can't seem to stop myself from falling deeper under his spell with every passing second. I know he doesn't feel the same. He wants a fake relationship to win the show. That's it. That's Rhett. Rhett is all about competition.

I keep trying to remind myself of that, but I feel like I'm losing it. I wonder if he can sense the shift in my emotions, how my breath quickens, and how my pulse races the closer he gets. There's some kind of undeniable connection between us, but is it real or make-believe?

I feel like a spark ignites every time we're this close. The song continues, and he pulls me even closer. I can feel the steady rhythm of his heart against mine. I inhale the crisp, clean scent of his cologne, and it takes all my willpower not to bury my face straight into his chest. I want to lose myself and forget everything else that exists. The competition. The fact that I miss my sister. Big Thelma. Wait. Why is Big Thelma in there? I'm not going to let her ruin this perfect yet fleeting moment.

His hand slides up my back, sending shivers down my spine. I find myself tilting my head up to look at him. His eyes are filled with an intensity that takes my breath away. I can feel myself being drawn in like a moth to a flame. I don't know if this is real. I don't know if he's faking it for the cameras.

In the back of my mind, I know I should pull away, that I'm only setting myself up for heartbreak. But at this moment, I don't care about any consequences. All I can think about is this man and how he makes me feel, which shocks me.

He was my rival just a few days ago. He was the guy I would tell everyone I hated from culinary school, and now I'm slow dancing with him in the kitchen in front of a television audience. As the song starts to reach its end, Rhett twirls me around. His movements are graceful and effortless, as if he's been taking dancing classes his whole life.

I let out a breathless laugh, my inhibitions melting away as I just surrender myself to the music and his lead. For a minute, I forget we're being watched and that this is all just a game. I'm allowing myself, for once in my life, to enjoy being lost in the sensation of somebody showing me attention because they want to.

Once the final notes of the song fade away, Rhett pulls me close. His lips are just mere inches from mine. My breath catches in my throat, and my pulse pounds so loudly in my ears that I wonder if he can hear it. I really want him to kiss me. I want the lines blurring between reality and fantasy to meld into one. But just before our lips are about to meet, he pulls away, leaving me suddenly cold.

"Looks like you've still got a few things to learn," he says, a teasing look on his face. I'm momentarily disoriented like I had oxygen, and then someone took it away from me. He releases me, and I think I've never felt such a void in my life.

RHETT

That was hell. Holding Savannah in my arms was like nothing I've ever felt before. Letting her go was painful.

As much as I want the home audience to believe there's something going on, I don't know if I could play pretend. Not with her.

When I let her go, I wanted to immediately pull her back and kiss her like no one's ever kissed her before. It took every bit of strength I have in my large body to let go of her hand.

Now, I can't hide. I feel like she *sees* me. And I never let anyone *see* me.

## SAVANNAH

We walk back upstairs into the room where Maggie is still happily sleeping. She lets out a loud snort and then turns onto her side. Thankfully, she's not snoring like a freight train when she's on her side. Do freight trains even snore? I don't know what to describe it as, but it's pretty rough.

Thankfully, once I'm asleep, I'm a pretty heavy sleeper. I don't know about Rhett because I never wake up in the middle of the night to check. I just know that he's looking at me every morning when I open my eyes. It's kind of unnerving.

What's even more unnerving is that slow dance we just had in the kitchen. I don't know what I was thinking asking him to do that. It just played right into his plan to make everybody think that we're in a relationship. I know that's what's happening. I know I can't let my mind run away with the idea that Rhett is somehow interested in me. I don't even know if I'm interested in him. I just know I'm not playing a game.

But Rhett has told me in no uncertain terms that he wants to have a fake relationship. So I know he's pretending. He's putting on a show for the cameras. All the women at home probably enjoyed that dance. *I* really enjoyed that slow dance in the kitchen, but I can't make it into more than it was.

We lie back down in our beds, staring at the ceilings as usual.

"I guess we should get some sleep."

"I guess so," I say. "Although I'm pretty hyped up on cookies and dancing."

He laughs. "Yeah, it probably wasn't the best idea to eat a bunch of sugary chocolate chip cookies right before we went to bed. We might be up all night."

"We can't be up all night," I say. "We have things to do. I don't know what they are, but I'm sure we have things to do tomorrow."

"You know they'll have us do some kind of public service thing since we have a few more days before the main challenge."

"Yeah, the main challenge. I wonder who will win this time."

"I don't know. I prefer not to think about it," I say. "It just gets me stressed out."

"When we were in school together, I always thought of you as somebody who couldn't be rattled."

I smile. "That's what I want people to think. I had to behave that way as a kid."

"What do you mean?"

"Well, I've told you that I was brought up by a

single mother who had addiction issues. I basically had to raise myself, and when you have to raise yourself, you become an adult pretty quickly. I always wanted people to think I was okay. I didn't want anybody to feel sorry for me. So I probably came off that way because of that."

"But now I see you get rattled on a pretty regular basis. Why the change?"

"This is an unusual situation," I say, laughing. "I never expected to be stuck in a house with strangers away from my sister, being watched by cameras all day. I think it's reactivated the anxiety I thought I had put away years ago. What about you? Do you find yourself acting differently in the house?"

He looks over at me for a moment. "I find myself acting differently with you."

"You have to stop saying things like that," I say, my face serious.

"Why?" He leans up onto his shoulder. "I'm just telling you the truth. I thought you liked that."

I push up onto my elbow and face him. "I do like that, except when it's about a *hippopotamus*. You *know* what I mean." I'm sure that people at home are completely confused by this comment, but Rhett knows what I mean. He knows that's our code word for fake relationships. It's a stupid code word, but there it is. "I know you're just doing things like a hippopotamus would."

"This is the silliest conversation I've ever had," he says, chuckling.

"Well, either way, you have to stop saying things like that."

"Well, I'm not going to. I do feel like myself when I'm around you, Sunny."

"Let's change the subject. What was your upbringing like?"

He falls back onto his back. "Yikes, what a terrible way to change the subject. I don't really want to talk about my family."

"Come on, I've told you about mine. I mean, there wasn't much of it."

"Well, I come from a very wealthy family, as I've mentioned. Doctor mother. Attorney father. We never wanted for anything. We had everything we could have possibly wanted. A couple of houses, the best schools, brand new cars when we were old enough to drive, family vacations."

"Wow, I can't imagine a life like that."

"Yeah, it looked good on the surface. I'm sure there were many people around us who were jealous of our family."

"But they shouldn't have been?"

"No, not really. What I learned from all of that is

that none of it matters. None of that material stuff is what actually makes you happy."

"So what makes you happy?"

He sits there for a moment, quietly pondering. "I think being here with you."

"What?"

"That is what has made me the happiest that I can think of. Being here with you."

I fall onto my back and stare at the ceiling, unsure what to say. He's got to be pretending. There's no way that Rhett Jennings is saying these things and being serious. He must be the world's best actor. I consider what I can say in return, but then I hear a breathing sound. I turn and look, and Rhett is sound asleep, with a smile on his face. He fell asleep? This guy who never sleeps, who has terrible insomnia, is lying beside me, chained to my arm, sleeping peacefully with a smile on his face.

# CHAPTER 18

RHETT

BEFORE WE GO for whatever our public service event is today, we have to eat breakfast. Thankfully, the producers have had it catered in for some reason. We have a whole variety of foods sitting in the middle of the long communal table by the time Savannah and I come down the stairs. There are hash browns with cheese and onions in them. There are cheese grits with bacon crumbled up in them. There are pancakes and waffles and French toast. Way too much food even for the group of us.

We sit down across the table from Connor because they're the only empty seats. I'm sure that's not an accident since probably no one else wants to sit across from Connor. Beside him is Lainey, who has become his twin. She acts just like him. That's *not* a compliment.

"Well, good morning, lovebirds," he says as we sit down. Several people around the table glance at us, but we decide not to give in to him goading us.

"Good morning, Connor," Savannah says with just about as much loathing in her voice as can fit. It makes me smile.

We start filling our plates with food. Savannah seems awfully hungry this morning for such a small person, but I'm not saying a word. I've learned never to speak about how and what a woman eats. It's not worth getting smacked in the face or something. I also pile my plate high with food because I don't know when we will eat again. Sometimes, these little field trips out of the house take a long time, and we don't get fed a real meal until the evening.

"So, Rhett, I have some questions for you," Connor suddenly says.

"Oh, goody. I was hoping you would," I say, looking down at my plate, trying my best to ignore him. He's impossible to ignore. He's like a fly buzzing around your face.

"I know you work on yachts with celebrities. Tell us who some of those celebrities are."

"He can't tell you, Connor. He signed nondisclosure agreements," Savannah says, obviously trying to save me. It's never going to be enough for Connor, though.

"Nondisclosure agreements. That seems a little silly, given that you're just cooking for them."

"Well, that's how business works," I say, biting into a piece of bacon.

"What kinds of yachts have you worked on?"

"What do you mean, what kinds? Like brands?"

"Yeah," Connor says, taking a bite of a biscuit that he has loaded with egg, cheese, and bacon.

"I don't know. I don't pay any attention to what the brands are."

Connor stares at me for a long moment. "Really? The brands are pretty important."

"If you say so," I say, sipping my coffee. I don't know what he's up to, but it's nothing good.

"So what do you do, exactly?"

"I cook desserts for celebrities. I thought that was pretty obvious."

"And that's it?"

"What else would it be?"

"I don't know. I just figured you'd have some other stories to regale us with. After all, riding out on the ocean in a yacht with a celebrity seems like it would give you plenty of stories to tell."

"Maybe I just don't want to tell them to you, Connor," I say, standing and leaning over the table.

I'm way bigger than this guy. I could snap him like a twig. If this came to a physical confrontation, I would have no question about that. But unfortunately, Connor likes to spar with words. He likes to get under your skin, and I'm not letting him do it.

"Connor, what is your problem?" Savannah asks, looking at him.

"This doesn't involve you, Savannah. I'm talking to your boyfriend here."

"He's not my boyfriend." The way she says it actually makes my heart hurt a little bit. I'm not her boyfriend, but maybe I would like to be. I don't know. I try not to think about it too hard.

"You know, one of my bosses in college had a yacht. Well, his uncle did. He was quite wealthy. He took me out on it a few times."

"That's a riveting story," I say dryly, still looking down at my plate because I really don't want to engage with this guy.

"So, what kind of water toys did it have?"

"Water toys?"

"Yeah, jet skis, things like that."

"Oh, I don't know. I don't really get to play around with *water toys* while I'm working." I make air quotes around the phrase "water toys."

"What kind of safety drills do you have to do? I'm

sure since you're out on them a lot, it must be pretty intense, especially with a celebrity on board."

"I'm not sure what you mean by safety drills."

Connor stares at me for a long moment like he's gotten me. He's somehow cornered me where he wants me.

"Really? You don't do fire drills, abandon ship drills, man overboard drills, medical emergency drills?" His voice trails off, and I can hear my heart beating in my ears. He's trying to pin me down. He's trying to prove that I don't work on yachts, and unfortunately, he seems to be doing a pretty good job of it.

"Connor, is this some sort of inquisition?" Savannah asks. She can tell that I'm uncomfortable.

"We do all kinds of drills, of course," I say, trying to make this whole thing disappear. "As every sailing vessel would do. Now, can we get back to eating our breakfast?"

"Sure," Connor says, "except I think everybody should know that you could not work on yachts and know so little about them."

My face is starting to burn. I want to stand up, grab him by his scrawny neck, and throw him down to the other end of the table where Maggie sits. But I can't. I don't want to get kicked out of this competition, and I'd hate to hit Maggie with Connor's body.

"Think whatever you want to think, Connor."

"Boys, boys. Let's just get back to eating. There's no sense in arguing about anything," Maggie says, being ever the motherly figure to all of us.

Connor shrugs his shoulders. "That's fine. I got what I wanted. I think we all know that Rhett is one big phony."

∾

## SAVANNAH

An hour later, after the awkward breakfast and changing our clothes, we're on the shuttle bus heading to a local food bank. Rhett has been very quiet since his confrontation with Connor. I can tell it got to him, but I don't know exactly why.

"You okay?" I ask as we go down the bumpy dirt road leading into town.

"I'm fine," he says, staring out the window.

"If you want to talk..."

He looks at me. "Talk? Yes, because it's so private to talk."

"Oh, yeah, right," I say, forgetting that we're miked up.

It's amazing how you can forget that microphones record everything you say and cameras record everything you do twenty-four hours a day. I guess Dan was right about that. You get used to it really quickly.

"Well, at least we get to go out and about today."

"To a *food bank*," he says.

His whole personality has changed even since last night. Since this morning. Connor really did a number on him. I understand how he feels.

"Listen, don't pay any attention to Connor. He's an idiot. He's annoying. I don't know how I ever dated him."

That gets a smile out of Rhett. "I don't know how you did either. I mean, you're all sunshine and rainbows, Sunny. Why in the world would you date somebody like that?"

"Like I told you, he was very different in the beginning. It was short-lived. I'm just glad it's over, and I hate to see him affecting you. Don't let him get to you like that. That's all he wants."

"Yeah, but..." he starts to say something, then stops himself.

"What?"

"Never mind. It's not important."

We continue down the road until we arrive at a small brick building that is seemingly out in the middle of nowhere. It has a little drive-through area, and several cars are waiting. People inside are leaning out the window with bags and giving people in the cars food.

I remember what that felt like. Going to the food bank was a regular part of my childhood. Sometimes, my mother would go with us, but often, it was just me, standing in line waiting for food to last us a week. I had to make sure Sadie was fed. She loved the juice boxes we got there. She also adored the boxed macaroni and cheese. The memory brings a smile to my face.

We get out of the van and head toward the building. A woman is standing in front with a big smile on her face. She's very petite, has bleached-blonde hair, and looks to probably be in her sixties.

"Hey, everybody," she says in her thick Southern accent. "My name is Lisa, and I run the Sweet Haven Food Bank. I'm so glad to have all of you here to help us today. Follow me."

She waves her hand, and we follow her like little baby ducklings into the building. It's pretty hot in here. I don't know if the air conditioning isn't working, but I immediately wish I hadn't worn long pants today.

When we get inside, she tells us that there are several tasks, and we will be split up to do them. Obviously, Rhett and I can't be split up, so we will be doing the same task. Some people will be sorting donations, while others will pack food boxes that are delivered to people who can't leave their homes. Some of us will be stocking shelves, and some of us will be helping hand out donations through the window.

Rhett and I have been assigned to stock the shelves. Maggie and Nate will sort donations, and then we will take those donations and put them on the proper shelves. We are the only two doing it, so at least we get some time alone. Well, except for the fact that the entire country could be watching us right now on the internet and later tonight on television.

When we finally get set up, Rhett is quiet. He's just picking things out of boxes and putting them onto the shelf without saying a word.

"Are you looking forward to getting unchained?" I ask, trying to fill the silence between us.

He shrugs.

I'm worried about him. I can't believe it. *I'm worried about Rhett Jennings.* I never thought those words would cross my mind.

"Are you sure you don't want to talk about what Connor said..."

He cuts me off, holding up his free hand. "No. Now stop asking me about it, please. Let's just do our job and get on with it."

"Okay."

We continue stocking the items in silence. Finally, he seems to shake it off enough to start chatting here and there. When we're finally done with our job a couple of hours later and reboarding the bus, Rhett seems like his old self again. I don't know what it was that had him so upset, but hopefully, it's gone now.

We have one more night of sleeping in the same room before we're unchained in the morning. Three days ago, I would have told you I would be excited for that moment, but I dread it. It was nice to have a built-in person to talk to, even if it's Rhett Jennings. He was nice. Most of the time, anyway.

"Oh, and to answer your question, no," he says as the bus pulls up in front of the house.

"What question? No, what?"

The bus comes to a stop, and we all stand up. He leans over, I guess hoping that I'm the only one who can hear him.

"No, I'm not looking forward to getting unchained."

RHETT

The rest of the day was spent in a workshop where we listened to Chef Alain talk about making the perfect crepes. I've never been a fan of crepes. It's not something I plan to make after this challenge is over, but I still had to sit there and act like I was interested in what he was saying. After all, irritating one of the main judges does me no good.

Savannah seemed to enjoy it but Savannah seems to enjoy everything. She's always smiling and happy, even when she's sad. Or at least that's what I assume.

After that, we had dinner, and we all sat out in the common area, talking and drinking bottles of wine that we found in the pantry. I'm not sure if we were supposed to be drinking them, but we did anyway.

I'm not much of a drinker. I don't like to feel out of control, so I only had a glass or two, but I noticed that Savannah was chatting and enjoying herself so much that she might've had way more than she was supposed to.

When it was time to go to bed for our last night of sleeping chained together, I was a little worried about her getting up the stairs. I helped her as best I could until we got to the room, and the producers agreed to unchain us so that we could change into our pajamas.

I'm pretty sure that tonight, we will not have the issue of being unable to sleep. Savannah is way too tipsy to stay awake, which makes me feel protective of her. While talking to everyone downstairs, she told me that she doesn't drink very much and that she's a lightweight. I can definitely see that. She's petite and is not holding her wine very well.

When she returns, the producer chains us back together, and I ask to speak to her around the corner where Savannah can't hear me. We stretch the chain so that she's in the room, and I'm a couple of feet outside of it. I don't think she's paying a bit of attention because she's so tipsy.

"Listen, I'm going to ask you to do something, and I hope you'll agree to it," I say, turning off my microphone before I start speaking.

"You can't turn off your microphone."

This is the producer that I see most often in the house, and she's not overly nice. She's all business, all about the rules, but right now, the rules don't matter to me.

"I'm turning it off because I don't want this recorded, and if this goes on television, I'm going to be pretty upset."

"I can't guarantee anything. There are cameras everywhere," she says, pointing around.

"I think you have some control over that. This is a conversation that needs to be private."

She sighs and talks into her little walkie-talkie, telling them to turn off the cameras where we're standing so that it doesn't pick up the conversation.

"You're not supposed to be talking to us about anything during the competition. Everything has to be fair."

"Yes, I understand that," I say, keeping my voice down. "But I need you to turn off the cameras and the microphones in this bedroom for the night."

"Excuse me?" she says, acting like I'm up to something nefarious.

"Savannah is in no position to be on national television when she's this tipsy."

"Well, I guess she shouldn't have drank so much, should she?"

"Look, I know you think this makes for good television," I say to her a little too pointedly, "but you could get in all kinds of legal trouble for showcasing this young woman on television when she is in a vulnerable state."

"Yes, and I could get in all kinds of trouble for leaving her alone in a room with a man she barely knows when she's in a vulnerable state."

"Okay, fine. Then turn the camera on but turn the microphone off."

"And how is that supposed to be something that the at-home viewers can watch?"

"Exactly. If this is about Savannah's safety and you just want to check in and ensure she's okay, then looking at her on the camera will be plenty. She doesn't need the audio to be aired nationwide."

"With all due respect, Rhett, you're really not in control of this."

I peek around the corner to make sure that Savannah is still standing there, and she is. She's playing with some wallpaper that is peeling off the old wall in the historic home.

"Again, she is in no position to be showcased on TV when she's tipsy."

"You mean drunk."

"She's not drunk. She's just on the edge of drunk. She's like in the suburbs of drunk."

The producer, whose name I think is Ellen, rolls her eyes. "I'll talk to my boss, but I can't promise anything."

"Listen, I come from a very wealthy family, and I don't like to bring that up often, but there is no amount of money that I will spare for an attorney to sue the pants off of this production company if they showcase Savannah on TV like this."

I don't even know what I'm saying. I don't have that kind of money. My parents certainly wouldn't give me that kind of money, but I hope these people don't know that.

"Again, I'll talk to my boss. I'll come find you in a few minutes."

"Okay, fine," I say, returning to the room.

I don't know why I feel so protective of her, but I do. I just don't think it's right that she had one night of enjoying herself and having some wine, and just because she's a lightweight, she's in this vulnerable position.

"Can we go to bed now?" she asks as I walk into the room.

"Yes, of course. Come on."

"Woo…" she says as she walks toward the bed. I'm afraid she's going to pass out, so I pick her up like a baby and carry her to the bed. I gently put her down, wishing I could lie down right beside her.

She crawls under the covers, and I pull them up to just under her neck, and then I crawl into the bed beside hers. There's a lamp on between us. Maggie hasn't come upstairs yet. I think she's still enjoying time down in the courtyard. Maggie can hold her own when it comes to wine. I have a feeling she drinks it often.

"Why don't you tell me a story?" Savannah says, her words slurring.

"I don't think so," I say, propping myself up onto my elbow and facing her.

"I like stories," she whines.

I swear it's like she's regressed to childhood.

"Okay, how about this one? Once upon a time, a beautiful red-haired woman drank too much wine with a bunch of strangers."

"Well, that's not a very good story," she says, sticking out her bottom lip.

"Savannah, you need to go to sleep. You'll feel a lot better in the morning."

"I don't know about that. I feel pretty good now," she says, laughing.

"I'm sure you do."

Without thinking, I reach over and brush a stray strand of red hair behind her ear. She catches my hand in midair and presses it to her cheek. Then, she wiggles down into her pillow, holding it there as she sighs and seemingly drifts off to sleep.

I don't know what to do. Do I pull my hand back and risk waking her up? I don't *want* to pull my hand back. I'm touching Savannah's skin. I can feel her breath coming in and out, in and out.

As I start to pull my hand back, thinking it's the right thing to do, she grips onto it harder, pulls it towards the top of her chest, and holds it there like a teddy bear. Even though I'm stretching for her to be able to do this, I don't want to pull it back. I want to just stay like this. I could stay like this all night, just holding my hand to the top of her chest and feeling her breathe.

As we lay there, suddenly, the producer walks into the room. She gives me the evil eye because I have my hand on Savannah's chest, and so I pull it back.

She walks over and leans down. "Microphones are off. Turn off your microphone packs."

I nod my head, and she walks out of the room. I turn mine off and then reach over to turn off Savannah's. At least we have some privacy where she won't be embarrassed at being basically out of her head on national TV. I don't want Savannah's future to be ruined because people are making her into memes on the internet.

I decide to go to sleep and try to get the fact that she's lying here next to me out of my head. Just one more night, and then we'll be unchained. I don't like it, but it is what it is.

I roll back onto my shoulder and face her, closing my eyes, and then I feel her reach out for my hand. When I open my eyes, her eyes are closed. She still seems to be asleep. She pulls my hand close to her and then puts it underneath her cheek, holding her hands in a prayer position around it.

"Rhett," she says in a low whisper.

I can't tell if she's awake. "Yeah?"

"Do you like me?" Her words still sound slurred and fuzzy, and her eyes never open.

"Of course I do, Savannah. You're my friend."

"Nooo…" she says, dragging out the word. "I mean, do you *like me* like me?"

Still, her eyes aren't open. She's barely talking above a whisper.

"I do," I say, hoping she doesn't remember any of this in the morning.

"But, I mean really like me or *hippopotamus* like me."

It makes me laugh that she can remember the code word at this moment.

"I *really* like you," I say, admitting it to her and myself for the first time.

She never opens her eyes, but she smiles and sighs, and then I can hear her barely snoring. I decide to stay this way even though it's uncomfortable with my arm stretched out. There's no place I'd rather be in the world right now than taking care of Savannah, even if my arm cramps up and falls off.

# CHAPTER 19

SAVANNAH

THIS MORNING IS A BLUR. I know I drank too much wine last night. I don't remember much. I have a vague recollection of Rhett helping me up the stairs and then him talking to somebody in the hallway while I picked at the wallpaper on the walls. I'm not sure why I was picking at it. It seemed very interesting at the time. Then I remember him helping me to bed, but not much at all after that. I suppose I just fell asleep.

I truly expected to wake up this morning and feel nauseous, but as I lay here, opening my eyes and looking around the blurry room, I don't feel too bad. I don't typically get a hangover from wine. I don't drink a lot anyway; I'm always working, but I do like the occasional glass of wine. Last night, apparently, I liked the occasional *bottle* of wine.

"Good morning." I suddenly realize that Rhett is still attached to my arm, lying in the bed opposite me. He's looking at me with such a softness on his face and a slight smile. I wonder how long he's been staring at me like this. I kind of like it, but I'm never admitting that out loud. "How are you feeling?"

"I feel pretty groggy," I say, still struggling to get my eyes to stay open. I use my free hand to rub one of them. "But all in all, not too bad."

"When you said you were a lightweight, I didn't truly believe you until I carried you to your bed."

I scrunch my nose. "You had to carry me to my bed?"

"You were a little woozy."

"I'm so sorry. I don't normally drink that much. If I didn't know better, I would've thought somebody spiked my drink with something."

"Yeah, I think that was all you, Sunny."

I laugh. "Well, at least you get away from me today."

"It hasn't been so bad."

We both slowly sit up, me because my head is still swimming a little bit and him because he's trying to make sure I don't fall off the bed. We're facing each other, and there's something different. I can't put my finger on what it is. The night starts to come back to me. The last few days. The slow dance in the kitchen. Did something happen last night? What if we kissed, and I don't even remember it? That makes me feel sad. What did I say to him? I vaguely remember us talking before I fell asleep, but I can't remember any of it.

"So, I guess we'd better be ready for the main challenge tonight," he says after a few moments.

"Yeah, I think that's why I drank all the wine."

"You'll do fine. You're getting better and better at each challenge."

"Are you giving me a compliment?" I say teasingly.

"You're very talented, Sunny. You shouldn't downplay that."

"Thank you. And for what it's worth, it hasn't been so bad being chained to you, either. I thought it would be the worst time of my life."

He chuckles. "Well, that makes me feel good."

Before we can continue, one of the producers walks in with a key and holds it up.

"Congratulations, you both made it to seventy-two hours. Oh, turn on your mic packs before we film this."

I look at Rhett with a confused expression. "Our mic packs? Why are they off?"

"I asked producers to turn them off last night."

"Why?"

"Well, you were a little vulnerable in your predicament. I didn't want them showcasing that across national television."

Something in my heart swells up. It's like that part in the Grinch cartoon that I watched growing up at Christmas time when his heart suddenly swells up; that's what this feels like. Rhett protected me when I couldn't protect myself. He made sure the mic was off and that nobody was using my vulnerability against me. Who does that?

"You made them turn the mics off?"

"Yeah," he says, shrugging his shoulders.

I reach across and put my hand on his knee.

"Thank you," I whisper, making eye contact with him.

He nods slightly. "No problem."

We both reach around and turn our microphones back on. The producer unlocks the handcuffs while the cameraman zooms in on our wrists. Within seconds, we're free.

Free of each other. No longer forced to do everything together. No longer sleeping next to each other at night.

Why do I feel so sad? I feel like I just lost something. I feel like I left Sadie all over again at the airport. This is a foreign feeling to me. I've dated several guys in my life, some seriously, but I never felt such a sense of loss knowing that I wouldn't get to spend all my time with anyone. Maybe I'm just lonely in here, missing my sister. Maybe that's all this is. But I don't think so.

Still, I don't know if Rhett is playing pretend or if this is reality. I can't imagine him having the depth of feelings that he seems to. This is Rhett Jennings. Rhett Jennings doesn't have those kinds of feelings.

It's all very confusing, and I suppose being unchained from him will make things easier. It will give me more time to think. Maybe I can talk to Maggie about it. And then I remember that everything I say is on TV. There is no privacy. There is no asking her for "girl advice." I have to keep this to myself and figure it out alone. If we're lucky, we have weeks left in this house, and I can't let these crazy thoughts derail me. I have to remember why I'm here: to win that money and change my and my sister's lives.

## RHETT

Another day, another main challenge. These are becoming old hat for us. I've won one time; Savannah hasn't won at all. I'm starting to worry a little bit about her longevity in the game, but since she still hasn't agreed to a fake relationship with me, she's kind of on her own.

It makes me worry. I don't want her to leave. I want her to stay as long as possible. Of course, I still want to win—I am competitive, after all—but I would like it to be Savannah and me at the end.

As Dan explained, today's main challenge is a mystery ingredient challenge. We can make whatever we want, but we must choose to use one of the crazy mystery ingredients on the table. They are wasabi paste, cayenne pepper flakes, and candied jalapenos. None of them are exactly helpful when trying to make a sweet treat.

This is the first time that I've been unchained from Savannah in three days. It feels weird. It feels like one of my limbs is missing, even though she's at the station right next to me, working away on whatever it is that she's making.

I miss her. I've never missed anybody in my whole life. Even when my grandmother died, and I was grieving that loss, I didn't miss her like this. This is like a longing, something I've never really felt before. Like I'm missing something I've never had but know that I desperately want.

I've dated a lot of women in my life. Being from a wealthy family gets you a lot of attention. You could be the ugliest guy in the world, but if you or your family has money, you will have dates. But I never felt like this, and that's scary because Savannah probably doesn't feel that way about me. She was just overly intoxicated on wine last night. She doesn't remember what she said. You can't take those kinds of feelings to heart.

I'm looking around the room and noticing every-body diligently working on their desserts. I crane my neck a bit, trying to see what Connor's doing, but I really can't tell. I have decided to make some wasabi white chocolate truffles. It's not the easiest thing to do, but I hope the judges will like them.

"Dang it," I hear Savannah say under her breath.

I'm not sure what's going wrong, but I immediately look over at her. "Hey."

She turns and looks back at me. "Yeah?"

"You can do this. You've got it."

What has come over me? I don't encourage other competitors. It's like my heart has a mind of its own and it's controlling everything I do. It's unsettling, and I don't like it. My brain needs to be in control. It is the only organ in my body that has ever been in control of everything. If my brain doesn't tell me to do it, I don't do it. But now, it seems like my heart has fought back and overtaken my mental capabilities.

I notice Connor looking in my direction. He has obviously heard me encourage Savannah. He shakes his head and rolls his eyes before returning to work.

The three hours fly by, and now it's time for the judges to walk around and give their verdicts. I think I did a pretty good job on my truffles, but I don't know what anybody else made.

They go to Connor first, who made wasabi white chocolate macarons. The judges seem to like them, but they're not nearly as impressed as I've seen them with Connor in the past. Maybe he got distracted watching me and Savannah.

Lainey made a spicy chocolate cake. That sounds disgusting, and the judges don't care for it. Maybe she'll go home. That would be one of the best pieces of news I've received in a while.

Zara made spicy jalapeno chocolate truffles. Chef Alain said they were innovative, but Marco said they were disgusting, so I don't know what to make of that.

Hank made wasabi vanilla cupcakes with orange buttercream. The judges were not amused.

Sophia created a beautiful cake with some kind of candied jalapeno icing, and Marco gagged. Tessa's face turned a shade of red I'd never seen before.

Finally, they come over to my wasabi white chocolate truffles. They compliment them and say they have an interesting taste but that they wouldn't necessarily order them to eat at a restaurant. Yeah, I'm not winning this competition.

They also go to Leo, who has made a candied jalapeno peppermint cake. What in the world? Why would anybody make such a thing? Needless to say, Leo is the one they target. He's obviously going home.

Then they finally come to Savannah, who has made a jalapeno pineapple upside-down cake. It was such an interesting thing to make, and I'm kind of proud of her for coming up with something so unique. The judges rave about it, telling her it's the best out of everyone's and proclaiming her the winner.

I'm more excited about her win than I was about mine. In fact, I find myself shouting out and clapping to the point where everybody turns around and looks at me. Leo is proclaimed the loser and will be going home. That's fine; I don't really know him all that well. As long as Savannah is staying, I'm okay.

Suddenly, I feel like she is my security blanket,

which seems very dangerous. I've never needed a security blanket. Until now.

SAVANNAH

I won! I won! I can't believe I won!

I scream like I've won the lottery and then run out from behind my station to join the others. On my way, several people high-five me. I don't know if anyone has ever high-fived me before.

Then I see him. Rhett.

He's standing there next to my station, smiling. He looks like a proud father who's just taught his daughter to ride a bike. He looks so happy, and it throws me off a bit. He seems happier for me than he was for himself when he won.

"Congratulations," he says, squeezing my shoulder. Electrical zaps ping around my body like the whole thing is shorting out.

"Thank you," I say softly.

"Can I buy you a sandwich?" he asks with a wink. We don't buy anything here, but I think it's his way of offering to make me a sandwich. It's kind of cute.

"Sure," I say, following the group back into the main house.

I sit at the breakfast bar with Maggie while the others disperse to different areas. Rhett goes to the refrigerator and sticks his head inside.

"Okay, ladies, I've got ham, turkey, and Swiss cheese…"

"I'll take turkey," Maggie says.

"Same," I say, enjoying the view of Rhett's backside a little more than I care to admit.

"Turkey it is!"

He pulls out the turkey, cheese, lettuce, mayo, and mustard and retrieves a loaf of bread from the pantry. I enjoy watching him do the mundane tasks of making a sandwich. It feels nice. Familiar.

I keep reminding myself that this isn't reality. It might be called a "reality show," but there's nothing real about being followed by cameras and microphones all day and knowing millions of people are watching your every move.

And there's nothing real about Rhett's caring for me. Even though I never agreed to be in a fake relationship with him, Rhett would do what he needed to win. This is obviously a part of that.

Now that we're not chained together anymore, he has to go out of his way to look like he's spending time with me. It's helping his game, I'm sure. Maybe it's even helping my game.

And I'm okay with it. He's being a nicer version

of himself, and I just won my first main challenge. Life is good right now.

"Congrats on your win, Savannah."

Life *was* good.

For some inexplicable reason, Connor is standing behind me. He just congratulated me, and it sounded authentic. Nothing Connor says or does is authentic.

"Yeah, thanks," I say, rolling my eyes. Rhett's jaw clenches as he pauses his work.

"And what else, Connor?" he says.

"What do you mean?"

"I know there's some snide remark waiting to fall from your thin lips." I want to laugh. Rhett is right. Connor has thin lips.

Connor sighs. "Look, man, don't try to start trouble with me. I was simply congratulating Savannah on a well-deserved win. That cake was super creative."

"Thanks, Connor." I say it just to get him to go away, and it works.

"What was that all about?" Maggie asks under her breath.

Rhett continues working on the sandwiches. "He's a snake. I wouldn't trust a thing he says."

"Oh, believe me, I don't. I know better than anybody that he's not to be trusted."

Rhett slides the sandwiches over to Maggie and me. He also pours each of us a glass of sweet tea and throws a bag of sour cream and onion potato chips between us before sitting down at the bar across from us with his own sandwich.

I take a bite. "Oh, this is so good, Rhett."

He laughs. "It's just a sandwich, Sunny. It would taste the same no matter who made it."

"He's so modest," I say to Maggie. She gives me a knowing smile.

"So, how do you feel about your big win?" he asks me.

"Great! I totally didn't expect to win, though."

"You should believe in yourself, Sunny. You have what it takes to go to the end." He bites into his sandwich, which gives me a chance to glance at Maggie. She's eating like the cat that swallowed the canary, looking at me with so many unspoken words in her eyes. She knows something is happening but has no idea it's a big game of pretend.

"Thanks," I say, biting into my sandwich again.

After we finish our sandwiches, it's time for bed. It feels weird not to have Rhett coming to my room with a chain hanging between us. I never thought I'd miss a chain.

Now, I have to sleep next to Lainey again. Lovely.

The three of us walk upstairs, passing Connor

and Lainey making out near the front door—ick— and head to the hallway of bedrooms. Maggie quickly escapes to the bathroom, leaving Rhett and me alone.

"Well, I guess this is goodnight," Rhett says. Do I hear nerves in his voice?

"I guess so."

"Congrats again, Sunny. You did great."

"You did great, too."

"But it wasn't enough to beat you," he laughs.

"We're even now." I let out a yawn I couldn't stifle.

"Go get some sleep. We have a lot more challenges coming up."

"Goodnight, Rhett."

"Goodnight, Savannah."

I walk into my room feeling like I just went on a very modest date, but I didn't. As much as my heart is fluttering right now, I convince myself I just need to see a cardiologist. It has nothing—and I mean *nothing*—to do with having feelings for Rhett Jennings.

This is dangerous territory. I want to win on my own merits. I don't want to win because I made at-home viewers think we're dating. I have to keep my distance from him as much as possible. It may hurt, but how can it hurt when it doesn't exist anyway?

# CHAPTER 20

MORNING CONFESSIONAL

*Producer: So, Rhett, how did you feel about Savannah's win last night?*

*Rhett, beaming with joy: I think she deserved it, and I'm absolutely thrilled for her. And proud.*

*Producer: Proud?*

*Rhett: She's a great person, and I was so happy to see her finally win a challenge.*

*Producer: Are you still claiming nothing is going on with the two of you? I mean, we did see you slow dance in the kitchen the other night.*

*Rhett: We couldn't sleep. You know, it's kind of hard to sleep when you're chained together.*

*Producer: Is that all?*

*Rhett: What do you mean?*

*Producer: Viewers want to know if you have real feelings for Savannah. Do you?*

*(A long pause. Rhett looks uncomfortable.)*

*Rhett: I do.*

*Producer: So you're dating?*

*Rhett: No. Not exactly.*

*Producer: Then what would you call it?*

*(Another long pause)*

*Rhett: I would call it me falling in love with Savannah, and her not realizing it.*

## SAVANNAH

It feels like the competition went into overdrive the last two weeks. At our third main challenge, Dan suddenly announced that we would have double eliminations from now on. Everyone was terrified of being sent home. The fewer people that are here, the more likely your chance of being sent home.

In week three, we had an edible art challenge. I made a vase with flowers. Rhett made a vintage car, which I still don't understand how he did it. Connor made some abstract art piece. Of course, Rhett won the competition. His was, by far, the best.

Unfortunately, Sophia and Hank didn't fare so well, and both of them went home. I really thought it would be me when one of my flowers literally flopped onto the counter while Chef Alain was talking to me. But the audience apparently saved me, and I don't know why.

Our week 4 challenge was to create macarons that were ocean or beach-themed. I created a tiki bar cake, while Rhett created a beach scene complete with umbrellas and lounge chairs. Again, it was amazing.

Sometimes, I wonder how in the world his family can't be proud of him. Rhett is talented and should have a cheering section at home. I can only hope that seeing him on TV will make them eat their words and tell him how they were wrong.

Tanya and Nate went home during week 4. Again, I was shocked because Nate had created a better cake than me, or at least I thought so. Tanya, on the other hand, had lost her way in the competition. Missing her kids had become unbearable, and I will always believe she threw that last competition so she could go home.

Sometimes, there are more important things than winning a competition.

Now that we're entering week five, I'm ready to push and win this thing. The only people left are me, Rhett, Zara, Maggie, Lainey, and Connor. Two more people will leave this week, and then the final four will battle it out in week six.

I guess Rhett was wrong about us needing to be in a fake relationship to win. I've reminded him of that several times—using the word hippopotamus so viewers don't understand—and he just smiles.

I think we've become good friends, and things are easier now that we're not chained together. Although I still feel those feelings sometimes, it's not hard to escape them now that the chain is gone.

"I still can't believe Nate got sent home," Rhett says as we sit on the couch in the courtyard. "Now it's just me and Connor in the room."

"Sorry about that," I say, laughing. Connor is still a snake. He tried to sabotage me in last week's challenge by stealing the mixing blade I needed. Turns out his congratulations the week I won was him trying to distract me from the fact that he wanted to sabotage me. Producers had a talk with him and gave him a warning.

"We're getting so close to the end that I can taste it."

"Yep. I can't believe I get to see Sadie in a couple of weeks. I hope I have good news for her." My eyes tear up.

"You miss her a lot, don't you?"

"So much," I say, my voice cracking. "Who do you miss?"

He pauses for a moment. "No one."

"Really? That makes me sad for you."

"It makes me sad, too."

"Why don't you do something about it then? Get on one of those dating apps?"

He waves his hand and grunts. "No thanks. I don't intend to be cut up into little pieces and put in someone's freezer."

I roll my eyes. "Oh, come on! Everyone does it these days."

"Do you?" he asks, looking at me.

"Well, no. But I've been too busy to look for love after my breakup. I've kind of enjoyed being alone."

"So you're swearing off love?"

"Maybe. For a while. I'm tired of getting my heart broken. I'm tired of being disappointed. I thought I'd be married with kids by now."

"Same."

"Rhett Jennings wants to be married with kids?"

He laughs. "Why do you always call me by my full name?"

"I don't know. It seems more dramatic."

"To answer your question, of course, I want to be married with kids."

"Why?"

"Why? What kind of question is that? Why do you want that?"

I shrug my shoulders. "I guess I want someone

who is always there for me. Someone to wake up to. Someone to cuddle while I fall asleep. Someone to be there when I want to vent or cry. Someone to share sunrises and sunsets with. A family. A real family that loves me, and I can love them."

He stares at me for a moment. "Ditto."

"You don't like to share your feelings much, do you?"

"You want me to share my feelings?"

"Yes. I think I do."

He gathers his thoughts for a moment and then speaks. "I want a woman who wants me. The real me. Not the version of me from a wealthy family. Not the version of me who can cook. The version of me that I don't show anyone else. The one that likes silly rom-com movies. Or the one that wants us to dress in matching pajamas for Christmas pictures. I want someone who wants to snuggle under the covers on Saturday mornings. I want someone who's excited to see me come home at the end of the day. I want someone who will encourage me no matter what crazy dreams I have, and I can do the same for her. Most importantly, I want someone who makes me a better man."

I'm stunned. I don't know what to say. If he's acting, he should win an Oscar.

"Wow. That was so poetic, Rhett. I'm sure you'll

find her, especially after this. Every woman in America just fell in love with you."

He smiles. "I'm only interested in one."

"Anybody wanna play pool?" Zara asks, walking over to us. We're still staring at each other like the two characters do at the end of one of those sappy rom-com movies. "Hello? Anybody here?" Zara waves her hand between our faces.

Rhett breaks our staring contest and clears his throat. "Sure, I'll play." He stands up and follows Zara to the table, looking back at me one more time. He winks, and I know. Rhett was talking about *me*.

RHETT

I can't even concentrate on this pool game. I keep looking over at Savannah until she goes back inside the house with Maggie. I want to follow her. I want to tell her this isn't fake. I want to say that I'm falling for her, and will she please just believe me? But I know she doesn't. She thinks I'm playing the game, and honestly, I don't even care about the competition anymore.

I realize that if I won Savannah, I wouldn't need to win anything else for the rest of my life.

I feel like such a weakling. I've never felt so confused and off-kilter as I do right now.

She can't find out that I said I was falling for her in my confessional. If she does, she'll think it was a game move, and none of this meant anything to me.

It means *everything* to me.

A part of me wants to quit the competition and run screaming for the hills. Of course, there are no hills here, so I guess I'd just run screaming into traffic.

The other part of me wants to beg the producers to chain me to Savannah again. It was the happiest time of my life to be chained to that woman for three days. I imagine what being with her all the time would be like.

That's it. I'm making an appointment for a mental health evaluation as soon as I get home. This isn't my brain.

I remember seeing those old 80's commercials that showed a fried egg and said, "This is your brain on drugs." Well, this is my brain on Savannah.

"Earth to Rhett." There's Zara's hand again. She's staring at me, obviously annoyed, as I look at the door instead of the pool table. Apparently, it's my turn.

"Oh. Sorry. I was just, um…"

"Why don't you just tell her?"

"Tell who?"

"Savannah. Why don't you just tell her you love her?"

My mouth drops open. "What are you talking about?"

"Oh, come on, man. Everybody can see you salivating over that girl. Everybody but her, of course."

"Not true."

"Liar," she says, putting chalk on her cue. "The great Rhett Jennings is in love with his pastry chef school rival, and she has no idea. The movie script practically writes itself."

I take my shot and miss. "You're wrong."

"No, I'm not. And it's okay if you're not ready to admit it. But you may only get one shot, Rhett. Don't miss it like you just missed that one."

SAVANNAH

Today is the reward challenge. For some reason, I woke up really missing my sister. Like the kind of missing someone where you could make a bad decision and leave the competition.

But knowing my sister, she would kill me. Like

literally go to prison for stabbing me with her little craft scissors if I came home early.

She would never let me live it down, and she would taunt me forever until I needed a restraining order. So, no, I won't be quitting.

"Good morning, contestants. Welcome to the week five reward challenge!" I don't know how Dan is always so chipper, day or night. I'd like to see what medications he takes and maybe borrow a pill or two.

"Good morning," we all say in unison like robots.

"Today's challenge is a decorating duel!" I have no idea what that means. "The judges have chosen a beautiful cake from the Internet. Your task is to replicate it exactly and finish with the fastest time. You have all the tools and decor items at your stations. Judges will be looking at your attention to detail. The cakes have already been prepared and have cooled. All you have to do is decorate!"

"What do we win?" Maggie calls out. She's gotten a lot more vocal and comfortable in this competition.

"Glad you asked, Maggie," Dan says, winking at her. I swear those two are flirting with each other all the time. "The top two contestants will get a very special reward today. I can't say what it is right now, but trust me, everyone wants this reward."

Ooh, mystery. I like a good mystery.

A few moments later, Dan counts us down, and we begin. We have ninety minutes to decorate a very intricate cake, and I don't know how any of us will do it.

The picture of the cake appears on the screen, and I want to cry. It's a replica of a Christmas tree, complete with detailed little ornaments on every limb.

I stare at the image for what seems like ten minutes before my hands finally start to move. Everyone is hard at work, and no one is looking anywhere but at the picture or their cake.

I'm curious about today's reward and want to win it. Being here has brought out a competitive side of me that I didn't even know existed. It feels good to strive for something and actually see it within reach.

"Man, this is going to be a challenge," Rhett says in my direction.

"Yes, it definitely is. Cake decorating isn't my top skill."

He looks at me and chuckles. "Don't you decorate birthday cakes in a bakery?"

"Not well," I respond as I pour the ingredients for my Swiss buttercream icing into the mixer.

The next ninety minutes are a whirlwind as I try

to recreate the cake on the screen. Every little detail matters. The gold-encrusted star on the top. The red and green ball ornaments. The meticulously crafted angel ornaments. Even the Christmas tree skirt at the bottom has a detailed Christmas village scene.

This is hard. Whoever wins this reward deserves it.

When the bell chimes, we all step back and drop what we're holding. There's nothing left to do.

The judges are impressed with everyone, but they're looking for the two people who came closest to the picture on the screen.

"Lainey, yours looks beautiful, but you forgot to put the gold leaf on your star," Chef Alain says, making a tsk sound.

"Dang it!" Lainey isn't happy. She hasn't won anything this season, but viewers keep her around as either eye candy or a source of amusement.

"Let's take a look at Connor's," Tessa says, craning her head in every direction as she looks at his cake. I swear, I think Tessa flirts with Connor sometimes. If she only knew what a dirtbag he is. "You did a wonderful job with the detailing on the tree skirt." Connor smiles. I can tell he's been using his teeth-whitening strips. If the lights go out, we can use his teeth to find our way back to our rooms.

"Still, the ornaments don't quite match the original photo," Marco says, leaning in. It looks like they might use a magnifying glass to point out the differences. Connor is fuming, which makes me want to laugh. Instead, I stick out my tongue like a three-year-old. That's when I hear Rhett snicker beside me.

The judges continue making their way around until they get to Rhett. They rave about his craftsmanship and how he duplicated everything so exactly.

"Look at this ornament. So delicate and fragile, yet you totally made it look like the original," Tessa says. She outwardly flirts with Rhett. There's no question about it. But he told me she's not his type and that her fingers are too long. I didn't know that was something men looked for—normal-length fingers. Learn something new every day.

"Wonderful!" Chef Alain says, and I know Rhett has to be one of the winners. I'm happy for him, which is something I never thought I'd hear myself say.

They move to my station, and I feel butterflies zipping around in my stomach. Why do I care about this one? It's just a reward challenge, but I really want to win it for some reason.

All three judges stand there for a moment, looking at my cake. Time seems to stand still because they aren't moving. They're just staring and then looking up at the image on the screen.

"Is everything okay?" I finally ask.

Marco smiles. "It's identical, isn't it?" He looks at the other judges.

"Savannah, your work here is superb!" Chef Alain says, his French accent on full display. "Our winner!"

I can't help but grin as Chef Alain grabs my hand —which is way too covered in icing—and thrusts it into the air. He pulls me from behind my station and walks toward Rhett. When he grabs Rhett's hand and pushes it upward, too, I know we've both won.

"Congratulations to Savannah and Rhett!"

Most of the contestants cheer for us, except for Lainey and Connor. Typical.

Once Chef Alain lets go of our hands, the judges return to the end of the room where Dan is standing.

"Congratulations to our winners! I'm sure you two want to know what your prize is?"

"Of course," I say, smiling. I'm so proud of us.

"You two have each won a five-minute video chat from a loved one!"

I immediately start jumping up and down, squealing with delight. I cannot wait to see Sadie's face. I can't wait to hear what she's been up to and just hear her happy little voice.

That's when I notice Rhett. He's smiling, but it's a

fake smile. That's not his real smile. He looks embarrassed or sad. I can't pinpoint what it is.

"...right now!" I only hear the tail end of what Dan just said, but suddenly, production is moving us toward the house.

"Where are we going?" I ask Rhett as we move.

"To have our video calls," he says under his breath.

I can't believe I'll be able to see Sadie in just a few moments. This is a dream come true.

# CHAPTER 21

RHETT

THIS IS A NIGHTMARE.

I know my mother will be on this video chat, and the whole world will see how much she disapproves of my life choices. Or, worse yet, she will pretend to be Mother of the Year. I don't know which side of her I'll get, but I'll surely get one of them.

Dan leads us to a room off the foyer that usually remains locked. He opens the door, ushers us inside, and closes it behind us. There are cameras on the walls and a speaker in the room where he can talk to us.

"Savannah, you're up first. Please have a seat in the chair."

I sit in a chair in the corner of the room, away

from the cameras, to give Savannah at least some semblance of privacy.

Moments later, she squeals. I crane my neck so I can see her sister's face. She has a head full of curly brown hair. They look nothing alike, except for the smile.

"Sissy!"

"Sadie!"

I feel like plugging my ears. They're talking several octaves higher than I do.

"You're doing so good! I watch every show, and I even catch the live stream when I can."

"You're paying for the live stream?" I can hear the worry in Savannah's voice. She sounds like a mother.

"It's not that much. We only have five minutes, so let's not waste it. How are you?"

"I miss you so much!" I hear Savannah's voice breaking.

"I miss you, too. Everything is good, though. We'll see each other soon enough. I'm so proud of how well you're doing!"

"Thank you."

"And that Rhett guy... he's a hottie!"

"Sadie! Hush up!"

"No, seriously, everybody is obsessed with you two!"

"Really? Why?"

"Because you're freaking adorable! The overflowing sink. The dance in the kitchen. All of it. It's so sweet!"

"But we're not…"

"Yeah, yeah, yeah. I know you keep saying that, but that man is in love with you. No joke."

She turns her head and looks at me, her face turning red. "No, Sadie. Everybody has it all wrong. We're just… friends."

"Friends with Rhett from pastry chef school? Um, no. That would never happen."

"But we're in love? We can't just be friends?"

"No! With that kind of passion, you either hate each other or love each other. And the audience has assessed the situation as being L-O-V-E!"

I don't know why she spells it out.

"Two minutes left!" The producer calls out. This feels like a prison visitation.

"Sadie, you're a hopeless romantic," she laughs.

"And you can't see what's right in front of you, sissy."

"All I see is a competition I need to win so we can change our lives. That's what I see."

"You're impossible," Sadie says, groaning.

"How's work?"

"It's work. Dull and boring."

"I'm going to do my best to win this for both of us, okay?"

"I know you will, sissy. You've never let me down a day in my life. Even if you don't win, you still haven't let me down. You're my hero."

Savannah wipes away some stray tears. I force myself not to walk over there and hug her.

What gets me is how Connor found her connection to her sister to be a bad thing. How is that even possible? Savannah and Sadie are best friends. I can see that with my own two eyes. Any man who wouldn't encourage the woman he supposedly loves to have a great relationship with her sister is a selfish jerk. And yes, Connor is definitely that.

The two of them continue chatting until a producer calls time and ends the video just as they are blowing kisses at each other. It's adorable, but I'm never telling her that.

"Okay, Rhett. You're up!"

Savannah walks over as I stand up to give her the chair.

"Glad you got to do that, Sunny," I say, smiling.

"Now it's your turn," she says, touching my arm. "Have fun!"

Sitting in front of the screen, I imagine what my mother will say. Will she say she's proud of me for the first time? I guess it's possible, but not probable.

Maybe my dad will be there. We're not close like you'd think a father and son would be, but maybe he's proud of how I'm doing for once.

After a few moments, I realize no one is popping up on the screen for me. Producers are huddled in the corner talking, but I can't tell what they're saying. I glance at Savannah, who gives me an encouraging look. Something isn't right here.

"Um, Rhett," the producer says as she walks closer, "unfortunately, we weren't able to connect with your loved one."

I sit there a moment, trying to take in her words. "What does that mean? There's a connection problem?"

She shifts back and forth on her feet like she's uncomfortable. "No, not exactly." Of course, a cameraman comes in close to get a good shot of the look on my face. This can't be good.

"What's going on?"

"Nobody showed up, Rhett."

I feel like my lungs have caved in on themselves. I expected my mother wouldn't be happy for me, and maybe she'd even say something negative on national television. Still, I never anticipated that no one in my family would *show up* for me.

"Oh."

I don't want to look at Savannah, but in this

moment of feeling alone in the world, I can't help it. She suddenly feels like a life jacket in the middle of a raging river. Nothing prepares me for looking over at her and seeing the sadness on her face. The empathy.

"I'll give you a minute," the producer says, leaving the room. It feels so dark and heavy here with just Savannah and me.

"Rhett, I'm so sorry." She stands and walks closer. I stand because there's no reason to sit. I'm not waiting for a video call. She reaches out to touch my arm, but I recoil.

"No. It's fine. Let's just get back to the competition." I try to walk around her, but her tiny little frame somehow stands in my way. She moves closer, puts her arms around my waist, and presses her cheek into my chest. There are no words. She's just *there*.

"You didn't deserve this, Rhett," she says softly. "You're worthy of people being proud of you. You're worthy of being loved just for who you are. You're worthy of people showing up for you."

I feel hot tears welling in my eyes, threatening to spill over and never stop. I haven't cried since my grandmother died, and even then, it was only at the funeral. I don't let myself get deep in emotions—any emotions—because I fear I won't make it back to shore. So, why does this feel safe right now? She's a tiny little woman, and she makes me feel so seen and safe.

"We need to go," I murmur, pressing my lips against the top of her head.

"We have time," she says without moving. So we stay there for several minutes. She feels so perfect in my arms. How will I ever let her go? Not just now but at the end of this competition.

I use all my strength to pull away enough to let her release her hold on me. The tears slide back down into their ducts, and I suck in a breath.

"Thanks," I say, unsure of what other words to use. I know what I feel but can't say it on TV. There is no privacy in this place.

"Are you okay? We can stay in here longer…"

"No, it's fine. I'd rather get on with it."

"Okay, if you're sure."

Why is she so dang nice? How does someone come from her background and still see the world in a positive light?

I open the door, and the light from the foyer pours in. I don't want to go back to where the other contestants are and answer a bunch of questions, so I turn for the stairs.

"Come on," Savannah says, grabbing my hand

and pulling me up the stairs. I have no idea what she's doing.

We reach the top of the stairs, and she pushes me into the bathroom. She's strong for such a small woman. A producer is hot on our heels, but Savannah stands between me and her in the doorway.

"What are you doing?" the producer asks.

"We need a moment," Savannah says, reaching around and turning off her mic pack. She points at me to do the same.

"You can't keep doing this!"

"Try to stop me," Savannah says and shuts the door. I'm in shock. "Is yours off?"

I nod. "That was pretty epic," I say, laughing.

"You deserve privacy after that whole fiasco. Who does your mother think she is, anyway?" She pulls me away from the door to the other side of the bathroom. We're pressed into a small alcove that should house a shelf but doesn't.

"She's never been proud of the path I chose. I shouldn't have been surprised."

Savannah puts her hands on my chest, and I feel prickly shivers run up my spine. What is this woman doing to me?

"I want you to know I'm proud of you, Rhett. I never

thought I would say that in a million years, but it's true. You're a good guy. You're talented. You're kind. You don't have to keep pushing people away. I just wanted you to know that without a bunch of cameras around."

I can't help myself. I pull her into a tight hug. No one has ever said anything like that to me, and I want to soak it in. I want to feel comfort in a way I've never felt it before. Everything in me wants to kiss her right now, but I know she doesn't want that. She's just such a nice person who wants to help.

"Thank you again."

She looks up at me. "You deserve all the good things, Rhett Jennings."

I want to tell her *she's* the best thing. The very best.

"Can I tell you something?"

"Sure," she says, stepping back.

"I haven't been honest about something with you. And it feels like I need to get this off my chest."

"Okay. What?"

"I don't work on yachts with celebrities."

She tilts her head slightly. "You lied about where you work? Why?"

"Because it's embarrassing."

"Rhett, I work in a grocery store bakery with a scary lady named Big Thelma. Not exactly a four-star restaurant. It's not likely I would judge you."

I take in a breath and blow it out. Why is this so hard to admit?

"I work on a cruise ship."

"And?"

"I work in the *kitchen* of a cruise ship."

"So?"

I can't help but laugh at her response. All this time, I was afraid of admitting I didn't work for some big celebrity on a yacht, and she did not react.

"I guess I just bragged a lot to make people think I was doing better than I was. My family also thinks I work on yachts."

"Why lie?"

I sigh. "I thought it would impress them. Make them proud of me."

"I'm so sorry that your family let you down today, but that's on them, Rhett. Working on a cruise ship is amazing! You get to go to all those beautiful places and meet new people. There's nothing wrong with that."

"Why do you always make me feel better, Sunny?"

She smiles. "I guess we were meant to be friends instead of enemies."

## SAVANNAH

If I knew what Rhett's mother and father looked like, I would hunt them down and smack them.

Who doesn't show up for their kid? Who allows him to show up on TV and be embarrassed?

As addicted as my mother was, I still knew she loved me. She couldn't do much but showed us love when she could. Her brain just loved drugs and alcohol more.

I can't think about it much because tonight is another main challenge. Two more people are going home; it can't be me and Rhett. This is week five. I just need to make it through this challenge to get to finals week. Then, I really have a chance at this money.

Rhett has been quiet after our bathroom meeting. I don't know if I did too much. Maybe I shouldn't have hugged him. Maybe that was too far. Not everybody likes physical touch.

"Penny for your thoughts?" Maggie sits down next to me on the outdoor sofa. There are so few of us here now. I remember when the courtyard was full of contestants.

"It's been quite a day, Maggie."

"I heard about Rhett."

I snap my head sideways. "What? How?"

"One of the producers told me during my confessional."

"No talking about production!" one of the producers says over the intercom. It's still so unnerving to know they're listening to our every word. It's also irritating that they shared Rhett's situation with another contestant.

Maggie rolls her eyes. "Anyway, I'm so sad for him. I like Rhett."

I lean my head back and look up at the sky. "I'm sad for him, too. And if his family is listening, you're a bunch of jerks!"

"I never had kids, you know. I wanted them so badly, but it just wasn't in the cards for me and my husband. I would give anything to have a son like Rhett."

"You would've been a great mother, Maggie. I know you would have given such unconditional love to your kids."

She wipes away a stray tear. "I would have. But you know God had other plans. Instead, I became an English teacher. I watched so many wonderful children grow up. Some of them still send me letters and pictures of their own kids. The circle of life and all that."

"I hope to have kids one day. First, I have to find the right man."

She looks over at me and smiles. "Honey, I think you already have."

"Connor? No way!"

"Not Connor. I'm talking about Rhett."

"Rhett isn't interested in me like that, Maggie. It just looks that way." I can't blow Rhett's cover. I can't let the audience know that he's just acting to get votes. It might ruin his game.

"Honey, that man is head over heels for you."

I laugh out loud. "No, he's not. One day, after this show ends, I have lots to tell you."

She eyes me quizzically. "I can't wait."

SAVANNAH

The kitchen is buzzing with anticipation. The tension in the air is palpable as the remaining contestants gather around Dan, who is standing at the front of the room. I can feel my heart pounding in my chest. This is the last challenge before finals week, and the stakes have never been higher.

Rhett, Lainey, Connor, Maggie, Zara, and I stand shoulder to shoulder, ready to face whatever the competition throws at us today. Dan clears his throat and raises the microphone to his mouth,

"Welcome to *The Baking Games*! This is the last challenge before finals week, and today, we have a special theme for you: holiday desserts. You'll design a dessert dedicated to your favorite holiday. That can be Christmas, Halloween, Easter, or even Arbor Day if that's your jam."

Even though what he said wasn't all that funny, there's a requisite laugh. Holidays mean comfort, warmth, and nostalgia for most people. So the other contestants, minus Rhett, of course, seem to be excited about this challenge.

For me, holidays were always a letdown. Christmas usually involved a TV dinner if we were lucky, and sometimes we would get a gift from a local charity of some kind, but most of the time, my mother would forget it was even a holiday. Never mind things like Halloween or Easter. I never went trick-or-treating, but thankfully, Sadie did because I took her myself. Once, I even set up an Easter egg hunt in our apartment. While sad to others, those days are among my favorite memories of me and Sadie.

The only time we got to celebrate anything was if the school had a party for it. Going home from school and leaving all the fun behind was always so upsetting. I knew other kids were going on Christmas break to spend time with their families, open their gifts, and sit by the Christmas tree drinking hot cocoa. We didn't even have a Christmas tree most years, but I don't feel bad for myself. It's just a stark contrast in these sorts of situations where I have to think of something holiday-related when that really hasn't been a part of my past.

Dan continues. "Let's ask a question of one of our contestants. Social media is buzzing with queries for you folks. Connor, tell us, what has been the most surprising thing that you've learned while you've been in the house?"

Connor suddenly gets a look on his face. A smirk. I know it well, and I know it isn't good. He steps forward slightly and turns to look at me and Rhett.

"Well, Dan, I was shocked to learn that Mr. Fancy Pants Pastry Chef over there," he points to Rhett, "doesn't actually work on yachts with celebrities like he told everyone. Turns out he's just a lowly cruise ship cook."

The room falls silent. I can feel the anger radiating off Rhett. I know this will throw him off his game, which is exactly why Connor has done it. My heart sinks when I see a look of betrayal on his face. He thinks I told Connor. I try to catch his eye so I can shake my head and tell him it wasn't me, but he's turned his head away, his jaw set in a hard line.

Clearly taken aback by this onscreen revelation, Dan tries to regain control of the situation. "Okay, well, thank you for that, Connor. Why don't we go ahead and get to the challenge? You have three hours to create your holiday-themed dessert. Remember, this is the last challenge before the final, so you want to give it everything you've got. Your time starts... now!"

We all rush to our stations, the energy in the room shifting straight to frantic. I'm trying to focus on my dessert and whatever idea I can come up with, but I can only think about what just happened with Rhett.

And then Maggie's words echo in my mind. She thinks Rhett is in love with me. I steal a glance over at him only to find him glaring at me. He is extremely angry, and I can tell his composure is shattered. I don't want this to be the reason that he goes home. I start to walk towards his station, and he holds up his hand and shakes his head. "Don't."

I realize that I'm doing this for my sister. I can't get distracted right now, even if it means that I have to talk to Rhett later if we're both still here by then. I'm sure we can work this out. But for right now, I have to focus.

I stand in the kitchen for a moment, close my eyes, and try to think of something that I can make. I finally come up with a Thanksgiving-inspired pumpkin spice cake with maple frosting. I will craft a Turkey out of fondant for the top, maybe even a small dinner table with food on it if I have time.

I take a deep breath and try to block out the noise. I have to concentrate. This isn't the time to get lost in thought. I gather my ingredients and start mixing my batter, but my hands are shaking.

"Hey, Savannah?" Lainey calls out from her station, which is now next to mine on the other side. Her voice is dripping with sarcasm. "You look a bit flustered. Everything okay?"

I force a smile. "I'm fine, Lainey. Thanks for your concern."

"You'd better keep it together. You wouldn't want to mess up in front of the judges."

I grit my teeth and go back to work. I start mixing my batter, and I can hear Rhett muttering angrily under his breath at the station next to mine. I look over and see him throwing his ingredients together carelessly. This is a rare sight because he's always so precise.

The minutes tick by, and I keep trying to focus on my own work, but my mind keeps wandering back to Rhett. Why does he think I would betray him like that? How can I prove to him that I didn't?

As I finally move to put my cake in the oven, I

catch Maggie's eye from across the room, and she gives me an encouraging smile. Her presence is always a comforting reminder that not everyone in this house is against me. I take a deep breath and decide I have to push through and handle things with Rhett later. I am determined to finish strong.

# CHAPTER 22

RHETT

I CAN'T BELIEVE THIS. My blood is boiling. I can hardly concentrate on the challenge. Connor's words just keep replaying in my mind over and over, each one like a knife, twisting deep into my gut. This humiliation is unbearable. My secret was exposed on national TV, and the one person I thought I could trust betrayed me—Savannah.

I don't know why she thought telling Connor of all people would be a good idea, but there's no other explanation. She's the only person here who knows. We have no access to the outside world, so it's not like Connor could have found out on his own.

This is why I don't trust people, and this is why I

don't let people get close. And now my family knows the truth. They know that I don't work on yachts with celebrities. They know I work on cruise ships, in the bowels of a ship, feeding thousands of people —not exactly what I hoped to do with my pastry chef education.

Logically, I know working on a cruise ship isn't a terrible occupation—for *most* people. But in my family, anything short of cooking for the President himself wouldn't be good enough. And even then, it would depend on *which* President.

I shake my head, trying to refocus on my dessert. I'm making a Halloween-inspired cake in the shape of a dark tower with all kinds of spooky things in the windows. I feel unsteady. My usual precision is gone, replaced by blind fury. I continue mixing the dough, but my emotions are mechanical because my mind is elsewhere.

"Focus, Rhett," I mutter to myself. It's no use. My mind is a storm, and there's no way to calm it. I glance over at Savannah, who is working on her cake. Lately, she's been the calm in my storm, and now she's the dark cloud hanging over me. How could I have trusted her?

She looks frazzled, but she always does. Still, I know she is responsible for what just happened, and

I've never been so disappointed in someone in my life.

SAVANNAH

The smell of spices fills the air as I pour my batter into the pans. I set the timer and then turn to my frosting. My mind is still racing with thoughts of Rhett. Maggie's words keep haunting me. Could it be true? Does he have actual feelings for me? And if he does, why would he think that I would betray his confidence like that? It's all too much.

"Come on, Savannah, you need to focus," I whisper to myself. I mix the frosting, the sweet scent of maple calming my nerves, but it's a temporary fix. There's so much tension in this room that it's almost suffocating. Lainey with her smug face. Connor with his sneer. Rhett's anger bubbling under his skin. It's all too much. I don't like conflict. I don't like drama. I don't know why I thought being on a reality show wouldn't have a bunch of both of those.

As I start to frost my cake, the door to the kitchen opens, and Dan steps in with the judges. It must be getting close to time. They usually leave us alone during the competition and then show up later, probably after eating something or drinking glasses of wine. I don't know what they do out there.

A few minutes later, the bell goes off, and we're forced to stop touching our desserts. The judges start to make their rounds. They start with Lainey. Her Christmas-themed spice cake looks like a work of art. I'm actually impressed. It's beautifully decorated with sugared cranberries and a dusting of powdered sugar that looks like snow.

Of course, hers looks good. She wasn't fixating on drama like I was.

"This is excellent work, Lainey," Chef Alain says. "This is exactly what we were looking for in a holiday-themed dessert. This is worthy of a magazine cover." Lainey beams, and her recently whitened teeth almost blind me.

Having been her roommate all these weeks, I've witnessed her morning and evening routines. These include whitening strips, all manner of face masks, and something that seems to freeze her whole face for a good half hour. I enjoy that time because she can't open her stupid mouth to talk.

Next, they move over to Rhett. He's made a Halloween-themed cake. The judges taste it and exchange glances. "The flavor is good, but this seems a little rushed. The icing is falling off here, and these detail pieces could be a little tighter," Marco says. "I have to say, it's not your best work, Rhett."

He looks irritated. I'm sure he was just trying to get through it after the drama with Connor before the competition. It has definitely thrown Rhett off, which is exactly what Connor wanted.

They continue around the room, looking at Maggie's Easter-themed carrot cake and Zara's Diwali-inspired dessert. They find hers lacking flavor and depth and say Maggie's is a bit dry, even though the flavors were spot-on.

Connor made a Valentine's Day sponge cake with more fondant hearts than I've ever seen. Honestly, it's not his best work and looks like something I'd make from a bag at the grocery store. "I think you went a bit overboard on the hearts," Chef Alain says, scrunching his nose like he smells something bad.

Finally, they reach my station. I hold my breath as they taste my pumpkin spice cake. "This frosting is wonderful," Tessa says, "but I feel like this cake is a little bit spongy and undercooked."

I nod. I feel the sting of disappointment, but I can't disagree with them. I wasn't exactly on my game. I knew I could have been. I knew I could have done better had I been able to concentrate.

Once the judges have finished their deliberations,

Dan steps forward. They open up the audience voting for about fifteen minutes while Dan stands around chatting and filling time. Finally, when they cut back to him, they are ready to announce the winner.

"The winner of this challenge is..." He pauses for dramatic effect, "Lainey with her Christmas-themed spice cake. Congratulations, Lainey! You are the first person to secure a spot in the finals."

Lainey beams, soaking in the applause. "Thank you. I knew Christmas was the way to go." She eyes all the other contestants who didn't choose Christmas.

Then Dan's expression turns serious as he addresses the rest of us. "Unfortunately, we must say goodbye to two of our contestants. Those who got the fewest votes from the audience and judges combined were…"

Again, another dramatic pause. "Zara and Maggie, I'm sorry to say that your journeys end here. Thank you for everything you've brought to the competition."

Both Zara and Maggie smile graciously, hug each other, and then walk around and hug the remaining contestants. Maggie's eyes meet mine, and she mouths, "Good luck." I'm going to miss her so much. I never realized how much I craved having a mother figure until I met Maggie. As they leave, Dan gives us a final nod.

"Get some rest, everyone. Finals week starts in just a couple of days."

I try to catch Rhett's eye as we leave the kitchen, but he's already storming off. I feel so guilty and frustrated even though I didn't do anything wrong. This was supposed to be a good time for us to get closer as friends if nothing else, and now it feels like everything is falling apart.

I head to my room, hoping to get a good night's sleep and wipe this day away. It will be lonely in there without Maggie. Rhett's anger keeps replaying in my mind. Tomorrow is a new day, and I have to find a way to fix this mess.

RHETT

I storm up the stairs as Connor's words repeatedly batter my brain. What he said in front of everyone echoes in my mind as my fists clench involuntarily. I can feel my blood seemingly boiling under my skin.

Savannah was the only one who knew. She had to have told him. How else could Connor have known about my work on the cruise ships? I wanted to keep that part of my life private. We took great pains to ensure our microphones were turned off when I told Savannah away from the prying eyes of national television. Now, it's out there for everyone, including my family, to judge.

I try to push my thoughts aside as best I can so I can go to sleep. I'm exhausted. I didn't do well in the competition, and I really just need a good night of sleep.

Part of me wants to pummel Connor for saying what he said, but I know that's what he wants. A reaction. He's probably hoping I get physical and get kicked out just before finals. It's not happening.

What I feel more than anything is hurt by Savannah, and I hate feeling vulnerable that way. After I get out of this house, I won't trust anyone again.

Before I can get into bed, I turn and see Savannah standing in the doorway. Connor brushes past her to come into our room.

"Oh, hey there, Savannah. I guess you're coming in here to try to defend yourself?"

"I want to talk to Rhett."

"Well, I don't want to talk to you," I say, turning over in the bed and facing the wall.

"Seems like your new boyfriend is mad at you."

"I want to know how you found out about that, Connor, because it certainly wasn't from me."

"Wasn't from you? Of course, it was."

"Are you kidding me? You must be kidding me. You're going to sit here and lie and tell Rhett that I told you that?"

"Well, it seems like maybe Rhett only told you, so how else would I know?"

"I don't know how you found out, but you know as well as I do that I didn't tell you anything."

I can hear them arguing back and forth. Of course, I'm not looking in that direction because I don't want to give either one of them the satisfaction of seeing my face right now.

This makes no sense. Why would Savannah have betrayed my confidence, and why would she have told Connor, of all people? She hates him. I hate him. But it doesn't make any sense. She's the only person I told. He would have no way of finding out that information on his own. I'm confused, I'm frustrated, and I'm tired. So I close my eyes and decide that the best thing to do is to go to sleep and worry about all this tomorrow.

∼

## SAVANNAH

Somehow, I manage to avoid Lainey like the plague when we go to bed. When I get in there, she's down the hallway with Connor, making out like a couple of high school kids. I can't stand either one of them. The best part of getting out of this house, besides seeing my sister again, is going to be getting rid of these two. Hopefully, I will never see either of their faces again.

I get a decently restful night of sleep once I actually fall asleep. Not having Maggie over there snoring is actually making me have insomnia. I guess I got used to her snoring as a white noise machine because I didn't know I would miss it so much. Thankfully, Lainey has moved to the bed on the opposite side of the room, so I no longer have to sleep beside her. I can't believe she won the competition this week. I think it was a fair judgment because her cake was better than anyone else's. So few people are left in the competition that it's almost easier to win.

There are only four of us going into finals week. From what I understand, there will be a series of challenges between now and the end. One person will be voted off in each of the next two challenges, leaving only the final two to complete whatever the final challenge is.

The only thing on my mind today is talking to Rhett. I need to make sure that he knows that I didn't tell Connor anything. I'm not sure how to convince him of that fact, but I will give it my best.

I get up and dressed, put on some casual clothes, and plan to lie around the house today and prepare for the upcoming competitions. I walk down the hallway to Rhett's room, but he's not in there, so I go downstairs, make myself a bowl of cereal, and wait until I see him.

Still, I don't see him anywhere. For a moment, I fear that he has left the competition and quit out of embarrassment. I honestly don't understand why he's embarrassed about working on cruise ships. I've never been on a cruise, but it seems like something that people with money do. People who have the means for that vacation. After all, I had never even seen the beach. I didn't get to go on cruises.

I would consider it a high honor if Rhett cooked for me on a cruise. I value our budding friendship. I miss him. I miss him talking to me, and I would gladly be chained to him again if I could. That sounds so silly when I think about it.

I finish my bowl of cereal and start walking around, looking for people. I see Lainey and Connor sitting in the hot tub and want to gag, but I don't see Rhett. I don't know where he could be. I walk around the house until I finally find him. He's in the side parlor where we originally all met as contestants. None of us ever go in there. It's a stuffy room with bookshelves. It looks like a place where a man would sit and smoke a cigar by the fire.

The lights are dim, and he's just sitting by himself in a chair in the corner. It's like the first time I ran into him in the bathroom. He likes chairs in corners.

"Hey, what are you doing?"

"I'm sitting in a chair," he says dryly, not making eye contact.

"Why aren't you in the courtyard or your room?"

"Maybe I wanted to be alone."

"I get that, but can we talk?"

"Well, I really don't have an exit plan, so I guess I don't have a choice."

I enter the room and shut the two French doors behind me. I sit in a chair on the opposite side of the room. This feels awkward and uncomfortable.

"Rhett, I didn't tell Connor anything."

"That's impossible, Savannah. You're the only person—literally the only person in the world—who knew that information."

"I know it doesn't make sense. He had to have overheard us."

"How? We weren't wearing our microphones. We weren't even standing near the door. We were whispering."

"I know that. It doesn't make any sense to me either, but I can promise you I didn't tell him anything. I don't even talk to Connor."

"I thought that was true, but maybe you and Connor have a separate friendship that I don't know about. Maybe you've been working with him to win this competition."

"Seriously? Connor and me? No. I can't stand him. That doesn't even make any sense. You know that."

"I thought I knew a lot of things, Savannah."

"I hate this. I didn't do anything wrong, and now you hate me."

"I don't hate you. I could never hate you," he says quietly. There's something about his voice. It makes me think about what Maggie said, that maybe she's right.

"Then you have to believe me. I didn't do this."

He looks up, a pained expression on his face. "I wish that I could believe you. I wish that I could trust you. I wish that I could trust anybody, actually. I opened myself up to you, and what did I get? Embarrassed on national television. Exposed to my family, who already judges me."

"You have to believe me, Rhett. I didn't do this."

"Can I just be alone?" He says it with such finality that it's jarring, but I want to respect his wishes. I stand up and walk to the door but turn back just before I exit.

"I've really enjoyed getting to know you, and I wish you all the best in the final, but I promise you, you can trust me. I didn't do this. All of this was real to me."

He says nothing, and I walk out the door, wondering if that's the end of my friendship... or whatever it is... with Rhett.

SAVANNAH

With nothing else to do, I decide to go to my room and start packing. No matter what, I'm leaving this house within a week. It will give me something to do while I worry about the upcoming challenges and what's happening with Rhett.

Unfortunately, Lainey is in the room, still wearing her bikini from the hot tub. She's painting her toenails a hot pink color while she sits on Maggie's old bed.

"I switched my sheets out so I didn't have to sleep on the old bat's sheets."

"Maggie isn't an old bat. Why are you so incredibly rude, Lainey? Did someone hurt you?" I say sarcastically. At this point, I don't care about making friends with her.

She sneers. "Don't take it out on me because your boyfriend is mad at you. Maybe he'll take you on a cruise. Oh, but he'll have to work in the kitchen, so he probably won't see you much." She laughs at her un-funny joke.

"Just shut up, Lainey. I'm not in the mood." I reach for my suitcase and unzip it.

"Going home already?"

"Just getting prepared for next week."

"You're never going to win this, Savannah."

"Again, you don't need to talk to me, Lainey. I could go the rest of my life without hearing your whiny voice."

"Geez, so moody. I thought you were all sunshine and lollipops, but Sunny has an edge, apparently."

"Stop calling me Sunny." In my mind, Rhett can call me that, but no one else.

"Is that only for your boyfriend?"

I throw my hands in the air. Why am I letting this woman get to me? "He's not my boyfriend! In fact, he hates me now. Just stop talking to me!"

"I don't get why he's so upset Connor found out about the cruise stuff."

"Because he thinks I told Connor. He thinks Connor and I are in cahoots, I guess."

"That's silly. Connor would never be interested in you again."

I laugh under my breath. "I dumped Connor, not the other way around."

"Whatever. And anyway, I feel like I need to be recognized in this whole thing."

I look at her. "What does that mean?"

"I told Connor."

My heart pounds in my chest. "What? How?"

"I was in the shower when you two numbskulls came into the bathroom."

I drop my suitcase on the bed. "What? Why were you in the shower?"

"I kept seeing you two sneak into bathrooms all season, so when I saw you pulling him up the stairs after the video calls, I wanted to see what was going on."

My face feels like it's on fire. "You stupid little…"

Lainey holds up her well-manicured hand. "No, no, no… we're on TV. No foul language, Sunny."

If I were big enough to put her in a headlock, I would totally do it. If I tried, I'd just hang from her neck like a necklace. For now, I'm just happy to know how all of this happened.

Without another word, I run downstairs looking for Rhett. Instead, I run straight into Connor at the bottom of the stairs.

"Whoa, whoa, whoa! Where are you going so fast?" He steps in front of me every time I try to get around him. I'm close to kicking him where the sun doesn't shine, as my grandmother would've said.

"Move, Connor! I need to talk to Rhett."

"He's in confessional. Probably talking about how you broke his heart."

"This is all your fault!"

"You're embarrassing yourself, Savannah. Running after a guy like Rhett? Seriously?"

I put my hands on my hips. "And why is that?"

"Because he'd never be interested in you. He's obviously just biding his time until he gets out of here. No guy with that kind of family money would ever lower himself to date a girl like… you."

"You dated me, Connor."

"And I didn't have rich parents and more money than I could ever spend. Rhett will leave you in the dust, and you'll be made fun of on social media for weeks after this. It's sad. You need to cut your losses now. He's not into you, Savannah. Can't you see that?"

"Just shut up, Connor. Honestly, your voice is the most annoying sound on the planet." I walk past him toward the kitchen.

"Hey, Savannah?"

I stop, but I don't turn around. "What?"

"I know I joke around, but I'm serious. We loved each other once, and I'd hate to see you get hurt."

I know he's trying to play me, but it's not working. I turn around and face him.

"Connor, if you tried for the rest of your miserable life, you'd never be half the man Rhett is. If you think I'm buying all of this, you're sadly mistaken."

"What's going on here?" Rhett suddenly says from behind me.

I turn and, without thinking, say, "Hippopotamus."

"Huh?"

"Hippopotamus, Rhett!"

His face suddenly registers what I'm saying. "I don't understand…"

"I found out how Connor knew about the cruise ship."

He glares in Connor's direction. "How?"

"Lainey was hiding in the shower when we were in the bathroom."

Rhett's mouth drops open. "What?"

I turn to face him, completely ignoring that

Connor is nearby. I place my hands on his chest, look up at him and wink. "See, sweetie? I would never have done anything to hurt you."

It takes a moment for Rhett to really get what I'm doing, but once he does, I see a smile spread across his face. "I'm sorry I didn't believe you, beautiful." He leans down and brushes his lips against my cheek.

Wow, that felt way better than I thought it would. I decide in this moment that a fake relationship with Rhett for the next week won't be so bad. I can live in the land of make-believe if I need to for one of us to win. It just needs to be me.

# CHAPTER 23

RHETT

When Connor finally slinks away, I pull
Savannah out into the courtyard. Since we're on
camera and she said our code word, I can't really ask
her why she changed her mind in the last week.

"Do you believe me now?" she asks when we sit
down.

"I do. I'm so sorry, Sunny. I had no idea that
Lainey would be so childish as to hide in the shower.
Who does that?"

She laughs. "This is Lainey we're talking about."

"True. Gosh, I feel like I can breathe again."

"I would never do anything to purposely hurt
you, Rhett." She reaches over and puts her hand on
my arm. Part of me wants to think it's real, but I also

know we're now fully pretending to be a couple. This might be the best week of my life.

"Can I ask you a question?"

"Of course."

"Well, since we only have one week left, if we're lucky, I'd like to ask if you'd go on a date with me tonight?"

Her eyes widen. "A date? Really?"

"Well, we *are* a couple…" I feel the need to remind her of this fact.

"I'd love to go on a date with you."

This is so hard. Is she looking at me that way because she's great at acting? Or is she looking at me that way because she has the same feelings I do?

"Okay, how about I pick you up at five?"

She laughs. "Pick me up?"

"I will arrive at your door at five o'clock."

"And how should I dress for this date?"

I smile. "You look stunning in anything, Savannah Greene."

Oh yeah. I'm in trouble here.

SAVANNAH

I stand in the bathroom, staring at my face in the mirror. I've never been one for lots of makeup, but right now, I feel naked. I wish I'd brought more than mascara and lipstick.

Suddenly, the door opens, and a crying Lainey basically falls into me.

"What on earth are you doing?" I yelp, pulling back from her. She stares at the mirror, mascara running down her face. She looks like a panda bear.

"Connor is a jerk!"

"Well, I could've told you that," I say, shrugging my shoulders.

"He broke up with me!"

"Oh no," I say flatly. "You must be devastated." My voice sounds like a robot.

She stares at me in the mirror. "Have some compassion!"

I sigh and lean against the counter. "Like you had compassion for me and Rhett when you hid in the shower and then gave that information to Connor?"

She crosses her arms. "Fine. I guess that wasn't all that nice." Her breath shudders as she tries to stop crying.

"Look, Lainey, we're not going to be best friends, but I never want to see anyone get their heart broken. Connor is a dead end. He doesn't have feelings like a normal person. Trust me, you dodged a bullet." I turn back toward the mirror and put on mascara.

"Why are you so nice all the time?"

"I guess it's the way God made me."

She sighs. "I don't think I'm ever going to find true love. What's wrong with me?"

I struggle with what to say without sounding overly mean. I'm not one to kick someone when they're down.

"Well, you're not always nice, Lainey. And you like to brag about yourself."

"That's just who I am!" she says, dramatically throwing her hands in the air.

"I don't think so. I think you act this way because someone hurt you. Somebody made you think it wasn't safe to be a nice person. Somebody taught you that you need to tear others down to build yourself up."

She stands there for a moment, sniffling. "What are you getting ready for, anyway?"

I grin. "I have a date."

"A date? With Rhett?"

"Yes. He realized I didn't betray his trust after he found out you were hiding in the shower."

"You know, he's not bad to look at," she says, smiling.

"Back off, Lainey. I *will* fight you."

She waves her hand at me. "Fine. I'm just joking, anyway. He's not my type. I like to be the best-looking one in my relationships."

"I can see that."

She stands behind me and looks at both of us in the mirror. "You can't go like this, Savannah."

I look down at my basic white t-shirt and tan capri pants. "Why?"

"It's a *date*!"

"I mean, it's kind of a date. It's in a house that we can't leave."

"You need to look hot!"

"I do?"

"Of course. What else do you have to wear?"

"Um, more T-shirts and pants? Pajamas?"

"Ugh. How did you ever snag this man?"

I want to tell her all I had to do was say hippopotamus, but I don't think she'd get it.

"And your makeup… or lack thereof."

"Okay, this is why people don't like you, Lainey."

She's dried her tears at this point and is now solely focused on me. "I'll help you."

"I don't need help…"

385

"Yes, you do. Now, come on. First, we'll look at my wardrobe."

RHETT

Why am I so nervous? I've taken New York socialites on dates. I've taken the daughter of the head of a NYC hospital to her college dance. I've even taken the daughter of a well-known DC politician on a coffee date. This is Savannah from pastry chef school, and it feels like the most important night of my life.

I walk up the stairs and pause at the top. My heart is thumping in my chest, and I feel my hands shaking.

For some reason, I can't figure out whether I'm nervous because we're playing pretend about our relationship for the audience at home, or if it's because I'm going on an actual date with Savannah. Either way, I don't want to be late, so I walk over to her door and knock.

When she opens it, I'm stunned. This doesn't look like the Savannah I normally see, with very little makeup and her hair pulled up into a ponytail. Instead, she's got it down, curled and flowing across her shoulders—her bare shoulders. She's wearing a red dress with the shoulders cut out, and the dress comes just above her knees. She has on a pair of black high heels. I've never seen her wear heels before.

Either way—dressy or plain—she's the most beautiful woman I've ever seen in real life.

"Wow," I say when she opens the door.

She smiles slightly. "Do I look okay?"

"You look great. It's just… different."

She laughs. "Yeah. Believe it or not, Lainey helped me."

"I helped her!" Lainey yells in the background, smiling from her bed.

"Wait, what? I don't understand."

Savannah holds up her hand. "We'll talk later. It's best not to ask questions right now."

I hand her the bouquet of flowers that I picked from the garden area, a mixture of purples, reds, and yellows. I have no idea what the flowers are called, but I thought they looked nice together. "These are for you."

"Thank you. These are beautiful." She leans in and smells them.

"I'll put them in water," Lainey says, walking up behind her. I don't know what happened between these two, but I feel like I'm in the twilight zone.

"So, where are we going?"

"I have some special things planned," I say. "Shall we?" I hold out my elbow like one of those men in an old movie, and she takes it. She looks back at Lainey and then walks out the door. We go down the stairs slowly because she's wearing high heels now. It's weird to have her taller. I'm used to looking way down at her.

I guide her to the garden area. Most people don't go out there because everybody spends a lot of time in the courtyard since it's way bigger, but the garden area is actually very nice. It's a small area off the side of the house that is surrounded by old brick walls. They're covered in ivy, and production has strung twinkle lights all over the area.

The ground is old pavers. I've had help setting up a small table in the center, and I spent the last few hours cooking us a special dinner. When we walk out, and she sees the candle in the middle of the table and hears music, she turns to me and smiles.

"You did all of this for me?" she says, putting her hand on her chest.

"Of course. Why wouldn't I?"

"I don't know. No one's ever done anything like this. I mean, I've been taken out to nice dinners before, but nobody ever went out of their way to set up something so romantic."

I look down at her and then run my thumb across her cheek. I don't know why I do it. It just feels natural. "Well, you deserve the very best."

She smiles, and then I lead her over to the chair, pulling it out so she can sit down. "So, what are we having?"

I sit down across from her. "Well, I planned a very special menu. I made stuffed mushrooms with garlic and herb cream cheese stuffing for our appetizer. And then, for our main course, I made pan-seared salmon with a lemon butter sauce. I also made garlic mashed potatoes and asparagus with a Hollandaise sauce. For dessert, I made my famous strawberry tiramisu."

Her mouth falls open. "Wow. I had no idea you could cook all of that."

"What? Did you think I was just a pastry chef? Of course, I can cook." I pour her a glass of sparkling water with lemon and mint. We also have a bottle of wine, but I'm saving that for dessert.

"Well, I'm sure I'm going to enjoy everything."

I stand and walk over to the table where the food is ready. I tried to convince the producers to get me somebody to serve us, but they weren't willing to go that far. I walk over to the table and uncover the mushrooms, handing her the spoon so she can dish them onto her plate.

As we eat, she compliments my food and we talk about all sorts of things. Our favorite TV shows as kids, our favorite books that we've ever read, our favorite movies. Even her favorite animal, which is a dog.

Everything she tells me about herself seems interesting. I hang on her every word. The audience is probably eating this up, but I don't care anymore. I'm just glad to spend this time with her. Every time I think about leaving this house and going back to our normal lives, I get a pain in the pit of my stomach.

Of course, she has no idea. She thinks we're just pretending. She'll return to her normal life with her sister, and I'll get onto another cruise ship with thousands of people I don't know.

The only difference will be that I'll be missing her. I'll be thinking about her for the rest of my life. So, right now, I'm happy to be sitting here and enjoying this time with Savannah. I'm already pre-grieving what it's going to be like when we leave this house.

∼

## SAVANNAH

I cannot believe he did all of this for me. Our dinner conversation is fun and engaging. We talk about all kinds of things. I tell him stories from when I was in middle school. He tells me stories from when he was in high school.

We laugh at how different our opinions are on movies and books. He likes to read; I do, too. He likes to watch movies. That's one of my favorite things to do, although I usually can't afford to see them in the theater. He loves action-adventure movies. I like horror movies.

I talk about Sadie, our past, and growing up with our mother. I also talk about my grandmother and how much I loved her. He talks about his grandmother, too. Learning to bake from our grandmothers is something we have in common.

Once we've finished eating and have dessert, we sit at the table, laughing and chatting. I will miss this when the competition ends, but I know it's not real.

I know he's just playing pretend for the cameras to get us votes, and I appreciate it. I would like to get to the final two and battle it out, just me and him.

But I'm going to miss this interaction. I have a feeling that once we leave, maybe we'll text a few times, and then I'll never hear from Rhett again. He'll be on cruise ships or working in a fancy restaurant. I'll be back at the grocery store bakery, or if I'm lucky and win the competition, I'll start my own bakery. We have very different lives and very different plans.

Our lives would never work together. Not that he wants it to, anyway. I think he's doing all of this to get votes. But still, it's the most romantic evening I've ever had, so I'm going to soak it in. Between the food, the conversation, the twinkling lights, and the soft music, I don't think I ever want to go upstairs again.

"So, tell me about Lainey. How exactly did she end up helping you get dressed? You two hate each other."

"Yeah, I thought so, too. Apparently, Connor broke up with her and told her he didn't want a serious relationship with anyone. Plus, he was mad that she told me about being in the shower. So she came into the bathroom crying while I was getting ready. We had a short conversation in which she asked why people don't like her."

"And did you tell her?"

"Yeah, I gave her the tip of the iceberg, so to speak. I didn't want to crush her completely."

He laughs. "You're a very nice person, Savannah. Nicer than most."

"I try to be. I think that Lainey has been led to believe that the only thing she has to offer is her looks."

"Well, her personality isn't exactly the best," he says, chuckling.

"True, but I think that's a defense mechanism."

"Maybe you should have become a psychologist."

I shrug my shoulders. "I've thought about it, but I like baking more."

"Well, you could be the baking psychologist. Ask people all kinds of questions about their problems, and then instead of giving them real advice, just give them a doughnut."

I laugh out loud at that. "That might be a good idea. People like doughnuts more than advice."

"Very true."

We sit there for a few more minutes when a slow song comes on the radio. "Oh, I love this song. It's one of my favorites," I say.

He stands up and reaches out his hand. "Shall we have our final slow dance in the house?"

I was hoping he would ask me. "Of course," I say, touching his large, warm hand. We stand up and walk away from the table a few feet beside the twinkle lights. I can't believe this is my life right now.

Rhett's arm slides around my waist, pulling me

close, while his other hand holds mine gently but firmly. My free hand rests on his shoulder. His *massive* shoulder. I feel the strength of his muscles under the fabric of his dress shirt.

As we begin to sway to the music, I'm acutely aware of every point of contact between us. I can feel the warmth of his hand on my back, the slight pressure of his fingers intertwined with mine, and the steady rise and fall of his chest as he breathes. The world seems to narrow down to just the two of us moving in perfect harmony.

"Remember when we used to argue about everything in pastry chef school?" Rhett says, his breath warm against my ear.

"Yes, I do. You were such a know-it-all," I say, resting my head against his chest. Wearing heels makes me much taller, so I can almost reach his shoulder.

"And you were so stubborn," he counters in a playful tone. "Still are, actually."

We fall silent, allowing the music and moment to speak for us. The rhythmic sway of our bodies feels like a silent conversation, one that's been building over the weeks we've been here. His hand on my back moves in slow, soothing circles, and I can't help but relax into his touch.

The song reaches a particularly tender moment,

and Rhett pulls back slightly, just enough to look into my eyes. The intensity of his gaze takes my breath away. There are no pretenses, no barriers between us at this moment. He leans in, his forehead resting against mine.

"I never thought I'd say this, but I'm glad we got to do this competition together, Sunny."

"Me too," I whisper, my voice barely audible over the music. Time seems to stop in its tracks as he tilts his head slightly, his lips brushing against my cheek, then my temple, in a series of feather-light kisses.

I have never felt my heart race so fast, but I'm not afraid. I close my eyes, savoring how it feels to be close to him. To drink him in. To smell his cologne.

Finally, in what seems like the longest lead-up in history, his lips find mine in a chaste, almost hesitant kiss. It's soft and sweet. There's the promise of something more. The simplicity of it makes my heart swell with emotion, and I realize how much I've come to care for this man who once drove me crazy. We pull back slowly, our foreheads touching again.

I open my eyes to see Rhett watching me, which makes my heart ache in the best way possible. The song ends.

"Thank you for the dance," I whisper.

"Anytime," he replies, his lips curling into a smile. "Literally anytime, Sunny."

We stand there for a moment longer, wrapped in each other's arms, letting another song start. This is a memory I'll always cherish, a glimpse of what could have been.

# CHAPTER 24

SAVANNAH

AFTER OUR DATE the other night, I feel like I've been walking on Cloud Nine. Rhett and I have continued to pretend like we're a couple, holding hands, snuggling on the sofa outside, and stealing the occasional quick kiss—nothing major, but enough to convince the audience that we're in a budding relationship. Do I want a deeper kiss where we maul each other like in the movies? Um, yes. But do I want my little sister to see that on national TV and taunt me for the rest of my days? No.

Whenever he gives me that quick peck on the lips, I wait for something more, but I don't think he wants to overdo it. He probably wants to do just the least amount possible to convince people to vote for us and not lead me on at the same time.

I'm willing to take whatever I can get, whether it's a hug or holding hands. I've never felt so connected to someone. Even after dating Connor for two years, we didn't have a connection anywhere near like this. The other bonus of us pretending to be a couple is that it's driving Connor insane. He can't stand it. He hates to lose and makes snide comments whenever given the chance.

Today is the first challenge where we will dwindle down to three contestants. I could go home today; any of us could. It's unnerving to make it this far and think that there's a chance you might be leaving in mere hours.

I'm standing in the industrial kitchen with Rhett on one side and Lainey on the other. Connor is on her other side. Of course, they're not speaking because they broke up. I don't think it was ever really official, anyway. Lainey just thought it was, but she's been much easier to deal with since their breakup. She's actually talking to me, and we've had some decent conversations. Lainey isn't as bad as we all thought she was. She just puts on a really nasty suit of armor, but slowly, I think she's letting that go.

"Good afternoon, contestants," Dan says. I like Dan. He's growing on me. His teeth aren't. They're the size of skyscrapers and way more white than anyone's teeth should be, but I don't mind him as much as I did in the beginning. "I can't believe that we are entering the last week of competition," he says, smiling at us. It's more of a genuine smile than it was when we started. I hated the fake smile he would do at the camera, although he still does it sometimes. He's the perfect TV host. In fact, I can't really think of another job that he could do without scaring people with those teeth.

"In our first competition, where we will lose one contestant, your challenge is to make an opera cake. Make it unique. The judges will look at the flavor and the little details you put into it. The audience, of course, will be voting at home. For those at home who don't know what an opera cake is, this classic French dessert consists of multiple layers of almond sponge cake soaked in coffee syrup and then layered with rich coffee buttercream and dark chocolate ganache. It's also topped with a smooth chocolate glaze. The cake is usually rectangular in shape and looks polished when it's done correctly. Contestants, your challenge is to do a new take on an opera cake. Switch it up and impress the judges. You'll have three hours to complete this task, so let's get started. Your competition begins in 3, 2, 1... go!"

We all run to our stations. I don't have time to

look at what anyone else is doing. I'm just going to focus on my own task at hand. I decide to think outside the box and do a raspberry and white chocolate opera cake. I will lightly soak the sponge cake in raspberry syrup. I'll use a raspberry buttercream made with sweet, fresh raspberries. Then, I'll make white chocolate ganache and use a raspberry glaze to give it a vibrant pink color. Hopefully, it will be enough to win.

RHETT

We are down to the wire. We only have three challenges left before someone is crowned the winner, and today, somebody's going home. At this point, it could be any of us. I think we're all on a fairly even playing field.

I've had the chance to watch what these other pastry chefs can do, especially Savannah. I know anyone could pull this out at the end. Impress the judges and the home audience, and you get to stay. Make one mistake, and you might be going home. It's a lot of pressure. I would hate to think I got this close to winning the whole thing and then got sent home before Connor or Lainey. If I lose to Savannah, I won't feel nearly as bad.

The last few days of faking our relationship have been the best days of my life. Holding her in the garden and dancing, finally pressing my lips to hers. These are things I never thought would happen, but they are the greatest blessings in my life right now.

It's not that I haven't kissed other women before. Of course, I have, but I've never felt anything as I did with just that simple little kiss on Savannah's lips. I hadn't planned it, but at the moment, it just struck me as the right thing to do, and she seemed to be okay with it. In fact, we've done it a few more times, but I haven't pushed it further than that.

It's bad enough that I asked her to fake a relationship. I don't want to feel like I'm pressuring her into something she's not interested in or ready for. So I have to be okay with just holding her hand, putting my arm around her, and occasionally sneaking a peck on the lips. Then I go take a cold shower.

Right now, I have to focus on making an opera cake. It's not something I've made a whole lot, and Dan made it clear that it needed to be innovative. So I decide to do a hazelnut and caramel opera cake. I'm soaking my sponge cake in hazelnut liqueur syrup. I'm making caramel buttercream and a milk chocolate ganache. The glaze will be a shiny caramel glaze that I think will really wow them.

I can't afford to look over at Savannah, or I'll stare at her. I'll watch what she's doing. I'll sit there impressed by her skills, and then I won't get my own cake done. Then, I'd be leaving here in a few hours. I can't let that happen, so I continue to work on mine.

This is it. We're coming to the end of this competition, and as much as I want to stay in this house with her forever, I also want to win. I want to get to the end. I want to make that money and start my life. But winning would mean Savannah lost, and that's something that's hard to deal with as well. One of us is going to win, and one of us is going to lose. There's no way around it.

## SAVANNAH

It seems like the bell rings for the end of the competition five minutes after it starts. I can't believe how quickly the time went. I like how my opera cake came out; it looks like Rhett's is good, too. I can't really see what Lainey made, and Connor is further down, so it's impossible to spy on him.

The judges come out and start walking around.

They start at Rhett's station. He explains his caramel and hazelnut opera cake. The judges each take a bite and nod.

Chef Alain speaks first. "This is a very beautiful opera cake with a wonderful, rich flavor. Well done, Rhett." The other judges seem to agree.

Then, they make their way over to Connor's station. Connor is smiling as if he's won the whole thing.

"And what did you make?"

"I made a raspberry pistachio opera cake," he says. His is not as pretty as Rhett's, or maybe I'm just biased. The judges try it.

"It's good. Definitely has some unexpected flavors," Tessa says. She's always flirting with Connor, so I can't tell if she really hates his dessert and just doesn't want to tell him or if she actually likes it.

Then, they move over to Lainey. Now that it's sitting on the counter, her opera cake looks very strange. It has a vibrant green glaze and looks like something that just came from a nuclear power plant.

"And what do we have here?" Marco asks, eyeing it carefully.

Lainey smiles. "I really wanted to think outside

the box, so I made a matcha and black sesame opera cake."

The judges' mouths drop open. "Tell us how you made that," Chef Alain says.

"Well, the sponge cake is infused with matcha powder, and then I soaked it in a light matcha syrup. Then, I used black sesame to make a buttercream and white chocolate ganache. I topped it with a matcha glaze, which is giving it this really cool green color." She seems quite proud of herself, but the judges don't seem impressed.

Tessa takes a bite and almost spits it out. "Did you taste this, Lainey?"

"Well, no. I was too busy making it."

"Yeah, this is not good. It tastes like the sesame seeds were burned, and there's a very bitter flavor."

Marco takes a bite at the same time as Tessa and looks like he's having trouble swallowing it. "Yes, I agree. This is not good, Lainey. Not good at all."

Lainey's eyes fill with tears. I think she knows what's about to happen to her, but she's probably hoping that my dessert is terrible. I hope she's wrong.

They walk over to my station.

"And what did you make, Savannah?" Tessa asks, taking a sip of water to try to get the taste of Lainey's cake out of her mouth.

"I made a raspberry and white chocolate opera cake. I lightly soaked my sponge cake in raspberry syrup, made a raspberry buttercream and a white chocolate ganache, topped with this vibrant pink raspberry glaze."

I stand there with my hands behind my back, waiting for them to taste it.

Tessa is first, and when she tastes it, an immediate smile spreads across her face. "This is lovely. So light and refreshing."

Each of the judges nods as they take their bite. Thank goodness. I know I have passed this round.

A few moments later, they give Lainey the unfortunate news that she'll be going home. I see tears streaming down her face. I actually feel bad for her. A week ago, I couldn't have said that. I walk over and give her a quick hug, the only one of the contestants who does that, and then she disappears out of the room.

"Well, congratulations, contestants," Dan says. "The three of you have made it to the next stage of the finals. I'll see you tomorrow for your next competition. Go rest up."

With that, we turn to walk out of the kitchen. Rhett walks over and takes my hand, which is becoming the most comfortable thing in my life. Connor glares at us and walks out. He can't stand to see it, which makes me laugh whenever I see it bothers him. One of the best things about leaving this house is that I'll never have to see Connor again.

SAVANNAH

Being in the house with just Connor and Rhett is like watching a before-and-after presentation. Connor is the before. The ugly thing you're trying to make pretty. The terrible thing you're trying to make good. The only problem is that Connor never changes. He has steered clear of me and Rhett, for the most part, staying in his room. He has now switched to a totally separate room from Rhett. The quicker we can get him out of this house, the better.

On the other hand, Rhett and I have spent lots of time together. We sat in the hot tub, played pool, and played checkers and chess. He's taught me card games, and we've cooked almost every meal together in the kitchen. It's like a very domestic thing we're suddenly doing, and I can't say that I'm not enjoying it.

For the first time, as much as I miss my sister, I feel a connection to another human being, and I will miss him too. It seems like no matter what I do in my life, I'll be missing someone. But I have to focus on the prizes: the cookbook deal, the wedding cake for the celebrity couple, and the $200,000 that I desperately want to see in my bank account.

While I'll always cheer for Rhett, I know that I need this money more than he does. Even though his family treats him as an outcast, Rhett is so skilled that he will get a fancy restaurant job somewhere. He just has to have that belief in himself. He will be running some fancy pants place before too long. But if I don't win this money, I'll work at the grocery store with Big Thelma for the rest of my life. I will *become* the next Big Thelma. Only they'll call me Little Savannah.

So, while I'm enjoying our time together, I'm also well aware that we are competing against each other, which is a strange place to be. Our next competition is tonight, and I can hardly wait. For the first time during this whole thing, I feel excited.

I'm ready to get behind my station and do my work. I'm becoming increasingly confident in my skills, and when I get back home, whether I win this money or not, I will look for a different job, something better than the grocery store. Hopefully, having it on my resume that I was on a reality TV baking show will help get me in the door. And if I win, even better.

"You know you can't do that," Rhett calls from the other side of the pool table.

"Do what?" I ask, playing dumb.

"You're supposed to call the pocket before you hit that eight-ball."

"You're just mad that I'm about to beat you."

"Maybe so," he says, laughing. "But you're still supposed to call the pocket."

"Well, I play by my own rules, Rhett," I say, walking over to him pretending to be seductive. I rise up on my tiptoes and kiss him on the cheek. "Do you have a problem with that?" I ask softly.

His face turns red. "No, actually, I guess I don't." He grabs me around the waist and picks me up, swinging me around in a circle. That's when Connor walks into the courtyard. He stops in his tracks, makes a gagging noise, and then hangs his head. "What's your problem?" Rhett says.

"My problem is that I'm stuck in the house with you two fawning all over each other. Why don't you just call in the justice of the peace and get married already?" he says, walking over and falling down onto the sofa.

"Are you jealous, Connor?" Rhett asks as he walks toward him, stalking him like prey. I kind of want to tell him to stop, but I also want to see what happens.

"No, actually, I'm not jealous. I've already been

with this woman, and trust me, if you're still with her in two years, you'll be desperate to get rid of her, too."

"Excuse me, Connor, but you didn't get rid of me. I got rid of you," I say, crossing my arms.

"Because you're obsessed with your sister, Savannah. Nobody is obsessed with their sister like you are. It's ridiculous. Nobody is going to put up with that."

"I would," Rhett says.

I look over at him. "You would?"

"I think it's wonderful that she's so dedicated to her sister and that she loves her like that. It's inspiring."

"Well, I didn't find it inspiring," Connor says, rolling his eyes and lighting a cigarette. "I found it annoying. When you're dating someone and about to marry them, they should be the center of your world."

"Well, it sounds like you're pretty obsessed with yourself, Connor. It's probably best that you be alone," Rhett says, taking my hand and walking me out of the courtyard.

"That was fun," I whisper to him as we enter the house.

"Yeah, it was pretty fun."

SAVANNAH

We're back in the kitchen again, awaiting instructions on the second of our three final competitions. Now that Lainey has gone home and left just the three of us, this competition is down to the wire.

Dan takes his place in the front of the room and brings the microphone to his mouth. "In today's competition, which is the last one before the actual finals, you'll be making a pavlova. Just like with the opera cake, we want to see a take-off on the pavlova and how you can make it different from how most people make it. For the at-home audience who doesn't know what a pavlova is, it's a meringue-based dessert named after a Russian ballerina. It features a crisp and delicate outer shell with a soft marshmallow-like interior. It's typically shaped into a large circular form with a slightly indented center holding different toppings. Many times, it's garnished with whipped cream and fruits. For our contestants here, we want a unique take on the pavlova. You will have three hours to complete this. Once you're finished, another person will go home, leaving our final two contestants to battle it out in the wedding cake competition."

That's the first time Dan has admitted that the last competition is the wedding cake for the celebrity couple. I have to start thinking ahead of time about what I'm going to make. I believe I can win this pavlova competition, but we'll see. I look over at Rhett, and he smiles at me, winking. It gives me butterflies in my stomach, but I can't concentrate on that right now. Instead, I have to pay attention to what I'm doing. I immediately decide that what I want to make is a tropical pavlova. I'll make a meringue base with a hint of coconut extract and then use a coconut whipped cream with a touch of vanilla. I'll top it with the tropical fruits of mango, pineapple, kiwi, and passion fruit pulp and then garnish it with toasted coconut flakes. I don't think anybody else will do something similar.

RHETT

The competition is heating up. Of course, I can't stop winking at Savannah. I really have to pay attention. I want it to be the two of us standing in the final, competing against each other. For some reason, I don't feel competitive with her. I just feel like we're working together. The only problem is that only one of us can win. My chivalrous side wants to let her win, but I also know she would never want that. She wants real competition. She wants to know that she can do this, and I want to know the same thing.

I look over to see what she's making, but I can't tell just yet, so I need to focus on what I'm doing. I opt to make a lemon and blueberry pavlova. I'll make the meringue base with a hint of lemon zest. Then I'll use a tangy and smooth lemon curd and top everything with a blueberry compote. I'll cook the fresh blueberries with a little sugar and lemon juice and then spoon it over the lemon curd. I can already taste it.

All I have to do is get through this competition, and then we can get to the finals. We can do the wedding cakes and see who will be crowned the winner, and then it's time to go on with our lives. But for some reason, I'm having a hard time imagining my life without Savannah every day.

# CHAPTER 25

SAVANNAH

IT IS time yet again for the judges to come around
and look at what we've made. They were very
impressed with Rhett's lemon and blueberry
pavlova. I have to admit, it looks delectable. I'm
hoping I can sneak over and have a bite once they
announce who's going home. They come over and
look at my tropical pavlova and rave about it. Tessa
says that she would expect to have it on a tropical
island at a fancy restaurant, which makes me feel
good. Marco says something similar, and he eats an
extra helping of it.

Then, it's time for them to go over to Connor. He's
standing there with a smile on his face like he's just
invented the wheel or something. "So what have you

made for us, Connor?" Chef Alain says, looking down at his pavlova with a questioning look on his face.

"I have made a matcha and red bean pavlova."

*Red bean? He made a dessert with red beans in the final competition?* What on earth is he thinking? I look over at Rhett, who is stifling a laugh. We both know that this can't be good.

"Exactly what is this?" Tessa asks, looking down at it.

"Well, I made a matcha meringue base infused with matcha powder for green tea flavor."

"Green tea meringue?" Marco says, looking at him quizzically.

"Yes, and then I made regular whipped cream with vanilla flavoring. But the unique thing about my dessert is that I made a sweetened red bean paste and then dolloped it over the whipped cream. And then I topped it with fresh strawberries," he says as an afterthought.

"Oh, my," Tessa says as she goes to take a bite. "I guess I must also try some of this red bean paste." She puts the bite in her mouth, and then the camera zooms in so that we can see it on the big screen. This isn't good. My heart starts to race. We might've pulled this off. They don't look like they are enjoying Connor's dessert, which would mean that Rhett and

I get to battle this out in the wedding cake competition.

Chef Alain takes a bite. "Oh my goodness." For a moment, I think that he might be impressed, that he will say that Connor thought outside the box and made a dessert that should go down in history. Instead, he turns and spits it into the trash can. They've never done that with anyone during this competition.

"You don't like it?" Connor says.

"No, I don't like it," Chef Alain says, wiping his mouth with a napkin. "What on earth were you thinking, Connor, using red bean paste in a dessert during a final competition?"

"I thought it was very outside the box," he says, crossing his arms.

"Yes, it was outside the box and down the street. It was outside of this universe. It was not good."

Connor's face starts to turn red. "I'm sorry, Connor, but this is terrible," Tessa whispers as if everybody on national television can't hear her.

"I think it's pretty clear that we have our two finalists," Chef Alain says, pointing across the room at me and Rhett. We both stand there staring at him like we don't understand the words. "Congratulations, Savannah and Rhett. You will battle it out in the wedding cake competition tomorrow, and we'll find out who wins *The Baking Games*!"

SAVANNAH

"We did it! We did it! I can't believe we did it!" I yell as Rhett and I reenter the house alone. We're the only two people here. We could run around like crazies if we wanted to.

I can't believe we started with so many contestants, and now it's just the two of us ready to battle it out. At the beginning of this whole thing, I thought I would be miserable being in the house with Rhett. I don't know how I never saw this side of him when we were in pastry chef school, but I'm glad I got the chance to do so.

Life will return to normal in a couple of days. I'll be back with my sister, and Rhett will be back on a cruise ship sailing in the middle of the ocean. I don't know which of us will win, but honestly, I would be happy for either of us.

Sure, I want the money. I want an easier life. I want to be able to breathe when the bills come in. I want to pay for college for my sister. I want to buy equipment and put down money on a lease for my very own bakery. I want so many things, but right now, I only want to spend as much time with Rhett as I can. Even if it's make-believe, it's been fun. He's very good at pretending.

"I know. I can't believe we did it either," he says as we sit down in the courtyard.

"Of course, you can. You believed you would win this whole thing from the moment you walked in the house."

"Yeah, some of that was a little bit of false brava-do," he says.

"I can't believe you're admitting that."

"It's true. When I first got in here, I was really surprised at the amount of skill that our fellow contestants had."

"Really? Well, you certainly didn't let on at the beginning."

"It would've ruined my reputation if I seemed like I was the least bit daunted by these other people."

"I can't believe we're the last two standing. Honestly, I thought I would go home very early. I'm not much of a competitor."

"I think you're a lot more of a competitor than you think you are, Sunny."

"Well, either way, we're almost to the finish line, and I want to say that you deserve this just as much as I do."

"Same to you," Rhett says, reaching over and taking my hand. "You deserve the world. I know you haven't had such an easy time in life, but how you approach everything with such positivity inspires me. I'm actually going to try to take a little bit of that into my regular life when we go back home."

It makes me sad to think about us not spending time together anymore. "Yeah, going home. I haven't really thought about it because it made me so sad to miss my sister, but now I will get to see her in a couple of days. It's going to be wonderful to be together again."

"I'm really happy for you," he says. "And I, of course, am jumping straight back onto the cruise ship. I was only able to get the six weeks off. So whether I win or lose, I have to fulfill my contract. I'll jump right back on the ship the day after this competition ends."

"Really? So you're not going to get any downtime?"

"No, I'm not. I have to go on at least one more run. If I win, then, of course, I'll quit. If I don't, I'll just return to my normal life until I can find something better."

"I know you'll find whatever it is that you're looking for, Rhett. You deserve it. Whether your family supports you or not, I do."

"And I thank you for that. I really do," he says, squeezing my hand. "I'm going to miss spending so much time together, and I literally never thought I'd say that about you, Savannah Greene."

"Ditto," I say, laughing.

SAVANNAH

The kitchen is alive with activity. We have more cameras, lights, and excitement in the air. Rhett and I are both positioned behind our stations, each of us nervously standing there, tapping our fingers or moving from foot to foot.

They finally get Dan miked up, the lights lit up before him, and it's time. This is it, our final competition.

"Welcome to *The Baking Games!*" he yells out. I can hear the theme music playing in the background. "Tonight, we are so excited to present to you the final competition of *The Baking Games*. This competition will last a total of four hours. Our last two finalists will make the wedding cake for celebrity couple Keaton Mallory and Keira Donaldson." Dan pauses for dramatic effect as if people at home stand up and clap.

"You can watch the full competition live online using streaming. Those who are watching this on TV will only see the last ninety minutes of the competition with a summary at the beginning of what's happened so far. Then, in the last fifteen minutes of the show, the audience will be allowed to vote, and those votes combined with our judges and our two special guest judges will determine the winner of this competition. So why don't we go ahead and introduce our two guest judges," he says, pointing at the judging table. They have fancied it up with twinkle lights and detachable curtains around the table.

Our three judges are sitting there. Dan points off through another doorway and says, "Please welcome Keaton Mallory and Keira Donaldson!"

Oh my gosh, the actual celebrity couple is here. Why did it never dawn on me that they would be the ones who would help judge the wedding cake? After all, we'll be making a cake that we would then have to recreate for their wedding in a few weeks.

Rhett looks at me, surprised as I am, but Rhett is not into pop culture at all. He has no real idea who these two people are. He's only seen them in passing on magazine covers or movie trailers, but he's definitely not a fan.

Me? I'm a huge Keira Donaldson fan. I've

followed her career since she started as a child actor. She's one of my favorite actresses. They walk out, smile, and wave in our direction.

Dan puts the microphone in front of Keaton. "So Keaton, what have you thought of *The Baking Games* so far?" He's very handsome, even more handsome in person than he is in the movies. He would put Brad Pitt to shame, and I love Brad Pitt.

"Well, so far, I have seen a lot of talented people," he says. Very diplomatic.

"What about you, Keira?"

She smiles broadly. "I'm a huge Savannah fan," she says. I feel like I'm going to melt into a puddle on the floor. I put my hand over my mouth. "I think she has done amazing and been such a sweetheart in the process. I would say that Rhett is a very lucky man," she says, winking in Rhett's direction.

He turns and smiles at me. "I would say you're right." Again, I don't know if he's pretending or being serious, but it doesn't matter. By this time tomorrow, we will both be back in our normal lives like none of this ever happened.

"So Keira, tell the contestants what you're looking for in your wedding cake."

"Well, I'm looking for something unique that speaks to our relationship or our own interests, something that will be a showpiece and can be showcased in photos when we have our wedding layout in *People Magazine*."

My heart starts to race. *People Magazine*? My cake could be featured in *People Magazine*. That's insane to think about. So much is happening at one time that I can barely take it all in.

"Great. Okay, contestants, are you ready to get started?" We both nod. "Then let's get this competition going in 3, 2, 1… go!"

As soon as he yells, we both start scurrying around our stations. As usual, Rhett grabs his sketch pad and starts drawing something out. I have no idea what he's planning. We didn't talk about any of it in advance. The one place I think I might have a leg up is that I know pop culture. I know a lot about Keira Donaldson and about her relationship. I know what she likes and what she doesn't like.

One of the things that stood out to me in an interview with her was how much she loves fairy tales. She plans to write children's books about fairy tales when they have kids. She even has a castle painted on her bedroom wall in her New York City apartment.

So I decide to do a fairy tale castle wedding cake. It will be very ambitious in the four hours allotted, but either go big or go home, right?

I start to work on the design. I will make a six-tiered cake, and the top will be designed as a castle turret. I'll even do sugar towers and flags. This will require detailed sugar work to create the castle walls, windows, and drawbridges. I'll use edible glitter and shimmer dust to give it a magical sparkle.

Each of the six tiers will have a different flavor profile. Tier one will be a vanilla sponge cake with blueberry and cream cheese filling. Tier two will be a coconut cake with pineapple curd and coconut buttercream. Tier three will be a carrot cake with walnut pieces and cream cheese frosting. I want to ensure carrot cake is included because it's Keira's favorite. Tier four will be a pistachio sponge cake with rosewater buttercream. And tier five will be a dark chocolate cake with a mint chocolate ganache. The castle turret will be made of white chocolate sponge and a raspberry mousse filling.

For the finishing touches, fondant in pastel shades will be used to create a fairytale look. Sugar ivy and flowers will climb up the castle walls, and I'll make tiny little sugar figurines of the bride and groom in their royal attire. If this doesn't win, then nothing I could make would. I'm very confident in what I'm planning and hope nothing goes wrong.

## RHETT

Savannah definitely has the upper hand on this one. I know she follows pop culture, which I don't. It's just never been my thing. I've seen these two celebrities before but don't follow their lives closely.

But still, I have skills. I know I can make an impressive wedding cake. I've done it before. Anytime someone gets married on one of the cruise ships, it's usually me sketching out the cake and making it with my crew, so I know I can do this; it's just coming up with an idea.

The fact that these two are celebrities immediately makes me think of Art Deco—something glamorous. After all, Kiera looks like she would enjoy that. She's wearing a very crisp, off-white pantsuit with beautiful jewelry. I have to believe that she'd love Art Deco.

For the design, I will do a four-tiered cake with very sharp, geometric edges. Each tier will be adorned with intricate Art Deco patterns, sugar decorations, and bold geometric shapes, including fans, zigzags, and chevrons, which will be all over the cake, painted in metallic gold, silver, and black. I will do a mocha sponge cake with espresso buttercream and chocolate ganache for tier one. And then, on tier two, I'll make a red velvet cake with cream cheese frosting with just a hint of vanilla.

Tier three will be a champagne cake with strawberry and champagne buttercream. Finally, tier four will be a dark chocolate sponge cake with raspberry filling and chocolate mousse. I'll put a striking black fondant base with gold and silver edible paint for the finishing touches, creating that Art Deco design. I'll even use edible pearls and crystal sugar shards to add extra glamor and sophistication.

I think I could win with this. I can't see what Savannah is doing, and I know it'll be great whatever it is. But I will put my best foot forward and try to win this competition. And who knows? Maybe if I win the $200,000, I can take Savannah on a very nice vacation and actually admit to her that this isn't make-believe for me; this is real life, and I want her in it.

SAVANNAH

The bell to end the competition dings. I can't believe that's the final bell for the whole competition. It's over. There's nothing else that I can do to change the outcome at this point.

I'm really impressed with my cake. I was working down to the final minute, and I thought I wouldn't finish it, but I did. It looks like a real princess castle, and I'm proud of myself. That's not something I say lightly.

I look over and notice that Rhett has made some kind of Art Deco cake. It's beautiful. It looks like a work of art. Now, it just comes down to the judges, the home audience, and most especially Keira and Keaton on which cake they prefer to have at their wedding. I really don't know.

Keaton and Keira are very into the artistic scene in New York City, so they could very well choose to go with Rhett's cake. Or if Keaton really wants to do what Keira likes, they'll choose my cake.

Either way, I'm happy I got to go through this experience, and if I don't win, maybe the notoriety of being on a reality show like this will help me get a better job than the one I work in now.

I don't think I've been as nervous as I am here waiting to be judged. Maybe I was nervous that time that Big Thelma stood behind me when I first started working at the bakery and made me make forty-eight doughnuts in a short period of time. She said it was a test. I'm not sure for what because she ended up taking most of the doughnuts home with her. Maybe she was testing how high she could get her blood sugar.

"Ladies and gentlemen," Dan says, "it's time for the moment that we've all been waiting for. For the last six weeks, our finalists have created exceptional desserts and proven themselves to be two of the top pastry chefs in the world. Now, they have designed two stunning wedding cakes, and our judges, along with Keira, Keaton, and the home audience, will decide the winner of *The Baking Games*. Let's get started with Rhett's Art Deco cake."

The judges, along with Keira and Keaton, walk closer. "Rhett, I have to say that this cake is visually stunning. The way you've made these geometric patterns is so precise, and the gold accents give it a beautiful elegance," Tessa says, leaning down and looking closer. Rhett has cut a piece for each of them to try. The judges, along with Keira and Keaton, each take a bite.

"Wow, the flavors you chose are bold. Can you walk us through them?" Marco asks.

"Of course. The bottom layer is a dark chocolate sponge cake with raspberry filling and chocolate mousse, the third tier is a champagne cake with strawberry and champagne buttercream, the second tier is red velvet cake with cream cheese frosting, and the top tier is a mocha sponge cake with espresso, buttercream, and chocolate ganache."

Keira smiles. "It looks so beautiful, almost too beautiful to eat. And with so many different flavors in the layers, it's hard to decide which one I like the most. The chocolate and raspberry combination is just divine. The bitterness of the dark chocolate is perfectly balanced by the tartness of the raspberry."

Keaton nods. "Yes, it's hard to pick which is my favorite layer, but I think it might be the red velvet cake."

"Well done, Rhett. You definitely brought your game up to be in the finals," Chef Alain says. "Good luck." Rhett shakes his hand and nods, looking over at me. Now they're walking toward my station.

"So, what have you made here?" Tessa asks as she walks up.

"Well, I made this fairy tale princess cake, which might seem a little odd for a wedding, but I chose it because I know that Keira loves fairy tales and plans to write children's books when she has kids. And I also know that she has a fairy tale mural on the wall of her apartment in New York City." Rhett looks over at me, surprised that I knew so much. He has a knowing look on his face, like he's almost proud of me.

"It is just gorgeous," Keira says, leaning down and

looking around all the little details. "Oh my gosh. Did you actually create little figurines of both of us?"

I nod. "I did. That took a while. I tried to make them look very similar to what you actually look like."

"This is amazing. I absolutely love this cake. It doesn't even look like a cake," Keira says.

"Yeah, it's really beautiful, and you really spoke to what Keira loves," Keaton says, putting his arm around her waist.

"Tell us about the flavors in your cake," Marco says.

"Well, it's a five-tier cake, obviously. The top tier is a vanilla sponge cake with blueberry and cream cheese filling. The second layer is a coconut cake with pineapple curd and coconut buttercream. The third tier is a carrot cake with walnuts and cream cheese frosting. The fourth tier is a pistachio sponge cake with rose water buttercream. And the fifth tier holding all of it up is a dark chocolate cake with mint chocolate ganache. The turret at the top is made of white chocolate sponge with a raspberry mousse filling."

All of them look surprised at what I could accomplish in such a short time period. Honestly, I feel like I need to go lie down and take a very long nap.

"This is absolutely amazing, Savannah. You really went above and beyond."

"Thank you."

"Okay, folks. We will give the audience at home fifteen minutes to go ahead and vote. We'll also show some unseen moments from the season while we wait for all the votes to come in, and then we will announce the winner of the first-ever *Baking Games* competition. Don't go anywhere," Dan says to the camera as we cut to a commercial.

"This really is beautiful, Savannah. I'm so impressed," Keira says.

I feel very starstruck at the moment. I want to ask her for her autograph, but I feel that might be out of place in this situation. "Thank you very much. I had a lot of fun making it."

"Good luck," she says, walking away. I look at Rhett; he nods at me, and I nod back. We both know that this is it. The thing we've been waiting for all these weeks, the thing we're both trying to get and only one of us can have.

After a very long fifteen minutes, Dan pulls the microphone up to his mouth, and I know this is it. Rhett and I are now standing next to each other, holding hands. I can feel him squeezing tighter than he normally does.

"We want both of you to know that this was a

very hard decision for the judges, and the audience votes were super close, closer than any other of the competitions this whole season. So, in the end, it actually came down to Keira and Keaton to make the decision. It is their wedding, after all. So we would like to congratulate the winner of *The Baking Games*, which is..." long pause for dramatic effect, of course, "Savannah!"

My eyes fill with tears of joy. I can't believe that I won. I know my sister is probably jumping up and down in our living room right now, watching me win. Rhett hugs me tightly. "Congratulations, Savannah! You deserve it. I'm so proud of you," he says, his lips against my ear.

"Thank you, Rhett. Your cake was amazing, too. I'm just so happy right now." Tears stream down my cheeks like a river.

"Well, there you have it, folks. Savannah Greene is the winner of *The Baking Games*. Thank you all for joining us on this incredible journey. We can't wait to see you all during season two next year!" Dan says as sparkly confetti falls from the ceiling. I won *The Baking Games*, and I can't believe it.

# CHAPTER 26

RHETT

SHE WON. Savannah won.

I know I should feel sad that I didn't win, but all I feel is happy for her. I imagine that money dropping into her bank account and how safe and secure she'll feel for the first time in her life.

I only want good things for my Sunny.

The competition ended last night, and Savannah spent the evening doing interview after interview through Zoom and on the phone. By the time she was done, we ate dinner and crashed. Our last night together wasn't nearly as romantic as I'd hoped.

I had hoped to talk to her without cameras around, tell her how I really felt, see if she felt the same, and exchange numbers so we could keep in contact. Instead, she fell asleep with her head on my shoulder, and we woke up early this morning in the courtyard. When she realized the time, she ran upstairs to finish packing.

"All packed up?" She's standing in the doorway of my room with her luggage in hand.

"Almost."

"When does your flight leave?"

"Later this afternoon. Yours?"

"In a little over two hours."

"Yikes. I guess you have to get to the airport soon then, huh?"

"Right now, actually. My driver is waiting."

"Your driver? So fancy, Savannah Greene, winner of *The Baking Games*."

She smiles. "Thank you for helping me get through this competition, Rhett. I couldn't have done it without you."

"Sure you could have, Sunny." I walk over and pull her into a hug, pressing my lips to the top of her head.

"I bet you're relieved," she says, her face pressed to my chest.

I pull back. "Why would I be relieved?"

"Because you don't have to pretend anymore, right?"

Then it dawns on me. Pretend to be in love with

her. Pretend that we're in a relationship.

"Right. No more cameras to worry about," I say, looking around the room. Production is packing up just like we are.

Suddenly, I freeze. To her, it was all make-believe. I can't admit my feelings and get shut down. It would shatter my already fragile heart even more than it's shattered right now.

"Well, I'd better get downstairs. Thank you so much for supporting me in this competition. Take care of yourself, Rhett. "

"You too, Sunny. Enjoy all that money," I say, forcing a smile. Why is this so awkward?

She walks down the stairs, opens the front door, and disappears.

## SAVANNAH

I'm alone outside in the hot Georgia summer sun.

My car is here, but Rhett isn't beside me. He didn't say he cared about me. He didn't ask me to be with him. He just agreed with me that it was nice not to have to pretend anymore.

This really was all a fantasy, and most of it was created in my own mind.

It was all for the show. He told me that, but I

guess a part of me wanted to believe that he was falling in love with me.

I refocus myself and remember that I did this for Sadie and for me. Now, our lives can finally start. Sadie is probably online filling out college applications already, and the thought makes me smile.

I did it. I made it happen.

Sure, the audience probably kept me around longer because they were obsessed with Rhett and me. But most of it I did myself. After all, I didn't agree to the fake relationship until last week. It was just the cherry on top.

"Ready?" my driver asks as he exits the dark SUV.

"Yep."

He loads my luggage into the back before opening my door. "Your chariot awaits, ma'am."

I climb inside and take one final look at *The Baking Games* house. This is the place where my life changed. Where I learned I'm worthy of being called a great pastry chef. Where I felt my heart open for the first time and where my heart was broken by the man I swore was my rival.

## RHETT

I run downstairs, determined to catch Savannah before she leaves. All I see is the back of a black SUV turning at the end of the road.

I missed her. I missed my one chance.

I didn't tell her how I felt while she was right in front of me.

What kind of an idiot am I?

Now, she's about to be on a plane headed for home, and I'm heading to my next cruise ship. I don't even have her phone number!

Maybe the producers will give it to me.

Maybe I will text her in a week and ask how she's doing.

Or maybe she thinks I'm a royal jerk.

I have no idea.

## SAVANNAH

I hate airports. There are way too many people everywhere, and somebody is always coughing or sneezing. I do not want to get sick. I want to go home, wait for my big check, sign my cookbook deal, talk to Keira and Keaton about their wedding in a few weeks, and see my sister.

It's going to be a busy time. Lots to look forward to!

But I can't stop thinking about Rhett.

His broad shoulders. Those blue eyes that look like ocean swirls. The way his cologne smells.

Ugh. Why can't things work out like the movies?

Why didn't he chase my car down the street? Why didn't he profess his love to me?

I consider myself somewhat of a feminist, so I suppose I could've professed my love to him.

Wait. I love Rhett Jennings? Is that true? It sure feels true.

I step onto the airplane and look for my seat, ready to get home and spend a few days relaxing with Sadie.

She can quit her job and focus on school. I can go tell Big Thelma I'm done being her punching bag. That makes me smile.

I find my seat and settle in. I hope no one sits next to me. I like having space around me. Having strangers pushed up against me is not my idea of a good time.

I start allowing myself to think of names for my new bakery. Will I stay in the suburbs or open it somewhere else? Somewhere with new memories to be made?

*"Good afternoon, ladies and gentlemen. This is your*

captain speaking. On behalf of the entire crew, welcome aboard Flight 1683, non-stop service to Atlanta. We are now ready to depart, and the cabin door is securely closed. Please make sure that all your carry-on items are stowed either in the overhead compartments or under the seat in front of you, and that your seat belts are fastened.

We ask that you turn off all electronic devices or switch them to airplane mode at this time. Please also ensure that your seat backs and tray tables are in their full upright and locked positions.

The weather en route looks favorable, but we may encounter some turbulence, so please keep your seat belts fastened whenever you are seated.

In just a few moments, our flight attendants will be passing through the cabin to perform a final safety check and to demonstrate the safety features of this aircraft. We appreciate your attention to this important demon-stration.

We are committed to making your flight comfortable and enjoyable. Sit back, relax, and enjoy the flight."

Time to go home.

**Four weeks later**

## SAVANNAH

I've done the hard part, but my heart is still racing. Being at a celebrity wedding in New York City wasn't on my list of things I would ever do. But here I stand next to Keira and Keaton, two of the world's biggest celebrities, while they cut their wedding cake.

I will be in their wedding photos, and the magazine spread about their wedding. How insane is that?

Sadie waves at me from across the room. Keira and Keaton were so kind to invite her, too. They really are the nicest people.

The crowd erupts as they push pieces of cake into each other's mouths. I slowly creep away, wanting to be out of the limelight. I had my fifteen minutes of fame, and that was quite enough for me.

"This is so amazing!" Sadie yells over music that just started blaring out of the speakers nearby.

"Can you believe we're here? I mean us! Nobody would've ever predicted the Greene sisters would end up at a fancy NYC wedding with two celebrities."

She smiles. "And all because you took a chance on yourself. I'm so proud of you, sissy!" She hugs my neck like she's done a thousand times since I got home. I thought we'd never let go of each other at the airport that day.

"Have you gotten any responses from the colleges you applied to?"

"A couple, but let's not talk about real life right now. Let's immerse ourselves in this dream life while we can!" She dances away from me toward a crowd of people and waves.

"What are you doing, Sadie?" I'm genuinely confused about why she abandoned me beside the punch bowls.

"Have you seen my hippopotamus, madam?"

I would know his voice anywhere.

I slowly turn, and Rhett stands there wearing a tuxedo, generally looking like the hottest man on earth.

"Rhett? What are you doing here?"

"Um, I was invited, thank you very much. I did come in second on *The Baking Games* behind a seriously sexy redhead."

I smile because I always smile around Rhett. "It's so good to see you." I step forward and hug him, pressing my cheek to his strong chest. Is it too much to ask to stay here forever?

He wraps his arms around me tightly. "I've missed you." He says it so softly that I barely hear him.

I pull away and look up at him. "You have?"

"You haven't missed me?"

"Of course I have! But you just said goodbye at the house like that was it. I figured I wouldn't see you again."

He looks truly shocked. "Why would you think that?"

"Because you were faking the relationship. Why would you need to see me after it was all over?"

He reaches out and puts his hands on my cheeks, cradling my face. "Sunny, haven't you realized by now that none of that was fake?"

"What?"

"I wasn't faking anything. Sure, I didn't know how I felt when I originally asked you to pretend with me. But the moment we were chained together, I knew."

I swallow the lump in my throat. He brushes his thumb across my cheek over and over.

"I knew, too."

A smile spreads across his face. "So, you weren't faking either?"

"No. Never." My voice is shaking.

He pulls me back into him. "Thank God."

"Wait," I say, pulling away again. "What happens now?"

"Well, for one, we do this," he says, pressing his

lips to mine in the most passionate kiss of my life. Warm lips, frantic movements. Hands in hair. His hand on my lower back. So much is happening at once, and I've never wanted to crawl into another person's skin like this.

Suddenly, someone clears their throat. We disconnect our hungry lips from each other and look sideways to see Sadie standing there, a knowing smile on her face.

"Excuse me, y'all, but did you forget this is someone else's wedding?"

I laugh. "Rhett, meet my sister, Sadie."

He smiles and shakes her hand, his face turning several shades of red. "Hey, Sadie. I've heard a lot about you."

# EPILOGUE

## SIX MONTHS LATER

Life is sweet in Sweet Haven. When it came time to choose a location for my brand-new bakery, I had a choice to make. Big city, suburb, or small town? I chose small town.

Sweet Haven doesn't have a lot going on, but it's close enough to Savannah to draw tourists, especially if it's being opened by the winner of *The Baking Games* and the woman who's besties with Keira Donaldson. Well, she's technically Keira Mallory now.

And we're not besties, per se. We are in my mind, though.

When Sadie got into her dream college in

Charleston, it seemed perfect for me to open the bakery right between Savannah and Charleston. Sweet Haven was a perfect fit and holds my best memories. Plus, it was nice to leave my childhood memories behind.

Sadie got her own place close to college, but I see her all the time. It's good for us to have our own spaces.

"To the left!" Sadie yells out as the poor sign man stands on a tall ladder trying to place our new sign.

"Here?" he calls down.

"Yes! Perfect!"

Sadie is bossy, and that is especially true when it comes to my new bakery. She wants everything to be perfect.

"Let the guy off the ladder, sis. It's fine."

"I can't wait for your opening next week. You totally deserve this, Sunny."

Yep. My sister now calls me Sunny, too.

"As long as Big Thelma isn't working here, I consider it a win," I say, laughing.

Big Thelma didn't take me quitting as well as I would've hoped. She threw a pie at me. An actual cherry pie. I left the store looking like I'd been in a horror movie, but I smiled all the way to my car.

Maggie and I talk all the time, and she rented a

place in an over-55 community in Savannah. She's playing golf and tennis, and she just met a new man who saw her on TV and fell hard for her. I love that she's getting another shot at her own romance.

I haven't heard from Connor, thank goodness, but I did hear from Lainey a few times. She got a job in California, working as a full-time pastry chef for a resort. It's the perfect job for her, and she seems happy.

The most shocking thing that happened was Rhett's mother reaching out to us. After the show was over, she called Rhett and explained that on the day of the video chat, she got called to an emergency in the ER. Turns out, she had been waiting to chat while I was on with Sadie, but had to leave before it was Rhett's turn.

To Rhett's surprise, his mother's friends were very impressed with him on the show and chided her a bit for keeping him a secret. Several of them requested that he travel to Boston to cater their parties and a few weddings. Rhett declined, of course. He said he wasn't leaving my side.

His mother met Rhett and me for lunch in New York City right after Rhett and I reconnected at the celebrity wedding. It was awkward at first, but I think she's warming up to me. She said she might even travel to Sweet Haven after the bakery opens. Baby steps.

"I need to run to the store to get those extra shelves you wanted for the walls. Oh, and the little centerpieces for the tables. I almost forgot!"

"You go, and I'll finish setting up the payment system if I can figure it out."

"Be back soon!" she shouts as she runs to my car.

I stand outside and stare up at the sign. I can't believe I did it. I went for it, and I actually got it.

My cookbook comes out next year, and I actually have a whole signing tour. People will line up to meet *me*. Crazy world we live in.

As I look up at the sign, I feel arms slide around me from behind. Either the mailman is getting frisky, or Rhett has arrived.

"Hello, beautiful," he says, pressing his mouth to my neck. Shivers run in every direction.

"Hey there," I say turning around. He plants a kiss on me that would make most women faint.

"I love the sign!"

"Me too. It's perfect, right?" I turn back around and look up at it while Rhett hugs me from behind.

"Absolutely perfect. It tells our story. I can't believe you get to do this right here where it all began, Sunny."

"It's a dream," I say, leaning my head back against him.

Rhett never left my side after we reconnected at the wedding. He quit the cruise line and worked at a local restaurant near where I lived. He even got an apartment in the same crummy building to be near me.

Once the money came in from the show, we decided together about Sweet Haven—me, him, and Sadie.

He adores Sadie. They fight like brother and sister sometimes, but he protects her. He encourages us to spend time together, and he always includes her.

Once we decided on Sweet Haven, Rhett applied to restaurants all over Savannah and got hired as a pastry chef at one of the top French restaurants in the south. He's so happy at his job, and I'm happy because he's happy.

"You know what today is, right?"

I turn and look up at him. "What?"

"It's Valentine's Day, Sunny."

I totally forgot! I've been so busy with the bakery that it slipped my mind completely. "Oh, Rhett, I'm so sorry. I didn't get you a card or anything. I'm a terrible girlfriend."

"That's why I don't want you to be my girlfriend anymore."

My heart suddenly leaps into my throat. He's breaking up with me on Valentine's Day? Dear God, could my luck with men get any worse?

"Wh… what?"

Before I have time to consider my next move, Rhett lowers himself onto one knee and holds up a turquoise-blue ring box.

"Savannah Greene, I've never met a more perfect woman in my life. You encourage me, challenge me, and make me laugh. Most importantly, you love me in a way I didn't know was possible. Would you do me the great honor of becoming my wife?"

Oh. My. Goodness.

I can't form words because I'm sobbing.

"Um, my knee is starting to hurt, so an answer would be good," Rhett says, his face contorting in pain.

I laugh. "Yes! Yes, I will marry you!"

I jump up and down as he stands up and slips the most beautiful diamond ring on my finger. He holds my face in his hands and kisses me deeply the way only he can do.

Suddenly, Sadie comes running from behind his car, squealing like a stuck pig.

"Congratulations!"

"How did you know?"

"Oh, sissy, who do you think helped him plan this? I was never going to the store!"

In all the days I've lived, there's never been a better one than this one. Standing in the parking lot of my new bakery with my fiancé and sister, I realize that families are made of parts and pieces.

Sometimes, you don't have all the right pieces right out of the gate. Instead, you assemble them over a lifetime. But if you don't give up, when the puzzle is complete, you're left with a tapestry of love that can't be broken.

"I love you, my Sunny girl," Rhett says, hugging me tightly.

"I love you too, Rhett."

The sign guy turns on my sign to test it, and we all smile. Nothing tells our story quite like a hippopotamus wearing sunglasses. "Sunny's Sweets" is ready for business.

Want BONUS CONTENT from The Baking Games, including recipes from the book, baking-themed bookmarks, and a character list? Go to https://Book Hip.com/LWPPQKV.

. . .

Be sure to join my interactive Facebook group of over 19,000 readers! I'm in there daily doing give-aways, polls, new book announcements, and other fun stuff! https://www.facebook.com/groups/ RachelReaders

Made in the USA
Columbia, SC
17 September 2024